JUST AMIGOS

GIGI BLUME

FIRST EDITION

Library of Congress Cataloging-in-Publication Data has been applied for.

ISBN: 979-8-9861828-5-8

Editing by Kristyn Fortner

Cover design and illustrations by Once Upon a Cover

For Cocoa and Cookie
You were, and always will be
my perfectly beautiful little ladies

"In the whole history of the world there is but one thing that
money can not buy…
to wit — the wag of a dog's tail."
-Josh Billings

JUST AMIGOS

Every kind of music is good,
except the boring kind.

-Gioachino Rossini

Chapter One

MATEO

Geronimo!

I've always wanted to holler that, especially while diving from a stage into the expectant hands of a concert-going crowd. The exhilaration of the jump. The pure bliss mixed with adrenaline. The feeling of weightlessness. It's the closest I'll ever get to flying, seeing as I'm averse to skydiving. But when the crowd splits like the Red Sea, it's considerably less safe than jumping out of a perfectly good airplane. The pub is packed and dark, but I have a feeling about the audience.

My band, The High C's, is the most popular sea shanty group this side of Melrose Blvd, and all the bodies smushed together on the dance floor make for an ideal crowd surfing scenario.

Somewhere between the time my feet leave the stage and my body is in mid air, my brain emerges from the whiskey buzz to remind me this might not be the best idea. The patrons at O'Malley's Tavern on this bonny St Patrick's Day evening are undoubtedly several beers and shots of Jameson ahead of me and are in no shape to catch a guy without much warning. They are way too inebriated to possess the motor skills necessary to pass me around above their heads. Either that or they're just jerks. After all, they did have the presence of mind to peel away from my airborne body. One guy even ducks down to protect his beer.

By the way the formerly enthusiastic audience bolts out of the way, you'd think they're running from an elephant instead of a human being.

Only one older woman remains in my path as I fall to the floor with a thud. The crowd gasps and the music halts abruptly.

I think I've killed her. Just for a second, though, as a million thoughts race through my mind. *I've crashed into a lady and now she's dead.* Until she squeaks from under me. I hear someone say, "You're crushing her, man. Get off."

When the woman glares at me with that scowl I recognize, I know I've stepped into my worst nightmare. My eyes bulge out, horrified.

"Sister… Monica?"

What the blazes is my high school math teacher doing here? Is she a sea shanty aficionado?

She shoves me off her and gets up on her own, adjusting the oversized green shamrock T-shirt she's wearing over her nunly frock—the kind my mom buys at Walmart (the T-shirt, not the nunly frock). No wonder I didn't recognize her.

I roll over onto the hard, beer-soaked floor of the pub, feeling the full humiliation of my tumble. Thank my lucky stars Sister Monica broke my fall. She's a hardy woman, I'll give her that.

The figure of one of my band mates, Desirée, looms over my body, hands resting on her hips. Her dainty little lips curl into her signature quirky sideways smile, and she's shaking her head, bright blue eyes twinkling with laughter.

"Seriously, Mateo," she says. "I can't take you anywhere."

"Clearly," I say, taking her hand as she offers to help me up.

A few guys surround Sister Monica, making sure she didn't break anything, when Heath, the pub owner, makes his way from the bar onto the dance floor.

"Are you okay, ma'am?" he asks, leading her away from the crash site.

"I've been better," she moans while giving me the side eye. "I think I'm not fit for the mosh pit."

Mosh pit? Where did this Irish Catholic nun pick that up?

I realize, as I try to come up with the best way to apologize to Sister Monica, that my knee hit the floor pretty hard.

I'm going to feel all of it once the adrenaline wears off. I hope I didn't injure the poor woman. And I can only imagine Saint Peter keeping me from passing through the pearly gates with one of Sister Monica's infraction cards in his hand. Every box is checked off with a red marker.

- *Non-compliance: check*
- *Disruptive behavior: check*
- *Inappropriate language: check*
- *Does not work well with others: check*
- *Dress code violation: check*
- *SEE ME AFTER CLASS: check*

Trying to hide a limp, I approach the nun, extending my hand as a peace offering.

"I'm so sor—"

She cuts me off with a snap of her wrist—her hand in the air between us like a formidable wall that shall not be crossed. The same hand she'd referred to as her 'holy hand' while writing equations on the chalkboard back in high school. "Watch me holy hand," she'd say with her Irish accent as she scribbled.

"I don't need to hear it, Mr. Precio," says Sister Monica. Then turning to Heath, she says, "I could use a wee dram, if ye don't mind."

Heath mumbles his apologies to her as they head to the bar, and in the hushed silence, patrons begin to leave or congregate in friend groups, grumbling the whole time.

"Not very festive, is it?" I quip, daring a glance at my band mates still on stage. Corbin, who plays mandolin, and our drummer, Jonah, are having a pow wow. I hope they're deciding on a good song to lift the drab spirits of the bar patrons, but they're probably discussing how they'll tease me later. All the guys in The High C's are straight up dudes, but Jonah's the most chill. He's also my roommate.

"Do you think they'll ever let me live this down?" I ask Desirée.

She twists her lips which makes her nose crinkle. "Well nobody expected that. I was all *'look out, he's airborne, get out of the way!'* FLUMP!"

She flops her hands over to demonstrate my flumping, as she calls it.

"Why don't you get your fiddle and pick something fun to play. I'll be right… oww."

My knee buckles and I stop in my tracks, embarrassed for Desirée to see me with any weakness. I guess it has to do with the older brother vibes I'm trying hard to project even though I fail miserably ninety-nine percent of the time. And since she's the only female in a band full of rowdy guys, I want to be the one she can count on.

So far, I suck at it.

"Are you okay? You want to sit down?"

"I'm fine."

The last thing I want is for her to fuss over me. I'm supposed to be watching out for her. Not the other way around.

"You don't look fine. Maybe you broke something, mister."

"I'm fine," I say a little too forcefully.

One of the groupies slides over to me and strokes my arm. Candy or Brandy or something.

"I was in the bathroom when one of my girlfriends came in to tell me you fell off the stage," she says with high-pitched meep. "Do you want me to check if you broke anything important?"

Desirée's eye-roll is so big, she could take out a set of bowling pins.

Candy/Brandy has the keen timing of making herself present whenever I'm talking to Desiree. And she ignores that she's standing right there every time. I'm convinced it's her mission to ensnare me somehow, since she's been with all the other guys in the band.

I made the mistake of agreeing to invite her and her annoying little friends over to our apartment one night after a show. She took off her shoes and did a striptease on our coffee table. Jonah was having the time of his life. I went into my room and locked my door before too many clothes came off.

I'm no monk, but I don't sleep with groupies. The way women hang around all the time, Desirée is convinced otherwise.

Ignoring Candy/Brandy, I turn back to Desirée. "I need to hit the head. Tell the guys to start without me."

Desirée cringes. "Can't you call it a bathroom like a normal person? Why do guys have to say head or can or john?"

"I shall convene to the water closet. Better?"

She squints at me. "I'll allow it."

I wait until she turns toward the stage before hobbling

away. Candy/Brandy has moved on to flirt with a group of preppy guys. Following the money.

The line to the… restroom… is atrocious, and I don't really have to go, so I make my way out the back door to the questionably safe alley. If I smoked, I'd light one up just to blow off some steam. But I can't stand the smell of cigarettes.

Taking my cell phone from my pocket, I send a text in the group chat between me and my seven siblings.

Me: *You'll never guess who I ran into at O'Malley's just now.*

More like *fell* into, but I'll leave that story for another day. A few seconds later, my phone pings.

Dante: *If it's Elvis, tell him he's on my kill list if he doesn't get back to the yard ASAP.*

My older brother Dante is a take-no-prisoners type of guy when it comes to running his towing business. A holiday like St. Patrick's is one of the busiest nights of the year, third in line to Thanksgiving and New Year's. Dante never gets a break it seems, working long hours, and when he doesn't get any sleep, stay far, far away from him.

Which is probably what Elvis is doing.

I'm not talking about the king of rock and roll. Elvis Wilson works for Dante driving a tow truck, and I'll bet he's taking his sweet time on a job or flirting with some poor woman with a flat tire.

Me: *It's not Elvis. Why don't you radio him? Or however you truckers communicate.*

Dante: **middle finger emoji*

Of course my recently married brother Ignacio takes offense to Dante's text. His new domestic life is making him boring.

Ignacio: Real classy, Dante.

I'm pretty sure Dante pocketed his phone by now. The man has no patience for group chats.

My little sister, Francesca, hops on. As the only female of us Precio siblings, she's taken it upon herself to keep us guys in line. No idea why she'd need to do that. Ahem.

Francesca: Who did you see at O'Malley's?

Me: Sister Monica.

Ignacio: No way.

Francesca: Who?

Me: She was wearing a shamrock t-shirt over her habit.

Ignacio: LOL what?

Francesca: Who's Sister Monica?

Ignacio: She used to teach math at Santa Ines.

Francesca: I don't remember her.

Ignacio: Watch me holy hand

Francesca: Oooooh. I've heard of her.

Sister Monica retired from teaching before Francesca or my youngest brother Sebastian went to Santa Ines High, but you better believe the other six of us went through her Algebra class and it's an experience we'll never forget.

My brother Enrique joins the chat.

*Enrique: *surprised Chris Pratt gif*

*Enrique: *single ladies hand gif*

Sebastian: Didn't you guys have PTSD after taking her class?

Ignacio: Shouldn't you be studying for midterms?

Sebastian is away at university so he can be a hotshot lawyer one day.

Sebastian: I'm on the can.

See? Guys are simple creatures. We say things like can or head. Not latrine, or water closet.

Francesca: *You're gross, Sebas.*

Sebastian's on East Coast time. And it's St. Patrick's Day. He can take a break from studying if he wants. The guy's on the honor roll anyway.

Me: *Gotta go do another set. Ciao.*

I silence my phone and slip it back into my pocket. My knee is killing me, but I'll ice it when I get home. I just need to get through this show and I'll have almost a week before the next gig.

But when I get back inside the pub, they're playing canned music over the speakers and my bandmates are almost done packing up.

"What's going on?" I ask, climbing onto the stage with a small degree of pain I cover up with a laugh.

"I might ask you the same thing," says Corbin. "What were you thinking, man?"

"I wasn't thinking, I just—"

"Exactly. You weren't thinking. And now Heath wants us out."

"Out?" I check my watch. "It's only ten fifteen."

"Nobody wants to see us play, Matt," he says. "Thanks to you."

"Woah woah, hang on. It was just a stage dive."

"You tackled an old woman."

"She's not that old. And she's built like a tank. Seriously, I've seen Sister Monica play football with the other nuns, and you don't want to mess with her."

"She's a *nun*?" Corbin's face blows up. "You stage dove into a nun?"

Okay, I know this sounds bad, but if these guys only knew all the epically embarrassing things I've done back in high school, they'd just nod and say, "Again?" and that would be it.

There was that time I left my skateboard in the hallway while I got a sip from the water fountain, and the dean slipped on it, falling on the hard tile floor. He sprained his wrist, and I had detention for a month.

Or when I ran into the quad in nothing but a towel after gym class because someone stole my uniform while I was showering. To this day, I'm 99.9 percent sure it was the water polo team. That incident earned me community service at the food bank, which did *not* count toward service hours.

But I'm not about to tell any of this to the band, of course.

By this time, the other guys rally behind Corbin and Jonah. Logan, who plays the tin whistle, Tegan, our banjo player, and Jeremy, who's only mediocre on the accordion.

Even Jonah's crossing his arms with disdain.

"Guys, it's fine. I'll go talk to Heath."

"You're the last person Heath wants to talk to right now," says Corbin.

"Might as well tell him." Jeremy says.

"What? Tell me what?"

Corbin sighs. "Heath wants us for our regular Friday night slot… but not you. He doesn't want you back."

"Wha… what do you mean? He can't do that."

"He wants us to replace you, Matt."

"You can't replace me. I started this band."

"I think he'll cool off after a while," says Jeremy. "Until then…

"Until then what?" I can't believe this.

Corbin gives me a cold stare. "We all agree, Matt. Maybe you should take a probationary period.

"Proba… what's that supposed to mean? You're putting me on *probation*? From the band? You're not serious. Logan? You on board with this?"

Logan dips his head down and nods solemnly.

I've worked so hard for this band, practically killing myself to get us paying gigs. I've poured my heart and soul into The High C's and now they want to cast me aside?

"Desirée? What about you?"

She bites her lip and shrugs one shoulder.

"Really?" I say incredulously.

"It's not up to me, Mateo," she says.

I look around the circle of guys who I thought were my friends. All of them with hard expressions directed at me.

"Tegan? Jeremy?"

"A break isn't a bad thing," says Jeremy. "It'll be like a vacation."

Tegan, a man of few words, just nods.

My hand twitches with anger so I run it through my hair to alleviate the urge to throw something. I settle for ripping the elastic from my ponytail instead.

"Unbelievable. Forget Heath. We'll get other gigs."

"Be realistic, Matt," says Corbin. "O'Malley's is our only steady gig. Ren Faire and church carnivals don't pay the bills. We need Heath."

"In case you haven't noticed, Heath is no George Martin. We don't need him. There are other pubs."

Corbin shakes his head solemnly. "Sorry man. We can't risk it."

"So that's it, then? You're gonna let Heath tell you what to do? Why don't you just twist the knife you stabbed in my back while you're at it."

"You just need to prove—"

"I don't need to prove anything," I snap. "I quit."

Without thinking about the ramifications, I storm out of the hot, sweaty pub and out the front door. The cool night air washes over me freely. It feels good. I only now realize that I left my guitar on stage, and I rode here in the van with Corbin. Great.

"Mateo, wait."

Desirée's voice reaches me before she comes into view. I don't know if I want to see her face right now, so I keep walking into the parking lot.

"Hey, hang on." Her boots crunch on the gravel at a faster pace, and she catches up to me, tugging on my shoulder. "Mateo, you need to chill. Why are you such a hot head?"

I'm not a hot head. Ignacio, maybe. Dante, definitely. But me? Chill is my middle name. But something has me on edge tonight, and even though Desirée is the last person I want to take it out on, I'm a little raw that she didn't stick up for me back there.

"Are you on board with this? Kicking me out of the band?"

Her enormous blue eyes grow even wider, like I'm the one who offended her somehow.

"No. Why would you say that?"

"I didn't exactly hear you vote in my favor."

Her cheeks puff out in defiance. "Nobody's kicking you out of the band, Mateo. You quit… like a… big toddler."

"A big toddler? Really?"

"Just go back in there and work it out with the guys. And maybe try to apologize to the nun again."

"Sister Monica never listened to excuses back in high school, she won't listen now."

"Please just go back and make things right. I'm sure Corbin didn't mean what he said."

"Corbin meant exactly what he said. He's been trying to squeeze into lead vocals for months."

She shakes her head. "He doesn't have the chops. Nobody can sing like you."

That's sweet of her to say, but you don't have to be Pavarotti to sing sea shanties. Any of the guys could step up to the mic if they wanted to. Now that I think about it, the signs were there.

"Not my problem anymore," I say. "I don't want to see Corbin's face again, let alone any of the other guys in the band for ganging up on me like that."

Desirée shoots me with a stabby glare.

"Mateo, I really don't need to deal with your male PMS right now."

"I beg your pardon?"

"Listen you wayward lothario. I never know what mood you're going to be in from one day to the next. You're like… Courtney Love on crazy pills."

"I don't think you're being fair to Courtney Love."

"That's true. You're way more unhinged."

"At least we agree on something."

She crosses her arms and paces back and forth in front of me. It's one of her tells. She wants to punch me.

"Rock me, Amadeus," I say, pointing to my cheek.

She stops pacing and glowers at me. "I'm not going to hit you."

The phrase *'rock me, Amadeus'* started when her brother, Ian and I were teenagers and she was about ten or eleven. Ian hid a bunch of plastic spiders under her pillow, on her toothbrush, in her doll house. Just lots of places. I thought it was kind of funny until I found out she's terrified of spiders. Tears were streaming down her face, and when Ian couldn't stop laughing, I told her they were fake, and that it was my idea. I don't know why I did that. I think maybe it was because I have five older brothers and knew what it felt like to get picked on.

Her face turned bright red, and her tears turned to rage.

So I told her to hit me. Right in the face. I turned my cheek to the side and said, "Rock me, Amadeus."

She hesitated at first, but after a half minute, I felt a soft tap of her little palm on my cheek. Then she apologized profusely, thinking she'd really done some damage. So to make up for the injury she caused on my face, she reached up on her tiptoes and gave me a super quick, barely there kiss on the cheek. When we got older, sometimes I'd tap my cheek and say "Rock me, Amadeus" for no reason, just so I'd get another kiss.

Just like I hope she'll do now.

"Come on," I say. "It's tradition."

She rolls her dazzling eyes and pokes me in the cheek.

"Poke, poke," she says, because she loves sound effects. Then she does what she always does and puckers up to kiss the spot on my face she just caused injury to. But I'm feeling cunning tonight. So I deviously maneuver my head so her kiss inadvertently lands on my lips.

Her bright eyes widen, and she stumbles back, blinking. But her discomfort is short-lived. She huffs out one of her breathy giggles, then shoves me in the chest.

"You're a rapscallion," she says.

"I hope so."

I toss her a wink for good measure. Because the truth is I *am* a scoundrel, a rogue, a scamp. All the silly nicknames she likes to throw at me from time to time. And maybe I lean into it more than I should. The 'accidental' kiss notwithstanding. I liked it. No. I *loved* it. Her lips are soft and dewy. It's everything I'd imagined how her lips would feel against mine. Like two perfect rose petals. And for an instant, my stomach swooped. And dammit, I want more of that.

But if I'm not careful, Ian will come at me with an ax to separate me from Mr. Happy, his brother Darrell and his other brother Darrell. I've grown quite attached to the brothers, so I best remember that getting involved with Desirée Grant is prohibited times a million to the power of eternity. Also, I'm not a fan of Ian rearranging my face, so there's that.

"Do me a favor," I say. "Take my guitar home with you. I'll pick it up tomorrow." I slug her arm (because I'm her completely platonic pal now apparently) and head down to the sidewalk.

"Where are you going?"

"Ordering an Uber."

"I'm not getting your guitar," she calls after me. "You'll have to go in there and get it yourself."

"See ya tomorrow, Paloma." I wave over my shoulder, resisting the urge to steal her away like the ending of The Graduate. We'd get on a bus and leave all this behind. No dip wad band, no drunken bar crowd, no irate siblings with axes. Just me and Desirée and the horizon. Doesn't sound so bad.

Until I remember I have absolutely nothing to offer a woman like her.

I'm not capable of being somebody's somebody.

I'm not like my dad, the way he's always there for my mom. Or my brothers who have it all together. How can I expect someone like Desirée to rely on a guy like me?

Nope. I'm better off living the single life. Footloose and collar-free.

Well, I might not rule out collars completely.

Without music,
life would Bb

-Unknown

Chapter Two
DESIRÉE

Grow a pair, Desi.

Get in there and deliver this pizza. You do not. I repeat, do *not* have the major hots for Mateo Precio.

Nope.

He's just a dude. Albeit a studalicious foxy dude, with just the right amount of ink on his arms, shoulder-length hair that curls at the tips, and a chiseled jaw that could cut glass. No biggie. He's got six brothers I've never felt anything for. But theirs is not the name I used to write all over my notebooks in grade school. Okay, also high school. And maybe once or twice in the bathroom mirror steam.

But I'm over it.

Mateo Precio is bad news with a capital B.

I'd forget all about him if it wasn't for the fact we were (until recently) in the same band. And until recently, he lived in an apartment with the drummer. So now he's moving back into his parents' house—next door to my house. And if that's not enough, somebody at the Precio household ordered pizza from the place I do deliveries for.

I'm doomed to have Mateo Precio in my life for all eternity. Maybe I'll move to Malta. I have no idea where Malta is, but it sounds nice to say it.

I slip off my helmet and shake out my hair, hoping my bangs aren't wonky. Checking the tiny mirror on my Vespa, I decide it can't be helped and dismount, unstrapping the insulated pizza delivery box from the rear rack. Five pizzas. One more, and the pimple-faced teenager with the Toyota Corolla would have made the delivery. I think the Precios know that.

I dare not hope it was Mateo who made the call. It was probably Dante, Mateo's older brother, whose truck is in the driveway. When my brother Ian joined the Navy, he made Dante promise to look after me. I'm not supposed to know about the arrangement, but I do. It's a little annoying, but Dante only comes around once a week for their family Sunday dinner. Except this week, because he's helping Mateo move.

I knock on the front door, expecting Dante, Mateo, or maybe their sister, Francesca. But a middle-aged man with a comb-over answers. He's wearing shorts and a tank top too tight for his round belly. I've never seen him before, but he seems comfortable enough to answer the door in his socks and scratch his belly button while looking at me like I'm delivering something other than pizza.

"Atomic Pizza delivery!" I chirp.

Just as I'm about to pass the boxes over the threshold, Mateo appears, puffing up his chest at the old guy.

"Don't talk to her," he growls. "Don't look at her. Don't. Touch. Her. Or her pizza. Don't even *think* about her pizza."

The man slinks away from Mateo, the height difference even more pronounced as the little guy slumps his shoulders and holds up his hands in surrender.

"I only answer the door muchacho," he says with a thick accent.

"Don't answer the door."

Oooh, was that a roar? *So very alpha of you, Mateo.*

"Okay, okay." The old guy backs away and disappears into the house.

"And don't call me muchacho," Mateo calls out, then adds under his breath, "Creep."

Um, not sure how to react to that. Why do I get the feeling it's not the pizza he's concerned about?

"Is… pizza supposed to be a euphemism for something else?" I question.

"Sorry about that guy," says Mateo, relieving me of the heavy stack of pizza. "Come on in."

"I… really should get going," I protest.

Mateo throws a sneaky glance over his shoulder as I trail behind him into the kitchen. Is that a wink? And darn it, he's so sure of himself that I'll follow him like a puppy dog. If I had a tail, it would be wagging right now.

"You're done working for the day. Right? We're your last delivery."

How did he know that?

"Ummm. Yeah." I don't have a better answer for him. We're not close per se. As much time as we spend playing in the sea shanty band, conversation with Mateo is like talking to an aloof James Dean. He doesn't tell me his business and I don't tell him mine. But somehow he knows my schedule. How when I get home from work, I don't go out much. How I prefer a quiet evening alone. I like my solitude. Reading. Drinking tea. And knitting. That's my Saturday night for you, folks. Woohoo.

Mateo ticks his head to coax me closer.

"Have a slice. We ordered your favorite."

"I noticed."

Yes, he knows my favorite toppings. Salami, mushrooms, and stewed tomatoes. But that could be anyone's favorite, right?

He's already serving me a slice when his mother stomps into the kitchen, mumbling under her breath in a mocking tone.

"Yes, may I help you! Yes, may I help you! Who does he think he is? *Fregón*." She stops grumbling when she sees me. "Oh hi, Desirée. So nice to see you. How pretty you look. Doesn't she look pretty, Mateo?"

Mateo's jaw ticks. "Yeah, Ma."

She huffs at him, rolling her eyes and gives me a hug. She's a good hugger.

"Nice to see you, too, Mrs. Precio."

"Are you staying to eat? I hope you're not too tired of pizza."

"There's no such thing."

"Good." She steals a slice from the box and takes a bite. "I'll go tell Dante the pizza's here. Mateo, take some out to Dad."

She's scuffling off with her mouth full before Mateo can respond. He casually rakes his hand through the long, wavy locks that fall over his eyes. When he does this in front of the band's groupies, ovaries explode everywhere. The way his tan forearm flexes, shifting the leather and beaded bracelets he wears, his tattoos flashing from the movement, and the black and silver rings on elegant musician's fingers, swishing through his hair… gah!

Did Mother Nature just turn up the thermostat?

I'm holding my slice of pizza close to my chest, gulping at the sight. I'll never tire of pizza… or watching Mateo Precio lazily comb back his hair.

Which is wrong on so many levels. So, so wrong.

Firstly, because I am not about to objectify a man when that would be a heinous double standard.

And secondly, because I'm proudly in my (hashtag) celibacy era. It's a huge movement right now among women claiming back their power. It's all over TikTok.

I'm just so frustrated with hookup culture; getting caught in a cycle of unfulfilling flings that leave me feeling unhappy, hurt, and disrespected. And the constant criticism from every boyfriend I've had. How they never even noticed I had a brain, or anything at all besides what I could do for them—preferably in the sac.

Newsflash: I am not a toy.

So, I decided to shut down shop.

"You okay?" Mateo squints at me.

"Uh… fine. I was just thinking about your mom. She seemed upset."

"Yeah, well." He picks up the box of meat lovers and a handful of paper plates. "That guy who answered the door? We call him Pancho Two, and he's staying with us while he's on house arrest. Mom can't stand him. But for some reason, Dad keeps giving him chances."

"House arrest. Wow."

Mateo leads me toward the back patio where the T.V. can be heard even from a distance.

"Didn't you see the ankle box under his sock?"

"I… no."

"He loves to say, 'Yes, may I help you?' to anyone who even looks at him. I think Mom is going to blow a fuse one of these days."

I still can't get over the house arrest detail. There's a criminal in the house! I wonder what he did.

"Is he dangerous?" I ask, a little too curiously.

Mateo pauses just before opening the French patio door, his hand on the doorknob as he thinks for a moment.

"No," he says at last. "I don't think so."

Lovely. That instills all sorts of confidence in me.

We head outside where Mateo's dad is watching baseball on a giant screen. He's clapping and chanting at the game.

"Let's go, Doyers."

Clap clap, clap-clap-clap.

As soon as the door opens, I'm greeted by a completely crazed Yorkie. Her little butt is wagging a million miles a minute as she scurries around my feet, crawls between my legs, and flops on her back for a belly rub.

"Hi puppy! Who's a good girl?"

I reach down to pet her, but she's too excited and bolts around the patio furniture, then back again.

"She's got the zoomies," says Mateo. "Lola, chill out."

She doesn't chill out. Lola covers the entire patio twice over. Did someone give this dog espresso?

The whole back patio is fitted to be an outdoor man cave, complete with a wet bar and a barbecuer's dream kitchen. I'm talking state of the art smoker, professional grill, and a wood-fired pizza oven. Which makes me wonder why they bother to order from Atomic Pizza. I suppose delivery is less work. Mateo's dad is watching the game from a cozy looking swivel chair.

"Hi, Mr. Precio," I say with my biggest smile. I really like this guy. He's always been a friendly neighbor, sometimes bringing over extra taco fixings when he makes too much for his family. "Is it baseball season already?"

"Spring training," he says.

"Oh cool," I say, then repeat his chant. "Let's go, Dodgers!"

Clap clap, clap-clap-clap.

We're both chanting now. Mr. Precio pronouncing his g like a y.

"Let's go, Doyers." *Clap clap, clap-clap-clap.*

"Dad," Mateo grunts. "Pizza." He's one of those guys who likes to be economic with their words. Whatev.

I sit down next to Mr. Precio and watch the game. The Dodgers are playing in a small ballpark instead of a big stadium. Fans are watching from grassy areas, sitting on blankets, having picnics. I'm not a big sports fan, but this looks like so much fun. Especially the picnic part.

One of the players hits a home run and Mr. Precio leaps from his chair, cheering. The ball goes over the fence, and fans jump up from their picnic blankets to catch it. They've got their baseball gloves reaching to the sky, and when one guy catches the ball, another fan congratulates him by bumping gloves together.

"A two-run home run!" hoots Mr. Precio. "Bravo!"

"Yes, bravo," I echo, applauding the play with my free hand.

Mr. Precio dips his hand into the ice bucket on the small table, where Mateo placed the pizza box, and digs out a bottle of Dos Equis.

"Cerveza?" he offers, holding it up between us.

"No thanks."

He shrugs and pops open the top, reaching for a slice of pizza with one fluid motion, and sits back down.

"Lola, *ven.*" He tosses a pepperoni to the dog.

The guy is in his element, joyously watching the game while chewing on his food, his little dog at his feet waiting expectantly for another slice of pepperoni. My own dad wouldn't know how to be so casual, even in his underwear.

Mateo slouches into a hanging egg chair and aimlessly swings in small circles. There's something off—he's exceptionally sulky, even for him.

Mateo's mom rounds the corner from the other side of

the patio. Her cheeks are rosy from running around the house, it seems.

"Has anyone seen Dante?"

"Nope," Mateo says, laconically.

She sighs, then eyes the pizza box on the table.

"Don't mind if I do."

She claims the chair on the other side of her husband and reaches for her second slice.

"Beer?" he asks her.

"Margarita?" she says, beaming at him.

"*Aye que la!*" Mr. Precio grudgingly lifts himself up and hobbles over to the wet bar to make his wife a cocktail.

"How are your parents, Desirée?" asks Mrs. Precio as she settles in, propping her feet on the ottoman.

"Fine," I say. "They're camping in Key West right now."

About two years ago, my parents signed the deed to my childhood home over to me and my brother Ian, bought a gigantic R.V., and have been roaming the country ever since. Recently, they invested in a sunny little house in Myrtle Beach, South Carolina where they have their hub whenever they want a rest from the road. Other than Christmas, they don't make it back to Los Angeles very often.

"*Mujer!* What the heck is this?" barks Mr. Precio, with one hand on the open box freezer lid. He's glaring at his wife.

"Nothing," she says innocently.

He presents the evidence above his head. "How many boxes of cookies did you buy, woman?"

"Put that away," she hisses. "I'm saving those."

"Do you really need… *un, dos, tres, quatro…*" he continues to count silently. "Twenty boxes?"

"It's not my fault the Girl Scouts deal their contraband during Lent."

Mr. Precio shakes his head and digs into the box freezer, plunking ice cubes in a glass. A minute later, he delivers his wife's drink and drops himself down into his chair with a grunt.

"I'd be afraid of the alligators," says Mrs. Precio, slurping her margarita.

"What?" I forgot what we were talking about for a second. "Oh. Right. Florida is pretty crazy," I say. "Although I think it's mostly crocs in the Keys."

"You should come to dinner on Sunday," she says, like the idea just occurred to her. "I don't like the thought of you alone in that house with nothing to eat."

"I have food," I say. Although cooking for one is kind of a drag. "I get all the free pizza I want."

It's mostly a joke.

"You're coming to dinner and that's that."

"Yes ma'am."

"And your brother? How is he?"

"Ian's fine."

Mateo snorts. "He feels the need for speed."

I roll my eyes at Mateo. He and my brother were best friends growing up. But after graduation, when Ian left for Naval Aviation School, they kinda grew apart. Now Mateo makes Top Gun jokes whenever Ian comes up in conversation.

"Is he a Maverick yet?" asks Mrs. Precio.

"Maverick? Oh, you mean a Strike Fighter? No. Not yet."

She considers this for a moment. "Are you sure it's not The Mavericks?"

"That's a movie, Mom," says Mateo.

"I know," she says. "A movie based on real life."

Mateo squeezes his eyes, like if he squeezes hard enough we'd all disappear.

Just then Dante barrels through the patio doors, whistling like a trucker for Mateo, "Matt, let's go for another load." He stops when he sees us gathered. "Why didn't anyone tell me there was pizza?"

He's about to reach for a plate when he notices me quietly sitting here. His expression immediately softens.

"Hello, Desirée. I didn't see you."

He comes at me for a hug but barely leans over before Mateo leaps out of the egg chair and slaps the back of Dante's head.

"Dude! You're dripping in sweat."

"I don't mind," I say.

Dante backs off, skewering Mateo with a sharp gaze. "Maybe if you didn't have so much sh–" he glances at his mom and alters what he was about to say. "If you didn't have so much *crap*, we'd be done by now."

"I don't have a *lot* of crap. It's just that my stuff is too big for my Stingray."

Dante helps himself to a slice. "Three truckloads is a lot of crap. Three… *if* we can fit it all this trip."

"Maybe you can have a garage sale," suggests Mrs. Precio. "You could use the money."

"I need all my stuff."

"How many amps and guitars and speakers does one guy need?" asks Dante with a mouthful of pizza. "I say you just leave it all at the apartment and let the other guys have at it."

Mateo glowers at his brother. "I. Need. My. Stuff."

Just as it seems the two brothers are going to get into it, Mr. Precio shouts at the T.V.

"Fly ball! Oops." Beer spills down his arm.

"Let's go, Dodgers," I chant.

"Just hurry it up, Matt." says Dante, stealing another slice to take inside the house. "I haven't got all day."

Mateo watches him disappear through the French doors before plopping back into the egg chair. This time, he rests his elbows on his knees and scrubs both hands over his face. It's here I notice the dark circles and bloodshot eyes.

"I better go," he says, resigned. He's not looking in my direction, but I know he's talking to me.

"Aren't you going to eat first?" I say softly. "The pizza's getting cold."

"I'm not hungry."

"You need to eat something," says Mr. Precio. "Now."

"I can't eat right now, Dad. "I'm good."

"You're not good," says his mom. "You've hardly eaten in days. I thought pizza would help. Especially Desirée's... pizza." She wags her brows behind her margarita glass.

What's with the pizza references in this family? Does pizza mean something else in Spanish?

"Why haven't you been eating, Mateo?" I ask as gently as I can.

"I'm fine. Just a headache."

"You said it was a stomachache," says his mom.

"Yeah, well. It's all connected." He's clearly annoyed by all this questioning, but now I'm really concerned.

"Are you sick?" I ask. "Do you need a doctor?"

"I don't need a doctor. I'm upset, that's all." Then he mutters under his breath, "Stupid, stupid, stupid."

"Is it because of the band?" I ask.

"The band, having to move back home. Sister Monica. Everything."

"Well…" I really don't know what to say, but I try to find words he'll be open to hearing. "Moving back home is just temporary. And like you said, you'll form another band eventually. Those guys are wieners anyway."

"I never liked that Corbin guy," adds Mr. Precio.

"Forget them," says Mrs. Precio.

"Yeah!" I rally, scooting closer to Mateo. "Forget them. You know what I do when I feel bad about something?"

Mateo doesn't respond with words. His tired eyes shift my way, sending pinpricks of awareness through me. Even looking like hell warmed over he's still hot. Darn him.

"Whenever I'm embarrassed or upset about something, I just think about other things I've done in the past and how I got through them."

He snorts, shaking his head. I'm guessing he has a lot of experiences to draw upon. I don't want to know.

"Who's your favorite band?"

His lip curls to the side. "The Beatles. Of course."

"Great. That's a great example. The Beatles did lots of stupid things and lived through it. Well, except John, maybe. Remember when Paul was asked how he felt about John Lennon's death and he said, *It's a bloody shame*' and the press had a field day? Or when John said they were more popular than Jesus and got a lot of flak for it?"

Mateo flops back into the chair. "It's not the same."

"All I'm saying is you can try it. You're going to laugh about this in a few weeks. Trust me."

He sighs dramatically and leans over, peeling a slice of pizza from the box. He doesn't bother with a plate. He takes a huge bite, more than half the slice, and throws the remaining piece on the table.

"There. Satisfied?" He's sulking as he chews.

"Take smaller bites, dear," his mom says.

Mr. Precio hands Mateo a bottle of water.

"And as for the nun," I continue. "I think she'll be okay."

He scoffs a humorless laugh.

"She has to forgive you," says Mrs. Precio. "It's her job."

"No, I really don't think so," he replies. "She once knocked off a few points because I farted during a test."

Mr. Precio laughs. "I don't blame her. Your farts were loud and proud. *Órale.* When he was in high school… *que pedoro!*" He waves his hand under his nose.

"Thanks, Dad. Real cool."

"Don't worry about it," I say. "You're an adult. What can she do to you now? Give you more homework?"

"You underestimate Sister Monica," he says.

"Hey. Dingleberry." Dante's peeking out of the door waving a cordless phone. The Precios are the only family I know that still uses a landline.

Mateo twists his head, responding to being called Dingleberry like it's his middle name or something.

Mrs. Precio licks the salt off her margarita glass and wags her finger at Dante. "Be nice, now."

"Sorry, Ma. *Mister* Dingleberry, the phone's for you. And guess who it is?"

Mateo perks up, half trepidation, half expectant. "Who?"

Dante smirks devilishly as he saunters over to pass Mateo the phone.

"Sister Monica."

The real problem
with reality is
the lack of
background music.

-Unknown

Chapter Three

MATEO

The nun's retirement home where Sister Monica lives is situated in a quaint neighborhood in San Dimas. The streets are uneven, brought on by years of wear and a few earthquakes, I suppose.

Lining the street on either side are tall, aged Jacaranda trees, a few palm trees, and giant Eucalyptus, the roots cracking the sidewalks. The houses are early twentieth century, maybe pre-World War Two. Or around that time.

It's quiet and suburban. A safe neighborhood, despite the age, and for L.A., that's saying a lot.

When I reach the address I was given, there's a long stretch of hedges in front of concrete privacy walls covered in Ivy. The wrought iron gate, barely hanging onto the hinges, rests open, wearily inviting. It seems more of a decorative installation than security. That rickety old thing wouldn't keep anything out.

As I navigate my Stingray around the long gravel path that serves as a driveway, I'm struck by the tranquil beauty of the grounds. The little road twists around grassy lawns peppered with rose bushes, trees that could be over a century old, and other plants of different varieties. There are several inter-connecting buildings with the look of early California Missions, each one adorned in bougainvillea and climbing star jasmine. The place is worn down, but it's peaceful here. I wonder what I'll find inside, though. It is a retirement home, after all. Are the halls filled with the sad cries of elderly nuns wanting to leave their rooms, needing assistance? Sister Monica doesn't seem to need any help. She could take on any of my brothers in an arm-wrestling match.

I leave my car in the back parking lot, where it looks like it's reserved for visitors. There are more cars here than I'd imagined. Somehow, that comforts me. As strict and stern Sister Monica was as a math teacher, I wouldn't like to think of her spending her golden years alone. Or do these cars belong to other guys who screwed up and have to atone for it?

Like me.

I still don't know what she'll have me do. Some kind of

community service task like picking up trash from the side of the road, or cleaning up graffiti? My brain doesn't really function this early in the morning to speculate.

I don't have to wander too much. Sister Monica finds me as I walk up the path.

"I was beginnin' to think ye weren't going ta make it, Maddy boy," she says, smiling bigger than anyone has the right to at this hour. "It's almost seven, don't ye know. We're about to begin."

Begin?

"You… said to get here before seven," I say tentatively. "Am I…"

"Ach, let me look at ye," she says, taking hold of my shoulders. "All grown up. Not that spindly little thing ye were in high school."

"No ma'am. Errr… Sister."

She gives me a look. "Well, get on in here. The good Lord won't wait all morning."

She leads me into the building, down some hallways. The walls are covered in things like bulletin boards, framed photos of nuns, all of them faded, like they were taken in the 70s and 80s and suffered sun exposure.

We turn the corner, past various rooms, although I don't have the *cajones* to look inside any of them. Then the hallway ends, and we go through a door which leads outside to a tiny, shady courtyard. There's a fountain and a few simple folding chairs, like it's a nice place to sit and contemplate your navel, or whatever it is nuns do to pass their free time.

We go across a path into another building. What strikes

me about this place is that it's so quiet. Where are all the people?

Then Sister Monica leads me to a pair of double doors and holds a finger to her lips before opening one. I follow her in, only to discover we've just entered the rear of a chapel. Rows and rows of women, all wearing brown polyester veils, kneel silently in the pews.

Sister Monica winks at me over her shoulder as she leads me down the aisle, to what I assume is her regular spot—only three rows from the front. I can feel the eyeballs of the whole convent on me as I walk past, completely out of place in my faded jeans, Doc Martens, and unruly hair. Thank goodness I decided to wear a long-sleeved Henley today, or the ink on my arms might cause a scandal.

Sister Monica shoos the nuns in our pew to scoot over, making room for me. I crouch down next to her, the kneeler making a creaking noise under my weight that echoes through the room like a firecracker in a library. There's just no way of slipping in quietly at this point.

Mirroring the bowed heads of all the nuns in my row, I dart my eyes around as surreptitiously as possible, wondering what the blazes Sister Monica has me signed up for. Am I supposed to pray my way into her good graces? Is this the kind of thing the nuns do all day? How many hours am I expected to stay here?

Then a door near the altar opens, and a priest in purple vestments steps out, and everyone stands. So... I guess we're here for Tuesday morning Mass?

This, at least, is familiar to me. I know the motions and all the responses. I also know, since there's no music, we'll be outta here in thirty minutes or less.

Once we reach the "peace be with you" portion of the service, greetings are a little awkward. I'm used to handshakes and arm punches from my brothers. But these ladies smile warmly at me with sparkling eyes and rosy cheeks. Most of them are quite elderly and have jolly faces. I'm taller than a lot of them. But there are a few, like Sister Monica, who come from hardy stock. I wonder if they all know what happened on St. Patrick's Day.

I have the answer to that not long after Mass ends and I'm invited for breakfast.

"Are you sure I didn't come too early?" I whisper to Sister Monica. "I feel like I should come back later."

She gives me a wry smile. "Have you had a balanced breakfast yet?"

To be honest, I can't remember the last time I've been awake for breakfast. I usually hobble out of bed around noon and snack on pretzels until my stomach's ready for a burger or something. I have to admit, that bacon smells amazing. There are probably eggs in those warming trays at the buffet table, too.

I shake my head, feeling a rumble begin to sound in my belly. "No, not yet."

"Then it's settled."

I just want to sneak out while no one's looking. Do I even know how to get back to my car from here?

I wonder if Sister Monica came home after the St. Patrick's Day catastrophe to tell the nuns all about it. I can just picture them standing in a circle, singing, *"How do you solve a problem like Mateo?"* all while making plans for my community service job.

Whatever that will be.

As long as I don't have to look after seven children, I think I can handle it. I inwardly scoff at my thoughts. My sister and her musical theatre obsession are rubbing off on me.

All through breakfast, the nuns at our table have a lively discussion about the scripture readings at Mass. When asked my opinion, I do *not* admit I wasn't paying attention.

All this talk of chastisement and punishment to help us *"be more disciplined"* is making my T-shirt collar feel tight. I've screwed up more times in my short life than anyone I know. I deserve whatever punishment I'm here for and then some, and I don't blame my parents for thinking this crazy arrangement is a brilliant idea. When I got off the phone with Sister Monica the other day and explained the plan to my parents, they practically cheered. I'm only surprised they didn't ship me off to a foreign country years ago. After the claw incident.

I still have nightmares about it. My little brother Sebastian, only six years old, scared and alone. Missing for hours and it was all my fault. Because I was selfish. Going on the Zipper with my friends instead of watching out for Sebastian. He still has a fear of small places to this day.

After breakfast, Sister Monica leads me outside to a gravel pathway, weaving between trees and various rose bushes. It's peaceful here, almost like we're not in L.A. anymore, like somehow we've been transported to a garden oasis.

Is this where she will have me work for the day? If I'm being honest, it's not too bad.

"So," she begins after a long stretch of walking in mutual silence. "How have ye been, Maddy? Except for the humiliation of flying off the stage the other night, that is."

If this is her attempt at humor, I don't know if I should feign a laugh or let it bomb. Nobody ever said comedy is in a nun's job description. I settle on a nondescript nod.

"Good, good. Great."

"Great, huh? You didn't seem so great when you left the pub the other night. You seemed rather out of sorts."

"Well, I've had better days. But that's life, right?"

"Yes, true. But something tells me you're not being truthful to yourself."

To myself? Or to her?

"You're not trying to sneak my confession out of me, are you?" I say with my own lame attempt at humor.

She winks and points to the sky. "I'm afraid I don't have clearance for that job, dear."

"Above your pay grade, then?" I joke.

This she does chuckle at.

"That is one way to look at it."

Here we reach a gazebo, small, but big enough for a bench, a kneeler, and one of the fourteen stations of the cross. The crucifixion, I think. Quite fitting.

I remember my brother Memo talking about constructing this as his Eagle Scout project years ago, but I was so young, my parents didn't care to take me to see it. I was only eight at the time. Before I turned into a misfit. The black sheep of the family.

Memo did a good job on the gazebo. Sturdy construction, even if it's now a little worse for wear.

Sister Monica places a hand against one of the pillars and taps it lovingly.

"The sisters were so happy to have this. Now I'm pleased to be able to enjoy it, too, now that I'm here as a resident. You should see it on Good Friday. It's such a sight."

"I'll bet," I say. I run my fingers over the wood. Maybe she'll want me to give it a sand and stain. I'm not much of a handyman, though.

"We were lucky to know such a helpful young man, your brother Guillermo."

She sighs wistfully, like those were the good 'ol days. Both teaching math and having the *one* good Precio brother in her class. After that, she must have been sorely disappointed with the rest of us.

I'm still trying to figure out what I'm doing here. I don't have the Mr. Fix-it talents like my brother, but if I have to, I can try, I guess.

Sister Monica wanders over to the gazebo bench and perches on the edge, patting the seat beside her. "Come. Sit"

I do as I'm told, because one always obeys Sister Monica, no matter who you are. Old habits and all.

"What is it you gave up for Lent?" she asks matter of factly.

I almost say, "Women," but think better of it.

I try to remember something, anything I might have inadvertently given up for Lent without even realizing it. Like chocolates, for instance. But no, that would be a lie. Maybe Netflix? Also no. *Think, think.*

"Ummm," I hedge. "Working on it. I'm making an effort to be nicer to people."

I'm so full of it. I should have just said chocolate. Everybody gives up chocolate.

"That *is* something we all need to do more of," she says, sighing.

After what seems like a full minute, she says, "I gave up chocolate."

"Oooh that's a good one," I say.

"Ha! Sister Ambrose would tell you otherwise."

"Why?"

"Let's just say 'being nicer to people' would have been a better choice for me. You don't want to get between me and my chocolate," she says wryly.

"You can always add that on," I say, hoping that showing kindness would make her ease up on my punishment. Whatever that is. I wish she'd just assign it to me and get this over with.

She seems to consider that for a moment, but then swats her hand down. "Ach, well. I still have my Guinness."

"That's one way of looking at it," I say.

She stands, sucking in a big breath of morning air. There's still traces of dew on the trees, and the spring chill hasn't quite burned off yet.

"I do wish the roses will come back this year. They haven't bloomed the way they used to for a couple years now."

I go over to the bushes in question and examine them.

"Well for starters, they should be pruned more often. It has to be done in the fall or winter."

"Oh but these usually give us a bloom twice a year at least."

I examine them closer. "A few of the branches have dry rot. They can go now. And the weeds are getting out of hand. They're choking any new growth."

"Our groundskeeper Lloyd. He doesn't like going near the thorns. He's been working here for over fifty years, so no one wants to tell him how to do his job."

"Fifty years! Shouldn't he retire soon?"

"Ach, no. He flat out refused. Stubborn old man. I told him he should at least hire some help. Preferably someone born this century."

I walk over to the other bushes, getting a closer look. The alocasia is suffering from yellowing leaves which probably can be fixed with fish fertilizer to balance the PH. Some nitrogen and enzymes in the soil will do the trick.

A few yards away, the sunflower bushes just look sad. The underside of the leaves are covered in a powdery mildew. The fungus infected part of the plant needs a good prune for starters. Then a baking soda treatment or cold-pressed neem oil could help revive it in time for the summer bloom.

The only reason I know these things is because when my parents were deciding on flowers for their garden, I was recruited to do the digging. Mom said getting close to the earth would be good for my soul. Black as it is. Anyway, I ended up going down a Google rabbit hole and now I know more about flowers than I'd like to admit.

If someone doesn't give this garden some TLC, there won't be much left of it come next spring. I can already identify some varieties of flowers that need to be replaced. The Bee Balm won't flourish in this environment. Lavender would be a better choice here. Or shrubby monkey flower to add a pop of color. And that Japanese Iris. Whose idea was that? Everybody knows they suck up too much water.

An herb garden would be nice and hopefully elevate the

cooking in this place. Breakfast was kind of bad. Humming-bird's sage, oregano, basil, and some cilantro would be a good start.

I find myself itching to dig my hands in the dirt.

"I'll do it," I say, turning back to face Sister Monica. "I'm not afraid of a few thorns."

Her face shines with a wide smile. As if all that talk about her blooms wasn't a hint. I'm here to do my community service, and it might as well be pulling weeds. Sure beats fixing that gazebo.

"You will? Really?" She claps her hands in delight.

"Well, yeah." I shrug like it's no biggie. "I could just go home for some gloves and come back…"

"No need. Lloyd has everything you need in the garden shed."

She slips her hand underneath the crook of my arm and leads me down the path. There's a rusty, old aluminum shed in the distance.

"It's not locked," she says.

"Okay then. I guess I'll get right to it."

"That is so good of you, Maddy. You're making good of that Lenten promise, no doubt about that."

"I guess God works in mysterious ways."

"That he does, lad. That he does. Well, I must be off. Those peanut butter and jelly sandwiches aren't going to make themselves."

"Is that what you're having for lunch?"

It would be an improvement on the overcooked bacon and eggs.

"Ach no," she says, swatting her hand through the air. "We're having tacos today. But a few times a week, we make sandwiches for the homeless. The fine folks at Catholic Charities come by to pick them up and pass them out on skid row. It's no gourmet meal, but at least peanut butter won't go bad very quickly."

"I love a good PB&J."

She winks at me. "Me too."

As she walks away, I can hear her mumble, "What was I thinking, giving up chocolate? Never again."

I head over to the garden shed and pry open the creaky door. These hinges could use some WD-40. Better yet, the entire structure could be improved on by some paint thinner and a blowtorch.

I go inside to find an unorderly array of tools, the bigger ones piled in corners. Old coffee cans line the shelves, and on closer inspection, contain things like rusty nails, mismatched bolts and nuts, and other miscellaneous items like paper clips and hooks. There are milk crates filled with crusty rags, other boxes I care not to investigate, and various loppers and shears that have seen better days. The whole shed has the smell of dust, lawn clippings, and something damp and musty.

"What are you doing here?" A scratchy, gurgly voice startles me, and I spin around to see the silhouette of a man in the doorway, beams of morning light and dust particles behind him, casting him in an ominous shadow.

I lift up my arms, because he's brandishing a weapon. Or maybe it's a rake. Either way, he doesn't seem afraid to use it against me.

"Sister Monica said I could find what I need in here. For the gardening?"

The man takes a step inside the shed. The space is as

tiny as it is. There's really no room for two in here. And he's blocking the exit.

"I told them I don't need any help. I've been working these grounds by myself for fifty-five years. Now they're trying to replace me? The hell they will."

This must be Lloyd. Charming.

"No no!" I say. "I'm just doing community service. Pulling weeds around the roses."

He grunts. "The rose bushes have thorns the size of hawk talons."

I want to tell him that's because the bushes haven't been properly pruned, but I won't dare it. Instead, I choose my words wisely.

"Doesn't bother me." My arms are still in the air, but he comes closer and as he gets right in my face, he pulls up a sleeve.

"See that?" He points at a few scabs. "This is from last month. And this one right around Christmas. I get cut, I don't stop bleeding. Damn old age."

"You should probably get that checked out," I say.

He snarls. "It is what it is. My skin doesn't heal like it used to."

"All the more reason to let me help you." I slowly lower my arms and slide up my sleeve, exposing my forearm. "My skin heals just fine."

"You have a lot of tattoos, young man."

I shrug. "I'm an art enthusiast."

That makes him kind of snort which I'll take as a chuckle. Then he curls his fingers around his collar and pulls it down. The faded blue of an eagle tattoo peeks from under his shirt. He gives me a hard look.

"Impressive," I say.

He fixes his collar, hiding the ink once more. "Don't let Mother Superior see your ink."

"Uh, okay." It might be too late for that, but whatever. "I was just looking for work gloves so I can pull the weeds. Then I'll get out of your hair."

What's left of it.

"You won't find any gloves here." He steps out of the shed and points for me to get out. "If you're going to pull the weeds, do it already and stop wasting my time."

I shuffle past him into sweet, sweet freedom, and head back to the rose bushes as fast as I can.

He grumbles behind my back, "Gloves. Ha. Pansy ass millennials." I hear the clunk of his boots stepping back into the shed, and I pick up my speed to put as much distance between us as possible.

I work for a couple of hours uninterrupted. It's surprisingly relaxing, pulling weeds. After I clean around the rose bushes, I find more weeds to deal with around the property.

Alyssum would flourish here, as well as California fuchsia. I could pick some up later this week. Not that I'll be coming back unless I have to.

I don't even notice the time until Sister Monica's shadow approaches me. Her cheeks are rosy and she has a smile on her face. Where was this smile when I was in high school? Then again… math.

"You're still here, Maddy. I thought you'd be long gone by now."

Uh, nobody told me what time I could leave, so…

"There are a lot of weeds," I reply.

"Well then, you can come in for lunch."

Was that a question or a demand?

She wags her brows. "I know you like tacos."

I look down at my dirty hands and the mud on my knees.

"Yeah, I love tacos, but…"

"Ach, we don't mind a little dirt on your dungarees."

My stomach is growling, but I don't think I can handle another meal with fifty nuns today.

"I better get going. But thanks for the offer."

Sister Monica sighs and ticks her head. "Well then, maybe next week."

Next week? How many weeks am I in for?

I nod and clap the dirt from my hands, startled as Sister Monica reaches over and places her palm on my forehead.

"May the sun shine warm upon your face; the rains fall soft upon your fields and until we meet again, may God hold you in the palm of His hand."

Riiiight. Do nuns have sin-reading superpowers? Like how Professor X can read minds? Because I'm not proud of a lot of things, and I'd rather keep them to myself. Like the thoughts I have when I look at Desirée. How I've memorized every tiny freckle on her face, every little laugh line, every inch of her body. Her eyes… so blue, they rival the Taco Bell blue raspberry freeze. She's my obsession. And also off limits.

There's no wonder why Ian asked Dante to look after her instead of me. I can't be trusted.

Sister Monica backs away and I clumsily cross myself, bowing stupidly. "Uh, kyrie eleison."

Kyrie eleison?

Maybe I should have said 'Amen' instead? What's the protocol for a nun blessing? My brother, Memo, usually just socks me in the arm or squirts me with holy water from a spray bottle like I'm a naughty cat.

Sister Monica raises one eyebrow. "Lord have mercy, indeed."

Oh yes. I totally know what kyrie eleison means. I'm just nervous for some reason.

"Yes. Mercy is… what the world needs now. Like love, sweet love."

Somebody stop me.

"So very true."

She smiles. I think I may have passed the test. Which is more than I can say for her math class.

"Well then, Maddy. I'm looking forward to our next meeting. And don't forget to bring your appetite."

"Got it. So… next Tuesday then?" I hedge, trying to get a feel for what her expectations of me are. She blinks, rears her chin back a fraction of an inch, and then her eyebrows rise up in delight.

"Yes. That would be fine. Just fine. I'll have the kitchen angels whip up an extra spicy salsa just for you."

That's what I'm afraid of.

The earth has music
for those who listen.

-William Shakespeare

Chapter Four
DESIRÉE

"How can you even classify Frankenstein in the same category as the Iliad?" cries Mateo in a heated conversation with his sister Francesca.

We're crowded around a long farmhouse table at the Precio house. Their colorful backyard is currently illuminated by hanging market lights as we sit on the patio for dinner—the special family dinner they have every Sunday, which I tried to decline in an effort to stay away from Mateo.

How can I swear off guys when Mateo makes me feel things I don't want to be feeling? This next-door neighbor thing is going to be a major test of my resilience.

But Francesca knocked on my door earlier to tell me if I didn't come, her mom would be offended. Then she dragged me by the arm until I agreed. Now I'm sitting between her and Mateo and caught in the crossfire.

"Homer influenced Virgil who influenced Dante, who influenced Melton, who is *referenced* by Mary Shelley," replies Francesca smugly.

"Just because there are references doesn't automatically qualify it on the same level," answers Mateo, huffing. "Next you're going to tell me Gilmore Girls is like Shakespeare because the teenagers act out a scene from Romeo and Juliet."

Francesca points her fork at Mateo across my face. "Don't you hate on my Gilmore Girls."

"How do you know about the Romeo and Juliet scene?" I tease Mateo.

"I've seen a few episodes." He shrugs. "So what?"

I try to hide a smirk. "Nothing."

I sink my teeth into my taco and almost die from delight, fluttering my eyes shut. It's that good.

"What's wrong?" asks Mateo, alarmed. "Is it bad?"

Oops. I might have been crossing my eyes.

Mateo's gloriously bronzed face is so close, I might have to close them again. "Uh, I was just having a romantic moment with this chicken."

His pupils flicker, and I swear he sweeps his gaze over me appreciatively. Then he licks his lips.

Licks. His. Lips.

Lord help me.

"Don't let Nacho hear you say that," he says.

"Don't let Nacho hear her say what?" barks Dante.

My face gets hot, and it's not from the salsa. But Dante's booming voice is so loud and dramatic, it gets the attention of the whole table, which until now, was rumbling with several conversations at once. Half of them in Spanish which I tuned out. Now all eyes and ears are directed at me and Mateo.

Ignacio, or Nacho as his brothers call him, stops what he's doing and glares at Mateo.

"Okay, Matt. Just say it."

He leans back confidently in his chair and twirls at an impressive handlebar mustache. "Jealous of the 'stache?"

Mateo snorts. "Yeah. If I wanted to join a barbershop quartet."

Ignacio's wife, Olive, grins up at her husband. "I like it."

"Olive's opinion is the only one that matters," says Mrs. Precio. "She's the one who has to kiss his furry face."

Nacho protests, "Dante has more hair on his face than me."

"But nobody has to kiss Dante," replies Mrs. Precio.

"Who would want to?" says another brother, snickering. His name is Nigel or Neil… I don't know him as well as the other Precio siblings.

"Shut up, Nate," says Dante.

Nate. His name is Nate. All I know is he's the one who surfs.

"Language." Mr. Precio shoots Dante a warning glare.

"Yeah, mind your tongue," says the oldest brother, teasing. I don't know him well either, but I know he's a priest. He leans under the table and brings out a water bottle, squirting a thin stream directly at Dante, chanting, *"Princeps gloriosissime caelestis militiae, sancte Michael Archangele, defende nos in proelio…"*

"Moooom!" cries Dante. "Memo got me in the eye."

"Guillermo!" scolds Mrs. Precio. "No holy water at the table."

Mateo's cracking up next to me.

Guillermo (or Memo, as they call him) sends Dante a little grin and hides the squirt bottle back under the table.

"Hey, Mat-feo." Their other brother, Enrique, calls to Mateo. "Tell us what you were saying about Nacho."

Mat-feo?

"Language," warns Mr. Precio. Guillermo looks like he's about to reach under the table for his squirt bottle again, but his mom gives him a stern look.

"I wasn't saying anything about Nacho," says Mateo, defensively. "Eat your beans."

"It was me," I say. "I was just telling him how good the food is."

"And I told her to keep it to herself so my fancy chef brother doesn't get a big head," adds Mateo.

"I, for one, love this dish," says Edmund. He's Francesca's fiancé, and he's trying so hard to fit in with the brothers. I find it endearing.

Mateo leans over to whisper in my ear. "Still sucking up, this guy."

"He's her fiancé," I whisper back. "Be nice."

"He's only her fiancé if he comes from the Fiancé region of France. Otherwise, he's just her sparkling boyfriend."

If Mateo wasn't being such a turd about poor Edmund, the soft flutter of his breath on my neck would send my lady parts on high alert. Where's that squirt bottle of holy water when I need it?

I jerk away enough to give Mateo a hard look while I say to Edmund, "You and me both, Edmund."

I take a dramatic bite. "Mmmm. Yum."

Maybe I should tone it down a few notches.

"What is that in there?" asks Mr. Precio. "Soya sauce?"

"Hoisin," says Ignacio.

A dismissive snort comes from the other end of the table.

It's that man who answered the door the other day. Pancho Two. The criminal. Mateo purposefully sat us as far away from him as possible when we came out for dinner.

"Taco meat should not be seasoned with soya sauce, *chamaco*," says the criminal guy.

One of Mateo's uncles grunts in agreement, even as he takes another bite.

Ignacio grits his teeth. "It's hoisin."

"Did you use the same marinade on my tofu?" asks Francesca.

Ignacio grumbles something under his breath.

"He says he did, but dusted the tofu with cornstarch first," says Olive.

"How is it you can translate for him when all he does is mumble?" asks Francesca.

Olive shrugs. "It's love."

"He doesn't deserve you," says Francesca.

"*Se falta chipotle,*" says the uncle with his mouth full.

"Chipotle would ruin it, Tío," shouts Ignacio from his side of the table. The uncle doesn't hear him, already engaged in a new conversation with Mr. Precio, the criminal guy, and Mateo's aunt Lucy, who keeps rolling her eyes at her sister's brother-in-law. I don't understand what they're saying, but the uncle keeps flapping his arms.

"So you never told me how it went at the nunnery," I say, trying to change the subject.

"Now who's referencing Shakespeare?" he says. "Get thee to a nunnery."

"Very funny, Hamlet, you know what I meant."

"It went so well, he has to go back next week to ring the bell tower," teases Enrique, curling his shoulder and distorting his face like the Hunchback of Notre Dame.

"Do that again so I can take a picture for your wife," says Mateo, pretending to take out his phone.

"No phones at the table," barks Mrs. Precio from across the long table.

"Where is January anyway?" asks Nate. "Sick of you already?"

"She's doing work for PETA," growls Enrique. "She'll be home in a few days—and misses me like crazy. You wouldn't understand."

"I'm free as the waves, dude. Just me and my board."

"Don't get so cocky about that, Nate," says Francesca. "One day… you'll see."

"So?" I continue. "Are you or aren't you ringing the bell tower next week?"

"There is no bell tower," Mateo says. "Sister Monica had

me do some yard work, that's all. Thought I might bring some fertilizer next Tuesday, maybe."

"How is Sister Monica?" asks Memo?

Dante chuckles. "Did she tell you to watch her holy hand?"

Enrique and Nate bust up laughing. Mateo just shakes his head. Soon, the laughter is contagious and Ignacio's cracking up so much, his face turns red. Even Francesca finds this amusing.

"What's so funny?" I ask the table.

"It's just something Sister Monica would say in her math class," says Mateo.

Dante holds back his laughter to give me an explanation. "Whenever she'd write out an equation on the chalkboard, she'd hold up the chalk and say—"

"Watch me holy hand," Ignacio supplies in an Irish accent. This busts everyone up again.

"She'd say that every time?" I ask.

Nate nods, tears streaming down his face. "Yep."

"You should ask her if she uses the same holy hand to wipe," chirps Mrs. Precio. Her cheeks are flushed from the wine.

"Mother!" warns Guillermo.

"Don't you dare think about squirting me, young man."

A grin splits across Mateo's face. I don't know the last time I've seen him smile.

"When are you going back, Mateo?" asks Francesca.

"I already said Tuesday."

"Every Tuesday?"

He shrugs. "I guess."

"How long are you in for?" Nate jokes.

Eyes shift over to that Pancho Two guy with the ankle bracelet like he'd be offended by a jail joke. He's not even paying attention to the conversation on this side of the table.

"So then what are you doing tomorrow?" asks Mrs. Precio.

Mateo sighs. "I don't have plans. Why?"

"Just wondering if you were going to look for a job?"

And there goes that smile. Gone like dust in the wind.

"I did that yesterday."

"Oh good. You got that out of the way. Now you can relax."

Mateo's shoulders slump. "You know what I mean. I'm waiting for some calls, that's all."

"Okay," she says, holding up her hands. "Just worried about you. It's my job."

I lean into Mateo and whisper, "What's going on? Are you okay?"

I thought he had some kind of trust fund. I know it's not any of my business. I just thought he was doing well—the way he blows cash like there's a hurricane in his wallet.

Whenever we'd go out to dinner or drinks with the band, it was always his treat. And he's the one who paid for the rehearsal space every week once we stopped rehearsing in his garage. He seems to have a new guitar every time I see him, and he's always dressed in expensive jeans or the newest designer sneakers. He may be a bad boy, but he's a rich daddy bad boy. But maybe I was wrong about it all.

He gives me a tiny shake of the head. "I'll tell you later."

"You're still going to play for my wedding, aren't you?" says Francesca. "That counts as a job."

"I wouldn't exactly call playing for Uncle Borris' cumbia band every once in a while a steady job," says Mateo. "But yes. I will play for your wedding, Panchita."

This family and their nicknames. Even I have one, apparently. But Mateo is the only one to use it. Paloma. I looked it up once because when I asked him what it meant, he only smirked in his lopsided way. According to Google, Paloma means dove—which is my favorite chocolate, incidentally. But it also means pigeon—which is... well, just a bird I guess.

I study his profile while he takes a sip of his water. The gentle slope of his forehead, the straight, perfect nose that could be sculpted out of marble, the masculine architecture of his jawline.

He catches me staring and hits me with a look that could melt my unmentionables. He punctuates it by biting his bottom lip as he rakes his eyes over me. I dart my eyes around, all agitated and squirmy, hoping his family doesn't notice. Lucky for me, nobody's paying him any attention.

"Hi there," he says with a rumble in his voice so deliciously gravelly, my ears are raw with fresh friction burn. Then he returns to his meal, casually taking a bite from his taco like he didn't just turn my insides to pudding.

"I still don't understand why you're getting married during Lent," says Guillermo.

"It's the only time Sebastian can get away from school," replies Francesca.

Guillermo huffs.

"You're going to officiate, right?" Francesca glares at Guillermo like he better say yes or she'll stab him with a fork. "Because I'm not going to wait for summer."

"Yes, of course, Panchita. First Corinthians seven nine says if they can't control themselves, they should go ahead and marry. It's better to marry than to burn with passion."

Edmund chokes on his drink and starts coughing. Dante slaps him on the back, and not very gently.

"Down the wrong pipe, Mr. Ed?"

Edmund nods and chokes out, "I'm fine."

Francesca throws a corn tortilla at Guillermo.

"I have an idea!" blurts Mrs. Precio. "You can go work for Dante. He's always complaining about how much work there is. You'd be a big help there."

Dante's head jerks up. "What now?"

"He can go work for you," she says cheerily. "You have a job for your brother, don't you?"

"Well, actually..."

"I think you need a special license to drive a tow truck," says Mateo.

"You can answer phones or something," says his mother. "Right Dante?"

Dante scratches his forehead, hiding his face behind those oversized hands of his.

"I don't want a handout," says Mateo. "I can make my own way."

"It's not a handout. Dante, tell him it's not a handout."

I can see sweat form on Dante's forehead.

"I have an announcement," Dante says, slamming his back against his chair with a resigned flop. All eyes and ears are trained on him like he just dropped a bomb. "I sold the towing company."

Silence falls over the whole table, even the conversation in Spanish (which I admittedly tuned out) has come to a screeching halt. For some reason, this seems to irk Mateo more than anyone.

His Dad is the first one to speak up, and he simply says, "Why?" with a small note of displeasure.

"Because it's draining me, Dad. I never get a break. Not to mention the dangerous neighborhoods we go into in the middle of the night. I was seriously considering applying for a permit to carry a firearm. Then I thought. What the heck am I doing with my life? I just can't do it anymore."

"Great," says Mateo. "Now you get to go job hunting too."

"I'm not going job hunting," says Dante.

Mateo laughs. "Oh you have to, brother. Just like I do. That was the agreement."

"Well I have something else in mind."

Mateo throws his fork down and looks around the table at his brothers. "Do you guys hear this? Unbelievable."

"Just hear him out," says Ignacio. "Dante, when did this all happen?"

"Why didn't you tell us sooner?" asks his mom.

"Because he didn't want to," says Mateo.

"Because it's still in the works," Dante growls at Mateo. "Elvis is paying installments. I'll be helping him transition as long as I can."

"As long as you can?" asks Mrs. Precio. "Why? Are you going somewhere? Is there something wrong?"

"Nothing's wrong, and I'm not going anywhere. I just… I want to make a difference. Help people. So I enrolled in an EMT training program."

"EMT. What is that?" asks his dad.

"They're first responders," Nate replies. "Like when the

ambulance came to help you that one time you thought you were having a heart attack."

"But it was just bad gas," adds Enrique.

"You guys will never let him live that down, will you?" says Olive. Then she looks at me like she's confiding something. "I wasn't even around back then but I've heard this story a hundred times."

"They were nice young men," says Mrs. Precio dreamily.

"So you won't be working while you go through training?" asks Ignacio. "What's the timeframe?"

"It could be up to a year," answers Dante. "I don't know. And then it might take a while to get hired, even after I get my certification. It's a long process."

Mateo's voice cracks. "Does anybody see the double standard here except me?"

"Matt, why can't you just be happy for him?" asks Francesca.

"Happy for him? I quit my job, it's the Spanish Inquisition. Dante quits his job and suddenly he's a saint."

"Don't be so dramatic," says Dante.

"Forget it." Mateo pushes himself from the table, scraping his chair on the floor with a screech and storms inside the house.

I expect someone to run after him, but after about three seconds, it's all business as usual at the dinner table.

Nate breaks the silence by clearing his throat, and leaning back in his chair as he says, "What's for dessert?"

When I was a little boy,
I told my dad,
'When I grow up,
I want to be a musician.'
My dad said:
'You can't do both, Son'.

−Chet Atkins

Chapter Five

MATEO

There's a soft knock on my bedroom door. At first, I think it's Francesca. My brothers don't knock, they pound. My dad doesn't even bother knocking at all. He just bursts in.

But this knock is different. And when Desirée's sweet voice calls my name, my anger dissolves like sugar in hot tea.

"Come in."

She quietly walks in and hovers around my vinyl collection, running her fingers over the cardboard sleeves, every once in a while, taking one out and feeling the weight of it in her hands.

After a few minutes, she sits on my bed. Not saying anything. Not judging. We sit side by side for a long while, and I can't thank her enough for it.

Finally, I ask, "How did you know where my room was?"

"I followed the smell of big dreams and unresolved teenage angst."

I chuckle. "Do you think I overreacted back there?"

"Not if you truly want to be taken seriously as a rock star. Rock stars are supposed to throw fits. It's expected."

"Yeah well. I doubt that will ever happen."

"Why do you say that? Of course it will happen."

She nudges me with her shoulder. It's just a friendly gesture, pure and harmless. But she's on my bed and she smells amazing. Her scent—so uniquely her. Honey and nougat, like a Snickers bar.

I turn my head to look right in her eyes. "They're only crazy dreams," I say, feeling a pang of loss, like someone ripped my hopes right out of my soul. "I'm a fool."

"The world needs fools who dream. Especially the crazy ones. Otherwise, where would we all be?" She takes a deep breath and starts singing The Rainbow Connection acapella.

She sings the whole damn song, and I couldn't be more mesmerized. Her voice is like velvet covered in chocolate. Rich and sweet with an earthy texture. She's the most perfect woman I've ever met. And the way the words and notes fall from her mouth, like the lyrics are tethering her to the stars and she might fly away any moment. She *should* fly away. Far away from me.

The last note rings in the air and she glances at me sidelong with the cutest grin. She lives in a musical, this woman, a place where bursting into song is no big deal.

"Feel better?"

"Oddly… yes."

That makes her grin spread wider, but there's a question in her eyes, and I hate that it's laced with pity.

"I know this is probably none of my business, but if you want to talk about what happened down there at dinner, I'm all ears."

"It's just my family. Nobody trusts me and it seems like they make up rules just for me."

"Why do you think they don't trust you?"

"I did something a long time ago. Something bad. I don't blame them for the way they feel. But that doesn't stop the way it stings, you know?"

"I'm sorry. But I do think maybe… your parents and siblings don't have it in for you quite as much as you might think."

"Okay, I'll tell you something. But you need to promise this is just between you and me."

She crosses her heart.

"My dad opened eight restaurants. One for each of us kids."

She nods, already knowing some of our history.

"Not too long ago, he decided to retire, and wanted each of us to take over for him. But I knew if I were in charge of a restaurant, that place would go out of business in a month.

And really, Ignacio is the only one who's qualified to run a successful restaurant."

"I kind of gathered that," she says.

"So we made a deal. Ignacio offered to buy us all out by paying a monthly stipend. But here's the clincher. They came up with a rule—that we had to hold steady jobs in order to access our money. This was so obviously directed at me."

"Okay, I'm with you on this. But why would they single you out?"

"Because my dad doesn't think music is a serious career."

"Isn't Francesca a musician?"

"She conducts the children's choir at church. And then there's Sebastian. He's in college and has to wait until he graduates. The rules are clear. No job, no stipend. Now Dante thinks the rules don't apply to him. Probably because they don't."

"So now that you don't have a regular gig anymore…"

"I'm flat broke. Back when we made the arrangement, I agreed to only take home half of what my siblings were, and put the rest in a CD fund. I wasn't worried about my expenses because I had something to fall back on. But now…"

"You don't have anything saved?"

"Some. But it's dwindling fast."

She squints at me. "Mateo, do you mind if I ask you a personal question?"

"All the previous questions weren't personal?"

"Well, I just don't want to upset you."

"Ask away. You can't upset me more than Dante does."

"You won't get mad?"

"I promise."

"Okay. Here goes." She squints, crinkling her nose like she's preparing for a blow to the face. "Are you... a shopaholic?"

"A whaaaat?"

"You promised you wouldn't get mad."

I suck in a breath. "Okay, okay. I'm not mad. And I'm not a shopaholic."

"Mateo, how much do you spend on guitars and rare collectable records and eating out?"

"I'm not a shopaholic."

"All right. I believe you."

"Good. And don't look in my closet. You might get buried under the avalanche of gold watches."

She curls her lips into a smile and flops backwards onto my bed, staring at the ceiling. I lie back, joining her shoulder to shoulder. The beginnings of a spring rainfall patter on my window and we stay in place, listening to the symphony of it.

"Do you ever just listen to the rain?" I ask. "It's music, you know. Like a drum."

She turns her head to face me and floods me with the most natural, artless smile.

"Like a piano," she says softly.

A pleasant warmth unfurls in my stomach and it hits me how all I'd need to do is lean in a few inches and we'd be kissing. Her hand barely brushes against mine as we lie on our backs, staring into each other's eyes. Somehow, this seems more intimate than a kiss ever could. I can see right into her soul. It's beautiful.

After a minute she starts laughing, giggling into the air, light and free.

"What are you laughing at?" I ask. I can't help but smile.

"I was just thinking how wet the tacos are getting."

That is a funny thought. I can just picture everyone scurrying to clear the table, rushing to bring the food inside the house.

"My large and obnoxiously loud family is coming inside the house, and soon we won't be able to hear ourselves think."

"You wanna come over to my house? You can pick up your guitar finally. Not that you need another one in here."

"I don't have a lot of guitars in here," I say.

"I counted ten."

"You should see the garage."

I use this as an excuse to wrap my hand around hers to lead her out of my room and down the stairs the back way to avoid my family.

We get a little wet as we run to her house, but it's not coming down very hard and it feels refreshing. Like a new start. Everything feels new with her.

She takes me inside her front door (which she kept unlocked to my chagrin), and I realize I haven't been inside her house in years.

"Your guitar is right through here," she says, leading me down the hall. We go into a room which I remember as Ian's room, but now it's fitted up as a killer recording studio. Black and white soundproofing foam covers the walls in a checkered pattern, a state-of-the-art audio interface, professional microphones, studio monitors, and almost every instrument you can imagine.

I whistle as I take it all in. "And you're calling *me* a shopaholic."

"I've saved up for years for this," she says. "And I only get what I need."

"How did I not know about this?"

She shrugs. "It's my happy place. Kind of like a secret garden. Corny, I know."

"Yeah. Corny but cool. Really cool." I run my fingers over the sound board. "You must do a lot of recording to have a setup like this."

"Yeah, I've recorded a few songs."

"Oh yeah? Anything I'd know?"

"Just some stuff I wrote. No big deal."

"Awww. I'm sure it's great. Can I hear?"

"You want to hear one of my songs?"

"Of course. I love your voice."

Her cheeks pinken.

"Well, there is this one piece I'm a little proud of. I used your guitar to fill in with some licks. I hope you don't mind."

I blink at her. "Fill in with some licks? I didn't know you played. I mean, I guess it's not much of a stretch from the mandolin."

Desirée used to play mandolin in The High C's. Then Corbin joined, almost squeezing Desirée out of the band. Until she surprised us all by bringing her violin one day. Now she tells me she knows how to play licks on guitar?

"It's not finished," she says, turning on the computer and setting up the sound system. "I was going to lay another track of guitar. Is it okay if I strum along? I like the sound of your Taylor better than my Yamaha."

She seems to know her stuff. My Taylor is a handcrafted builder's edition and plays like a dream.

"I can't wait to hear it," I say.

She plugs in my guitar, sets herself up with the track she's been working on, and smiles shyly.

"It's a work in progress. Don't judge me too harshly."

"Never in a million years."

She clicks on the dashboard to play the track, hands poised on the guitar to accompany what she'd already recorded.

I don't exactly know what I was expecting, really. I suppose something acoustic with simple vocals. But what I hear is something so complex and sweepingly majestic, I hardly have words for it. It's a waltz, but not in the traditional sense. Just the time signature and the flow of it. The music is fluid, buoyant, like we're on a ship in the middle of the ocean, and the waves are dancing. I'm transported to another dimension, this powerful rush leaving me feeling lightheaded. The vibrations of the music rise up my spine, leaving goosebumps in their wake.

Desirée closes her eyes and sings along to her own voice, layering in another harmony. There's a tiny smile on her sweet lips. This is her happy place. She's so beautiful, completely in her element. And my heart cracks a little, knowing I'll never be good enough for her. No. I'd be outright bad for her. I'd ruin her.

Then, like an explosion into the clouds, the time signature changes to 5/8, building into intense and desperate pressure and my insides turn to honey. The cacophony of rhythms, the marriage of opposing genres, the sweeping strings mixed with techno beats and folky guitar—it shouldn't make sense. But it does. It's everything a song should be and more. My entire body is wound up, my chest tightens, and yet I've never felt more mystically at ease.

I'm sinking into a warm bath—no—I *am* the warm bath until the music subsides and I melt into weightlessness.

I stand in stunned silence, even after the song ends and Desirée blinks at me in her bashful way.

"You didn't like it," she says after a long stretch of time.

She clicks off the mixing board with her shoulders slumped.

"No!" I force myself out of the stupor I'm in. "I love it. It's… wow. Are you in another band I don't know about?"

"No. It's just me."

Just her. She did everything?

"You're telling me… all the instruments on this recording are played by you?

She shrugs. "Yeah. So?"

"And you wrote this song?"

She shrugs again. Her bluer than blue eyes darting around the room, like she's uncomfortable with the questioning.

"I had no idea you played so many instruments."

"It's really no big deal. I taught myself when I was four."

"When you were four? Even the cello?"

She snorts. "Not the cello. Just piano. And violin. The cello and other instruments came later. Once you learn one instrument it's easy to learn another." She gestures at me. "*You* know that."

"No, I don't know that. I can play guitar. Maybe a little bass. That's it."

"That just means you've spent time mastering it. Instead of fooling around with so many. Like me."

"Sounds to me like you've mastered quite a few."

She shrugs the guitar off her shoulder and presses it to her chest with her eyes fixed on the floor. How had I not known this about her? She's a freaking virtuoso.

"I don't get it," I say. "You could be playing at concert halls. You could have gone to Juilliard. Or anywhere you wanted."

"That's ridiculous. I've never taken any lessons. It's just a hobby."

"But you're good. You're really really good." I swipe the sheet music off the stand, waving it between us. "This. This is a major composition. You're like… Mozart."

"Don't be silly."

"I'm serious. You're self-taught. When you were four. There's a word for that. What's that called?"

"Bored." She takes back the sheet music and gingerly places it back on the stand, running a hand to smooth it over. "It's called being a bored kid."

I snap my fingers. "Prodigy. You were a child prodigy."

She snorts. "Pah-leeze."

"Surely your parents could see it. Why didn't they give you lessons? Send you to some prestigious school?" I know they could afford it.

"My parents are not really into the arts. It's hard to explain."

"Try me."

"You have a very artistic family. Your sister. You. Even your brother's cooking is like an art. You wouldn't understand why my parents are the way they are. I mean, they bought some of my earlier instruments after I begged and pleaded for nothing else for birthdays and Christmas. Mostly just to humor me, I guess. But they'd never support the idea of music as a career."

"I understand more than you know."

"It's different for you. Your parents want you to pursue your dreams."

I scoff. "They have a funny way of showing it."

"I'm serious. They're cool."

"Cool? Did you not hear me when I said they cut me off?"

"They're just upset you quit the band. You said yourself they'll give you access to your trust fund when you get another job."

I don't want to talk about that at all.

"Job," I say a little salty.

"I think they're prouder of you than you realize. They go to your concerts. And you're so talented, it's crazy."

"So are you. More than I am."

She looks at me with those insanely blue eyes. So big and innocent, like she's seeing everything for the first time and is just now taking it all in. Always so wide open.

"Look, I know my music isn't for everyone, and I'm okay with it. Nobody wants to hear some weird genre bending wackadoodle music. It's super niche and to be honest, not really that good."

"Says who?"

"My parents, for one."

"Not me. I'd never say that. You have more talent in your pinky finger than most people have in their entire body. And that song that you just played... it's beyond good. It's phenomenal."

I can't believe the way her parents just ignore the genius she has. It makes me irrationally angry. Any bozo can tell she has insane talent. What kind of parent holds their child back like that? Desirée's talent comes once in a hundred years. She could be one of the greats and the world would never know.

It makes me feel like an ass. Here I am feeling sorry for myself, feeling pissed off at my former band mates when this woman is better than all of us put together.

"Have you played this for Corbin or any of the guys yet?"

"No. You're the only one. I'd never play it for anyone but you."

I'm the only one. My chest swells with pride to hear that. Even though it's not right to keep her to myself.

"You need an agent. Or at least put it up on Spotify."

She shakes her head vehemently. "No. No way."

"Why not?"

"Matt, I don't have big dreams like you. I'm just fooling around. Experimenting."

"What did people do to you to make you feel like you're not a frickin' genius? You had dreams once. You wear them all over your face when you sing and then stuff them down when you think someone's looking. Whoever stole that from you doesn't deserve you."

"Well... I don't know about that." She hitches one shoulder and twitches her brow. "I write songs for me and I think I'm a big enough audience."

She's wrong. But I know I can't convince her how brilliant she is in one night. I give her a resigned smile.

"Okay. At least you have the High C's. Just do me a favor. Don't tell them I moved back into my parent's house."

Desiree blinks at me. "I don't plan on seeing those guys any time soon."

"Why not? What about Wednesday night practice?"

When we outgrew my garage, or rather when my dad complained too much, we found a practice space with a Wednesday night available. The walls are supposed to be soundproof, but you can hear the muffled sounds of drums and electric guitars in the next room. It was the only place we could afford—we just ignored the sticky stains on the carpet and couches.

Desiree does that thing, looking up and to the left. Those bluer than blue eyes her tell—how she'd rather not answer my question.

"Desi. What about Wednesday night practice?"

"I… quit the band."

"You *whaaaat*?"

"I didn't care for the way they treated you. And why would I want to play without you?"

"So you just quit? Because of me?"

She shrugs. "Pretty much. Yeah."

My hands reflexively go to my scalp and pull at the roots of my hair. I'm pacing in this little room. Two steps. Spin. Two steps. Pivot.

"No."

"No?"

"No! You don't just quit a band because I quit a band."

"It's already done."

"Well you shouldn't have done it." I stop pacing and wave around the room at all the instruments. "You are a musician. Musicians need to play for people. That band might not be the best in the world, but it's better than hiding your talent from the whole world."

A terrible thought claims the front of my mind. "Did something happen? What did those guys do to you? I swear I'll rearrange Corbin's face."

"Nothing happened. Sheesh. Why does your brain go there first? I quit because I wanted to quit. In solidarity with you. For you."

"In solidarity? For me?"

She hitches one shoulder. "Yeah."

There has to be something more she's not telling me. She should be performing. Not standing up for me. Lord knows I don't deserve it.

"I don't need your pity quit," I say, almost snarling, though more at myself than her.

"It's not a pity quit," she says, taken aback. "It's a stick-it-to-the-man quit."

"You want to stick it to a man? Then get your music out there. Show the world how good you are." I growl through my teeth. The thought of Desiree sticking it to any man makes my head explode like in those cartoons. Smoke's coming out of my ears.

I step into her space, toe to toe, hovering so close, I can feel the soft heat of her. I take hold of her hand where she holds the neck of my guitar, wrapping my fingers around hers. Firm. Grabbing my instrument without letting her let go. I like the feel of her hand on it—her fingers all over my fretboard. I want to take possession of them and never let go. I'm all up in her face now, breathing heavily from the anger I hold against the band, her parents, and anyone else who shot down her self-esteem along the way.

And then there's the buzz I feel when I'm around her. Particularly this close to her, our noses almost touching. Those eyes of hers widen just so. The whites allowing more room for the perfectly blue circles to sparkle. Doesn't she know what that does to me? And the way her pretty little lips part. A touch of natural pink forming a small O. So kissable. So deliciously kissable.

My fingers tighten around hers and the scrape of her palm against the strings causes a dull chord to ring. She sucks in a little breath, dipping her eyes down to where our bodies almost touch, snagging them briefly at my lips.

I want her.

It comes to me how very much alone we are in this house. Her brother is off somewhere doing Navy things. My family is probably having dessert in the living room, my uncle passed out on the couch. No one will bother us if I just give in and take her lips right now. It would only take one inch until we're pressed against each other. One tiny inch. Yet it might as well be a mile. She might be my next-door neighbor, but we're worlds apart. She is of the heavens and I'm leather and dirt. What would it cost to take a slice of her? To own her lips—her body—for only a little while? For tonight. How amazing I'd feel for the first time in forever. To get lost in her softness, to bury my face in her hair. Those long, dark waves keeping the light out so I could just forget, just for a while, how messed up I am. She could save me—for one night.

But I'd hate myself even more tomorrow. Just the thought of it makes me sick. She's an angel. I don't deserve an angel. Especially when she quits the band for a devil like me.

For one brief second, I dip my head down, hovering my lips over hers. Her eyes flutter shut.

With the breath we're sharing, I say through the burn in my chest, "I don't want you to fight my battles, Paloma. You'll soil your pretty wings."

Her eyes flash open, and the hurt I see in them is like a hundred knives in my chest. She doesn't need to know I put them there myself. It's the only way I can think of to keep me from pinning her against a wall.

"What's that supposed to mean?" she asks. Her hand tugs slightly on the guitar neck, but I'm stronger and I hold it there between us as a promise. What kind of promise, I don't know. For now, it's all I can do to not throw it to the ground so I can use this hand to pull her against me. With each passing moment I find it harder and harder to come up with a reason why I shouldn't. As I mentioned before— we're so very much alone. Dangerously so.

Music is indeed the mediator
between the spiritual
and the sensual life.

-Ludwig van Beethoven

Chapter Six
DESIRÉE

Mateo's strong, capable hand swallows mine around the neck of the guitar. But it's the magnetism of him that holds me in place. He's a live wire, all zingy and electric. I could plug into him to power my whole recording studio.

People like Mateo spark with creative energy. He's wild and unpredictable, so alive with his music it just oozes through his pores. It's no wonder women flock to him after the shows. His very sweat is like a song. Each drop a note hanging in the ether. I don't know if all those groupies hear the crunchy, grungy chords that seem to follow in his wake whenever he enters a room. But I do. He is rock and roll. He is twisted metal. He is a Prince solo riff gone crazy.

But he's a bad decision waiting to happen. And right now, I don't even care.

My palm is hot on the fretboard. The heat of him surrounds me. I can hardly breathe. So close. His mouth is so, so close to mine. I can smell the wine from dinner on his breath. Mixed with his regular scent of clean shampoo and leather, it's a cocktail of lady killer perfume to my brain.

The tungsten rings on his fingers press hard against my knuckles, a stark reminder of the fire I'm playing with here. I know he'll break my heart. Love me and leave me, just like all the others. Now I'm beginning to understand those people who jump off of cliffs in flying squirrel suits. For the thrill of it. This flutter low in my belly—it's an adrenaline rush. And my survival instincts flew off that cliff ahead of me.

Screw it. I'm jumping over.

"I don't want you to fight my battles, Paloma," he says, with a hot breath against my skin. "You'll soil your pretty wings."

Soil my pretty wings? Can he read my thoughts about the squirrel suit thing?

"What's that supposed to mean?" I ask.

He takes a moment to answer. For a split second, I swear his lips get closer to mine and I think he might just kiss me after all. But then he ruins the moment.

"It means… live your own life. And stay out of mine."

Crack. That's the sound of my heart breaking a tiny bit more. There's a chip in it the size of a grain of rice from that time I realized Mateo only saw me as his friend's punky kid sister. Okay, I was eight years old, but still. Ever since then, a hairline crack has grown out of that tiny chip—kind of like windshield glass. It's only a matter of time before the whole thing shatters.

He remains for another moment, face as hard as stone, but with something more in his eyes. As his lips hover over mine, I can sense one of those angry kisses coming on. You know, the kind you see in movies right after the main characters fight. And for a second, I think I could get into that. But then my brain switches back on.

"I think you need to leave now," I say as calmly as possible. His Adam's apple bobs as he swallows hard. And just like that, he nods, lets go of my hand, and leaves. I don't even bother telling him he's left his guitar behind. Again.

Maybe I'll just keep it indefinitely.

I speed walk over to the window in time to see Mateo storm into his house. Once I can no longer see him, I lock the front door, go back into my studio, and angrily play "Magic Man" by Heart until my throat is too sore from belting.

All the good music
has already been written
by people with wigs and stuff.

-Frank Zappa

Chapter Seven
DESIRÉE

Avoiding Mateo Precio was a lot easier when he lived across town. But ever since he's been back in his parent's house, I see him every single day. Okay, so I peek out my window when I hear the rumble of his car. Or the sound of his voice. Or any noise, really.

I'm pathetic that way. Just because he's a brat, doesn't mean he's not a hot brat. For the last few days, I've spotted him leaving in a suit and tie. He looks super uncomfortable with his hair bound back and the collar buttoned all the way up his neck.

On Tuesdays, he leaves at six thirty, which is definitely not in character. On those days, he wears beat up Dickies and a long-sleeved T-shirt. When he comes back, he's covered in dirt and glowing with sweat. Not that I notice the way wisps of hair cling to his neck and face, or how his broad shoulders slump from exhaustion. I wonder what kind of work he's doing at that convent.

Nope. Not my business. And as he made it ridiculously clear, I'm to stay out of it. And I shall. Just until he leaves the house again.

The Precio house has been a hotbed of activity in preparation for Francesca's wedding. Every now and then I see men unloading stage equipment, tables, chairs, and other rental supplies. Before I leave for work, I wander over to ask if there's anything I can do, but I don't find Mr. or Mrs. Precio. Instead, Francesca is there, sitting on a homemade swing that hangs from a tree. She seems pretty chill for a girl about to get married. When she sees me approach, she smiles brightly.

"Wow!" I say. "This is a lot of stuff in your backyard."

"Is it too much?" she asks. "Sorry to be the obnoxious neighbor."

"Not at all. And thank you for inviting me."

Now I wish I had made more of an effort to get to know Francesca over the years. I was more of an introvert while she seemed so cool. Now that she's getting married and moving out, I feel the loss more acutely. Life is weird like that. Or at least I am.

She sighs, glancing over the yard wistfully. Maybe she's feeling nostalgic, now that she's leaving.

"Do you want some limeade?" she offers, getting up from the swing. She ambles over to the patio bar, where there's a pitcher and glasses on a tray. It's like she was ready for a visit as if we're living in the South in the eighteen hundreds and there's nothing for women to do but wait on callers.

"It's organic and fresh squeezed. I used limes from our tree."

She pours me a glass and I thank her. I'm not one to turn down anything made by the Precio family. They seem to have magical culinary powers.

When I take a sip, my tastebuds explode. It's the perfect mixture of sweet and tangy.

"This is amazing," I say. "Where do you find the time to squeeze limes and make wonder potions while planning a wedding?"

She grins, showcasing her adorable dimples. Mateo has dimples, too, but they're understated while hers sparkle.

"I would have been happy with an intimate, family thing. But then I remembered my family could populate a small island. So we decided on a backyard reception."

"You seem pretty calm about it." I say.

"I'm trying not to be a bridezilla. Would I prefer a Broadway showcase instead of my uncle's cumbia band? Yeah. But that would be a lot of work. And really, Edmund and I just want to get married. We've waited a long time." She widens her eyes ridiculously and looks into the middle distance. "A *looong* time."

"He's a good guy," I say, even though I don't know him well.

She beams. "He is, isn't he?"

I like this. Francesca is easy to talk to. But at what point is it appropriate to sneak in a question about where Mateo might be going every day?

Luckily, I don't have to because Francesca opens the floor on the subject.

"So what's going on with you and my brother?"

I realize I'm not actually prepared for this conversation and regret being so nosy.

"Uh, your brother? Which brother?"

"Mateo. I'm not blind. He's been acting weird all week. Ever since he came back without his guitar."

Oh that.

I shrug, trying to be casual. "He decided I could keep it for a while."

Lies. I'm a liar now.

"When he came home, he slammed his door. My dad was not happy about that."

"Oh. Well… He did mention something about getting a job and feeling some pressure. And I think he's more upset about leaving the band than he lets on."

Whether he's upset about himself or me quitting remains to be known. I'm just gonna keep that bit to myself.

"He shouldn't have quit," she says. "But he's such a hot head. I'm surprised he lasted that long."

"I won't argue with you there."

"Anyway, we were all hoping you could calm him down. But I guess he's not one to be tamed. We'll all have to wait until his frontal lobe is fully formed. Which might be never."

"If it makes you feel better, my brother flies fighter planes and I'm not even sure he has a frontal lobe."

She lifts her glass in a toast. "To brothers."

"I'll drink to that," I say, clinking my glass to hers. She takes a swig, then winks at me.

"You know what would make these better? Tequila."

"That sounds awesome. Too bad I have to work in a bit."

She mock frowns. "Too bad. But promise me you'll have a drink with me at my party."

"I will try to make my way to you through your enormous family."

"I'll be watching for you."

I lap up the rest of my limeade wishing I didn't have to go to work. I'd much rather hang out with Francesca all afternoon and whoops… just happen to still be here when Mateo comes home. Yes, I'm still mad at him and I know I vowed to stay far, far away. I'm just curious, that's all.

"Is there anything I can do to help?" I offer before I go. "Like stuff Jordan almonds in little baggies?"

"Nah, I think we're good. Unless you want to play with the cumbia band."

"Yeah, that's not gonna happen."

If there's one thing I will never, ever do again, it's being in a band with Mateo Precio.

Francesca surprises me by pulling me into a hug. "I can appreciate that. But maybe you can keep an eye on Matt when I'm gone. I don't trust my other brothers to tell me anything."

I give her a little squeeze. "To brothers."

"To brothers," she repeats. "Can't live with 'em, can't kick their butts."

After an uneventful pizza delivery shift, where I definitely don't think about Mateo's butt all day, I come home, run my rabbit around the yard for a while, and take a nap. It's going to be a long night with my Stealthy Yarners group, and I don't expect to be back until the sun comes up.

It's close to one in the morning when there's a banging on the front door. My Spidey-senses are on high alert because I already know it's Mateo.

"Go away," I cry through the door. "I'm sleeping."

"No you're not. All your lights are on and I heard your blender running."

Darn blender and my love for late night smoothies.

"I'm blending stuff in my sleep. Goodbye."

He knocks again. "Desiree, open up. I need you."

"You don't need me. You want me out of your business, remember?"

I hear an exaggerated sigh and a thud, like he banged his head on the door.

"I'm sorry," he says. "Will you let me in?"

"No. I'm walking away now."

I go into my room for my stuff, checking to see if I have everything I need in my tote bag. I tap on the doorbell camera app on my phone, and sure enough, Mateo's still on my porch.

I talk into the app which sounds through the speaker

outside. "You do know my parents and brother have access to the camera."

He turns to the source of my voice and presses his finger on the doorbell.

Ding dong. Ding dong. Ding dong.

He's relentless.

I storm over and bang on my side of the door.

"Stop that."

He rings it again.

"I will if you let me in."

Grrrrr.

I open the front door for no other reason than to get him to stop pressing the dang doorbell, but I'm blocking the entrance and there's no way he's coming inside.

"I can't stand another minute in that house with Pancho Two," he says as if that's an acceptable greeting. "Can I crash here?"

In his dreams.

"No. Are you crazy? Go home."

I begin to shut the door, but he steps into the threshold.

"I can't sleep."

"Not my problem."

"Listen, you won't even know I'm here. I'll sleep on the couch."

"Go. Away."

"If Ian were here, he'd let me in."

"Well, my brother *isn't* here. I am. And I'm alone, so get lost."

"Your brother doesn't have to know."

Such a player thing to say.

I bumble to come up with another reason why Mateo

and me alone in my house is a terrible idea. "Dante wouldn't jive with the idea either," I say, crossing my arms.

"Dante? Why Dante? Is there something going on I should know about?"

"What? No." Just the thought of me and Dante Precio... no. Just no. It would be like dating my cousin. Bleh.

"You like him?" he presses. "Is that it? Because you'll be disappointed."

"No. I do NOT like him. Wait. Why would I be disappointed?"

Mateo half laughs. "My big brother's not exactly a ball of sunshine. Definitely not boyfriend material. A lone wolf. All he cares about are engines. Besides, he's not romantic. Not like me."

"Oh, *you*?" I snort. "YOU'RE romantic? HA! Mister..." I check the time. "Mister *'Late Night booty call'*. That just *screams* romantic."

He leans toward me, pressing against the doorframe with a wink. "This isn't a booty call. But if it were, I'd show you just how romantic I can be."

I close the door another inch. "I have news for you. Taking home a different girl every night is not romantic, dude."

"I don't do that." He plasters a wet puppy dog expression on his face, playing the offended card. Like I'm going to fall for that.

I make a show of rolling my eyes so he'll get a clue. "Oh no? You forget I was in the band, too. All those groupies. Please."

"I *don't* do that. Can I just come in?"

"No."

I swing the door to shut it in his infuriatingly beautiful face, but he stops it with his foot. Even in the streetlamp light, one can see the ink bounce and pop over the flexing muscle.

Lawd have mercy.

In an effort to keep him out, I plaster myself against the doorframe, as if my smallish body could block his entry.

Big mistake. Big.

With a foot still stopping the door, he leans one arm above my head, looming over me. I press myself as close to the threshold as possible, trying in vain to escape the brush of his shirt. Even the faintest touch—even his clothing—will set me on fire. Why does my body react to him like this? Brain. Where are you?

"If you won't let me in, I'll stand here," he says with a gravelly voice. "I'll stand here, and we can talk."

I gulp. "I don't want to talk. I'm going to bed."

"Fully dressed? With those shoes?"

I glance down at my Doc Martens. They're my Stealthy Yarners shoes. Mateo hooks one finger around the thin strap of my purse crossing over my chest. It's so tiny and light, I forgot I'd already put it on.

"Where are you going this time of night?" he asks, almost teasing. "What's his name?"

"None of your business," I say. "Now kindly step aside."

If possible, he leans in even closer, trapping me under his arm. It's chilly outside, but this pocket Mateo has created in the doorway of my house is warm. I want to squirm away, but the way he's caging me against the threshold is annoyingly thrilling.

He lowers his mouth and whispers hot against my ear, "Maybe I don't want you to go. It's late. Maybe I'm your guardian angel."

I snort. "More like a devil."

"That's right. And as a devil, I know other devils. Any guy who expects you to come to him at one o'clock in the morning has very bad intentions. So no. I'm not gonna… step aside."

"I never said I was going to see a guy. Your brain just went there."

"Okay, so where are you going?"

I sigh. "If you must know, I'm meeting some friends downtown."

"Downtown where?"

"At the civic center."

He lowers his voice to sinister levels. "Why?"

"To do… something."

His eyes narrow as he tilts his head like he's trying to decide if I'm crazy or just plain lying to him. After a minute, he pushes himself off the doorframe but doesn't budge otherwise.

"Okay," he says casually. "I'm going with you."

I half-laugh. "Uh, no you're not."

"There's no way I'm going to watch you scuttle into the night all alone on your scooter. I'm going with you."

I can tell we're at an impasse here, so I compromise.

"Fine. But I'm putting you to work."

I suppose that tall frame of his (not to mention those biceps) could be put to use.

A small, satisfied grin spreads across his fine face, and it takes a moment to compose myself in order to gather my things.

My rabbit fell asleep between a throw pillow and the arm of my sofa, so I gently pick him up and place him in his cage. He doesn't seem to like me disrupting his sleep for this, wiggles out of my arms, and hops into my bedroom.

"I guess he's okay in there," I say, scooping up my keys. "Let's roll."

We head outside as I lead the way to my Vespa, but Mateo makes a full stop.

"No way," he says. "I'll drive."

I flop my arms up. "Get your car then. Just hurry. I'm late already."

"Late for what? How do I know your schedule if you won't even tell me anything?"

"Something beautiful. That's all you need to know."

"Is it something illegal?"

I shrug. "Maybe."

"Great. Just great."

He storms toward his house, stops short, and spins back over to me. "My dad's truck trapped my car in the driveway. If I start either of them up, it'll wake my whole family."

I'm already strapping on my helmet as I swing my leg over my Vespa.

"Whatevs. You coming or not?"

Mateo stands there, looking at my ride like it might fall apart any minute.

"Stop being a namby-pamby and hop on."

He grumbles something under his breath and reluctantly takes his place behind me.

"Are you sure this tin can will hold our weight?"

I start the engine. "Nope. Hold on."

He lets out a little yelp as I twist the gas handle to advance out of the driveway. His arms wrap tightly around my waist while I navigate out of the neighborhood out into the city streets.

"We're not going on the freeway, are we?" he shouts, squeezing me tighter.

I'm acutely aware of every place his body touches mine. His inner thighs against my backside, his hard chest along my back. And those sturdy, muscular arms. The hands which are so competent on the guitar now pressed on my belly, his palms burning through my sweater.

I don't do freeways. Not on this two-wheeler. But he doesn't have to know that.

I don't answer him, leading him to wonder and cling to me a little scared even though he'd never admit it. When we arrive, his fingers are clenched around the fabric of my sweater.

"You can let go of me now," I say, popping down the kickstand. He doesn't move for a moment, inhaling my hair before disentangling his fingers.

"Just give me a sec, okay?" he says shakily.

"Too scary for you?" I tease.

He rasps a shuddery breath. "No. The opposite. I need a minute. Don't make me explain."

Oh… OH!

"Sure," I say in the most casual way I can. "Okay."

He scoots back an inch, putting distance between our bodies and curses something under his breath. Then, he gets off the Vespa, shakes his legs out, and clears his throat.

"Thank you," he says. "I'm good now."

"Not going to blow your load?"

He coughs so hard he almost chokes. "Whaaaat?"

"Ya know. Throw up." I make a barfing gesture.

"Oh. Um… no."

"Great. You're going to meet my friends now. So be nice."

He flashes that million-watt smile. "No promises."

With a nod, I secure my tote bag over my shoulder and lead him into the square where my friends are waiting. The gang's all here with their stuff.

Tootsie, my closest friend out of the group, leans against a lamppost while Duckie and Cheddar sit on one of the benches. This is all part of our installation, so I'm surprised they didn't start without me. Our window of time is limited and closing by the minute.

When they see me approach with Mateo, they give each other a look and glance back at me with curiosity.

The only guy in the Stealthy Yarners stands behind the girls holding up a ladder. I can't read his expression when he looks Mateo up and down, but he's harmless.

"Hey everybody. Sorry I'm late. We… had a small transportation hiccup."

Tootsie wanders over to me and Mateo, checking him out appreciatively.

"No worries. New member?"

"Um, no. Just my friend." If you could call him that. I point individually at everyone as I say their names. "This is Tootsie, Cheddar, and Duckie. And the guy with the life-saving ladder is Mr. Busy."

Mateo grunts and does one of those guy chin things at Mr. Busy.

"Everybody, this is... um..." I look up at Mateo. "I forgot you need a nickname."

"Why do I need a nickname?"

"We don't use real names," says Cheddar.

"May I ask why?"

Mr. Busy props up his ladder and comes over. "So we can't rat each other out... in case one of us gets caught."

Mateo's eyebrows shoot up. "Caught? Caught doing what exactly?"

"Well..." I say.

"Giggles didn't tell you about our graffiti gang?" says Mr. Busy.

Mateo gives me a look. "Graffiti? Are you kidding me right now?"

I bite my bottom lip.

"And Giggles? *That's* your nickname? Giggles?" He looks around. "There's a hidden camera somewhere."

Duckie hopes up and shakes Mateo's hand. "Nice to meet you, Amigo of Giggles. Should we get started?"

Cheddar snaps her fingers. "Amigo. That will work."

Mr. Busy slaps a hand on Mateo's shoulder. "Sounds good to me, Amigo. Let's do this."

Mateo stands stunned as the group starts to prepare their things.

"What is happening?" he says to me.

I shrug. "They just gave you a nickname... *Amigo*."

"Great. That's just great. Illegal activity *and* racial profiling. And here I was thinking I only asked to crash on your couch tonight."

"Why *did* you come over anyway? Having nightmares?"

"I told you. Pancho Two was making noise, laughing obnoxiously at some show he was watching in his room. And I swear he was talking on the phone with someone. I don't trust the guy."

Mr. Busy clicks his tongue to get our attention. "Amigo. You're with me."

"I don't get why your dad lets him stay at the house. He's a criminal."

"Criminal? You're the one defacing public property. *And* taking me down with you into your life of crime."

"Relax. We're making art. It's a beautiful thing."

"Is that what the kids are calling it these days?"

I dig into my bag and hand him a pair of crafting scissors and a small ball of yarn.

"What's this?"

"For the yarn graffiti," I say. "Actually, it's called yarn bombing, but tomato tomahto."

He stares at me incredulously.

"Yarn? Bombing?"

I take my creation out of my bag. It's a cover for the bench. I'm super proud of it. Crocheted entirely of colorful granny squares, I made it exactly to the bench's measurements.

Whoever sits here is going to be blessed.

I picture a girl on her lunch break, having her sandwich outside to get some sunshine after too many hours working under office fluorescent lights. Or maybe a couple of lovers meeting at this bench for a weekend rendezvous. Or an artist looking for a place to sit and dream. This bench cover will give them joy.

"Yarn bombing. Yeah. I didn't make up the term. Just go with it."

Mateo makes a show of overly rolling his eyes. "This is your idea of breaking the law? By… *knitting*?"

"And crocheting. Just go on. Mr. Busy will show you what to do."

I shoo him away and get started on the bench. Tootsie wanders over to help me tie the pieces into place with yarn scraps.

"Soooo," she says. "Are you gonna spill the tea about that tall, dark honeypot or do I have to go poke him myself for some answers?"

"There will be no poking."

"Oh, I think there's plenty to poke," she says. "I can poke some tea right out of that—"

"There is no tea. He's my neighbor. He saw me leaving my house and wanted to come with. That's it."

"Wait a minute. Is that the same neighbor with the magic fingers?"

I give her a hard stare. "I have never. Ever. Used the phrase *magic fingers*."

"Oh haha. Yes you have. It's him, isn't it? The guitar player in your band." She wiggles her fingers. "Magic man."

Heat rises to my cheeks at the image her words (and gesture) convey. "One, please remove that from your vocabulary. And two, I know lots of guys who are talented with their fingers—uh, on guitar."

A smirk plays across Tootsie's face. "If you say so, Giggles."

"I say so."

We resume our work, tucking and tying the yarn installation, then move over to the lamppost, which was one of Tootsie's projects. It's a simple sleeve-like design, but she did an ombre rainbow pattern that looks like someone painted it on. So gorgeous. I stand on a small step stool and hold the yarn in place as she snips and adjusts. She wants to get the yarn tie-offs just the right color. While she works, I steal a glance at Mateo on the top rung of the ladder, helping Mr. Busy install his intricate tree branch masterpiece. There are yarn sleeves for almost every branch of that tree. I can't wait to see it once it's done.

Mateo's tying pieces together on a branch above his head. The muscles in his shoulders flex and shift while the tattoos of his arms dance and twist with every movement. From this angle, I can see a peekaboo sliver of skin when his T-shirt lifts up from the waistband of his jeans. Even at night, in the dim light of a few streetlamps, I can see how deliciously smooth his skin is there. And if I were to tilt my head just so, I might catch a glimpse of—

"Earth to Giggles," says Tootsie. I turn back to her only to notice I failed to hold the sleeve in place, instead stretching it all wonky as I ogle Mateo and his bulgy arms. "Are you enjoying the view?" She wags her brows.

"Just making sure Mr. Busy is getting the help he needs," I lie.

"Speaking of Giggles," she says.

"Don't even go there."

"I wonder if a certain set of magic fing—"

"Stop. We're just friends. Actually, not even friends. He's a guy who used to play in the same band as me, but now he doesn't and happens to live next door. I don't even talk to him that much. Or *like* to talk to him, really. I don't even like him as a person. And he certainly doesn't like me. Not in that way. Or any way. Not that anybody asked. I'm just saying. Actually, I'm not saying anything. Nothing at all."

"Okay, okay. Quit rambling and help me out with this so we can find Cheddar and Duckie for the big install."

"Right. Sorry."

I get back to the task at hand but steal one last look at Mateo. It kind of warms my heart, seeing him hanging a yarn installation. It's so out of character from his bad boy rock and roll facade. Sometimes I wonder if he wears it like a costume. Or a mask. Like it's Halloween every day for him—just as long as nobody sees the real him.

He turns his head to look my way, catches me staring, and flashes a devastating smile. Then he absolutely kills me with a wink and my heart does a flip floppy thing. I lose my footing on the step stool, and while I try to regain my balance, I somehow wobble long enough for Mateo to race to me before I fall to the ground. And instead, I fall into his arms. His strong, hard as stone, arms.

I love to sing,
and I love to drink scotch.
Most people would rather
hear me drink scotch.

—George Burns

Chapter Eight

MATEO

"You got here so quickly," she whispers. "How?"

I'm in tune with her every move. That's how. I knew she was about to fall before she did. Before anybody.

"You're a slow faller," I say. "Are you okay, Paloma?"

Desirée nods, her wide, blue eyes locking on my own. Is that a look of surprise? Or something else. Desire? Perhaps. It's her name, after all. Her lips call to me. Her lashes flutter like she's some damsel in distress. I want to kiss her so badly, I could burst. There's electricity between us. It's undeniable. Or maybe it's just her. She's pure voltage, and I'm just some crusty orc in her energy sphere.

"Can you get up?" somebody asks behind me. Cheese girl, or Cheddar, or Tootsie Roll. Honestly, I forgot they were here for a minute. I wish they weren't.

Desirée blinks, turning her gaze from me. "Yeah. I'm fine."

I help her to her feet, and her friends all clap. Like she just escaped the jaws of death or something. They're ridiculous. Especially that Mr. Busy guy. I don't like the way he looks at Desirée. I don't even like the way *I* look at her, let alone some bozo who knits sweaters for trees. He elevates the term tree hugger to a whole new level.

"Maybe we should stick to ground level installations," says the mousy one. What's her name?

Desirée assures her with a smile. "It's okay, Duckie."

Right. Duckie.

"We have to do the big installation. It's our only chance."

Cheese Face and Duckie exchange a look. Are they afraid of getting caught?

Tootsie Roll chimes in. "Amigo, we need you to be the spotter for Giggles. Make sure she doesn't fall again. Mr. Busy, you and I will direct the installation. Cheddar and Duckie, you'll tie the strings together. Got it?"

She stretches out her hand palm down.

The others in the knitting gang all form a circle, each one placing a hand in the center.

Desirée ticks her head from me to the huddle.

"Well, Amigo? Will you join us?"

I'd rather not, but the way Desirée asks so nicely, I can't resist. I place my hand over the pile of hands. Desirée's hand, unfortunately, is not the one directly below mine.

"On three," says Tootsie. "One, two…"

Everyone joins in at once, "Stealthy Yarners!" and flings up their arms.

Yay! Stealthy Yarners.

This has got to be one of the weirdest things I've ever done. And I've done some weird things.

Desirée leads me to a pathway lined with trees. There are a few benches on either side, and some flowers in between. I imagine it would be a nice place to sit, but the trees aren't very lush, so it wouldn't offer much shade on a hot day. Overall, much like the rest of this concrete town square, it's overwhelmingly unremarkable.

"We're going to make a canopy," explains Desirée. "Each of us knitted a few triangle sails. We're going to tie them together, hook them on the trees, and make this into a magical shady walkway. Whatta ya think?"

I look around. I don't see anyone else, but that doesn't mean the police won't come around soon.

"I think we better get this over with," I say.

"That's the spirit!" Desirée chirps and bops my nose.

Bops. My. Nose. With a '*boop*' sound.

For the next half-hour, we're piecing the triangle sails together, taking turns climbing up to attach an end to a tree. Desirée measures the yarn by holding one end to her chin and stretching it out the length of her arm. She juts her chin out as she does so. Why do I find that so adorable? She's not even trying to be cute. She's just quirky and guileless.

And her laugh. She just laughs her way through life. The kind of laugh that makes you want to laugh with her, just to be able to hold onto that bright, sweet smile. It's no wonder everybody likes her.

When we're done with the canopy installation, Mr. Busy sets up the timer on his phone's camera and we all pose like loons. He promises to send it to everyone. I'll have to get a copy from Desirée later.

It's close to four o'clock when we get back to her house. I insisted on driving her scooter with her behind me this time. I won't put myself through that torture again —Desirée's back nuzzled against me while I try my hardest not to think about how good it felt to have her close.

When we get back to the neighborhood, there's a VW van parked on the street between our houses. It wasn't there when we left, which considering the time of night, is somewhat suspicious.

But before I investigate, I walk Desirée into her house, making sure she gets in safely. I go around her whole house, making sure all the windows and doors are locked.

"What are you doing?" she asks, half amused.

"Making sure you're safe. There's a van outside I don't like the look of."

"The surfer van? I've seen it before. Probably just the neighbor across the street getting ahead of street sweeping day."

"You've seen it before?"

"Yes. Mateo, it's fine. You don't have to worry."

"This is L.A., Paloma. You didn't lock your door the other day."

"I promise I won't let that happen again."

She gives me the softest, sweetest look. She's basically a Desirée sugar sculpture covered in Jelly Bellies and that colored icing they put on cake. It's a look that I might mistake to mean '*stay*'.

But I won't stay. I swear, I won't stay. Even if she really wants me to, which she doesn't. This is all in my head.

But I'm a little jazzed up from the crazy time we just had, and I'm feeling more alive than I have in a long time. It's silly, I know. Who would have thought? Yarn bombing is surprisingly fun.

"So, do you do this a lot? Madcap yarn graffiti in the middle of the night?"

I want to add that I hate the idea of her running around Los Angeles when there are more weirdos out and about than in the daytime. How she better not go again unless someone drives with her. Preferably me.

"We do this every few months, yeah."

Act casual. Act. Casual. Do not smother her. Because she's a brilliant, independent woman who would absolutely fry my *huevos* for coddling her.

"Can I go with you next time?" I ask. "We can take my car."

A bright smile forms on her face. "You liked it?"

"Well, I'm only offering because you could fit a lot of yarn in my trunk."

She shoves my shoulder. "You loved it. Admit it. You had fun."

"Yes, okay. I had fun." *But only because I was with her.* "I can't believe we didn't get caught," I add. "I even saw a patrol car go by. My heart almost stopped."

Desirée smirks. I know that look. It's her *I've got a secret* look.

"What's that?" I ask. "What are you hiding?"

An impish glint sparkles in her eyes. She's holding in her laughter, but the pink in her cheeks soon turns to a fierce red, so she turns away to hide it.

"Tell me what you're up to."

I reach for her, spinning her around by the shoulders to face me. It's here that she busts up, hardly able to contain herself. I can't help but chuckle along. She's just so contagious.

"What's so funny?" I ask, even through my own mild laughter. I want to be in on whatever she's thinking. I find myself wanting that more and more.

Finally, she snorts, wiping her eyes. "We…" she snorts again. "We… have a…"

"A what? We have a what?"

At this point she doubles over, and when she straightens up, she fans her face.

"I'm so sorry," she says. "It's just…"

"What? What?"

"We have a permit." She forces a serious face and looks at me with those stunningly wide eyes. Then spits out another giggle. "I'm so sorry."

She's not sorry at all. Generally, when someone says sorry in the middle of laughter, they're the opposite of sorry.

"A permit? A permit for what, exactly?"

She takes a few deep breaths which calms her giggle fit a little.

"For the yarn installations. We were never in danger of getting caught."

She presses her lips together trying to contain a howl which explodes once more out of her mouth.

"You were all playing a joke on me. The new guy. Making me almost crap my pants whenever I saw head-lights in the distance."

"No! No, really. Tootsie and I are the only ones who know this. Cheddar, Duckie, Mr. Busy… they all think we're some sort of rogue knitting gang. It makes them feel like they're part of something grand."

"Wonderful. And here comes *Amigo Mateo*, just a chump to amuse you and Tootsie."

"I couldn't tell you without ruining it for the others. I swear."

She crosses her heart, and I grab her pointer finger and hold it between us. I don't want to let go.

"Is that why they call you Giggles?" I say softly.

She shrugs. "I guess I giggle a lot."

"Ya think?"

I'd never noticed it before, too caught up in my music, the band, the gigs. And there were always girls around. But none like Desirée. No one even came close.

I tug on her finger to bring her closer to me. Her booted toes tap against mine. I want to kiss her so badly. I've been wanting this for a long time. I screwed up royally the other night. I won't do that again. I know I don't deserve her. I know I'm no good for her. But by the way she's looking at me right now… that can go right out the window. I'm going to kiss her, and I'm going to kiss her good and well.

I release her finger and place her hand on my chest.

The fact that she allows it is a huge step. What do normal guys do with a girl like her? Do they ask *permission* to kiss her? Do they woo her for a while? I'm guessing good guys don't do the things I'm thinking of doing right now. Like grabbing fistfuls of her hair or thrusting her body onto the sofa.

I hook my thumb under her chin and lift her lips up. She parts them for me like the good girl she is.

"That's right," I mumble as I stroke her jawline with the backs of my fingers. Back and forth. Back and forth. "Look who's not giggling now."

She sucks in a breath. Her eyes, now the deepest, darkest blue imaginable, gloss over with want.

This could either be the best kind of bad or the worst kind of good. Either way, kissing her would be wrong. I'd ruin her—because if we do this, there's no going back. She'll be mine and that's it. I don't share, and I certainly don't let go of what's mine.

She swallows hard. "I… can't think of anything funny enough."

"Oh? Then maybe you should be doing something else with that quirky little mouth of yours. I can think of a few things."

"You mean, like sing?"

"You gonna sing for me, Paloma?"

"Ma… maybe. Sing or—"

"Shhhh." I place my thumb on her lips. "That's enough talking."

What was the reason this was a bad idea?

I can't remember.

I bend down to her, my mouth ready to take hers in eleven different ways... when she squeals. Her eyes perk up, and she hops back.

"Anthony!"

Anthony? Who the flip is Anthony?

"Anthony Hopkins. Bad bunny. No nibbling on my pants."

She takes another step back and bends down to pick up her rabbit.

"You named your rabbit Anthony Hopkins?"

"Yeah. Sometimes I just call him Mr. Hopkins."

"Clever."

Now can we go back to where I was about to kiss her?

The damn bunny starts squirming in her arms.

"Awww. He wants to go with you," she says before shoving the thing on my chest. I reflexively catch him and hold him there like a dodo. I've never held a rabbit before. Is it like a dog? Does it like belly rubs?

I wiggle its little paw and wave it at Desirée.

"Quid pro quo, Clarise. Have you any... fava beans?"

Desirée laughs and scratches Anthony Hopkins on the back. "He likes you."

He *is* kinda cute, actually. Nuzzling into me. "Yeah. I think you might be ri—"

Something warm and wet filters through my T-shirt and sticks to my skin.

"Oh no!"

I grab him by his furry little scruff and hold him out in

front of me. There's a pee stain on my shirt and it feels gross.

"Mr. Hopkins," scolds Desirée, taking him from my hands. "Bad bunny."

She wags her finger at him all the way to the cage.

"I'm sorry. You can clean off your shirt in the sink."

Clean off my shirt. I need a shower. Not to mention a mood killer. Maybe I can salvage this situation. Make margaritas out of lemons. Or in this case, a ruined shirt.

"You can wash your shirt in the kitchen sink," she says.

I head over, and slide off my shirt, but I'm pretty sure I'll never get the smell out. When I get home, I'll dump it in the trash.

When Desi returns, she stops in her tracks and stares at my chest. She's so obviously checking me out. The way she bites her bottom lip.

Clearing her throat, she says, "Some dish soap should do the trick."

"I think I just want to get this pee off my chest for now."

"Oh. Right."

She turns on the faucet, squirts some dish soap on her hands, and starts lathering me up. She swishes her hands all over my chest, creating so many suds, they drip down my belly button and down into my waistband.

I stop her wrist.

"I think I'm clean enough. Thanks."

"Oh, okay." She looks down at her soapy hands and back at my torso. "I'll help you rinse off."

She cups her hands under the steam of water and splashes me repeatedly.

"Whoa whoa, what are you doing?

"Well can you get closer? Lean over the sink."

"Desiree, you're making a mess."

There's a puddle on the floor now, and the front of my jeans are soaked. Not to mention the cold. I step away and slip off my belt to air out my jeans. I find a towel and dab myself all over. And now I look like I peed my pants.

"I'm just gonna finish cleaning up at home," I say.

She's mortified. "I'm so sorry. Your boxers!"

I look down. Yeah, my jeans dipped an inch or two without my belt, and the waistband of my boxers are showing. This is not the way I imagined revealing that little detail to a woman.

"They're a little wet," I say. "It's fine."

I can't help but smile at her reaction, the way her eyes rake over me as she bites her bottom lip.

"I don't know what got into Mr. Hopkins," she says. "He's usually a very good bunny."

"Maybe he doesn't like Silence of the Lambs references."

She giggles. "I don't blame him."

"Can I help you with…" I point to the puddle on the floor.

"No, I'll mop it up."

"Okay then. I'm just gonna…" I hook my thumb over my shoulder. "See ya later."

"See ya later, alligator."

"I'll see myself out. Don't forget to lock the door behind me."

"Gotcha," she says with gusto, then salutes me.

Taking my leave with my shirt in one hand and my belt in the other, I open the front door but to my surprise, I almost run into the figure of a broad, solid man with a stunned expression on his features and a Navy duffle bag at his feet. Ian's face is a rock, the tick in his jaw the only movement in his whole body.

His hand is frozen where it was poised with the house key to unlock the door, and in the flash of a millisecond, I see the moment awareness sets in.

His gaze falls to my naked chest, then down to the pieces of my clothing in my hands. He doesn't say a word— just fixes me with a hard scowl. And the next thing I see is his fist flying at my face.

Go ahead and play the blues
if it'll make you happy.

—Homer Gimpson

Chapter Nine
DESIRÉE

I know I probably shouldn't splurge on a manicure when I can paint my own nails for the price of a dollar ninety-nine bottle of polish. But I'm down to my last nerve and could use some pampering.

My brother stayed a day longer than he originally intended, and in that time he's been a complete booger. After he jumped to conclusions, he gave Mateo a shiner, which turned into a mini brawl. I had to hose them down to break them apart. So Mateo went home even more soaked than before, and Ian lectured me for an hour. Did he believe me when I explained things to him? Of course not. He's a bigger hot head than Mateo. He better not tell Mom and Dad. That's all I've got to say.

But I digress.

Ian left this morning to get back to his fleet, thank goodness—but not without several attempts to 'have a few words' with Mateo. But what do ya know? Mateo hasn't been home since that fateful night of getting punched in the face. He's probably at some girl's house, getting his wounds nursed. Ian did hit him pretty hard.

No amount of screaming or crying could hold back my brother's rage. And no matter what I said by way of explanation (why there was a half-naked Mateo in my house at four o'clock in the morning) could I convince him it was all rather innocent.

Mostly innocent.

You see, Ian is a lot like my father. Stern. Overprotective. A throw punches first and ask questions later kind of guy. Except in this case, the only questions he had were for Dante. Mainly of the interrogating variety.

For the last few days, there has been too much Ian and not enough Mateo in my life. I texted Mateo a few times— to make sure he didn't go blind or anything. His only reply was a black heart emoji.

Since then, it's been crickets.

So here I am at Classy Claws getting gels on my short nubs so I don't look like a feral animal at Francesca's wedding.

The nail technician swipes a second coat on my nails,

asking me personal questions, which I reply to with rote answers, just like always.

"No, I do not have a boyfriend."

"Why not? Because men are difficult."

"Thank you for telling me I'm pretty, but I still don't want a boyfriend."

"I'll pass on the facial hair wax, thanks anyway."

There's a bit of a ruckus at the front of the store, where the owner of the salon is loudly shooing someone out.

She's yelling, "No. No. We don't want."

I crane my neck to see what's going on, and all I see is the owner swinging a broom at a dark-haired guy in a starchy suit.

Is that? No way.

"Mateo?"

Starchy suit guy turns his head at the sound of his name, sees me, and hits the floor out of my line of vision. I get up just in time to see him crawling out of the shop.

"Mateo, wait," I cry, running after him.

The nail technician calls out, "You forgot top coat!"

"I'll be right back," I say. I don't want the owner to think I dipped without paying. She might come after me with a broom, too.

I catch up to Mateo in the parking lot, out of breath from chasing him.

"Hey. What's going on? Why are you running?"

"I didn't want you to see me like this."

"Like what Dapper Dan? Totally dressed up and handsome?"

"Like a guy getting chased out of a nail salon with a broom."

I wave my hand behind me at the salon. "Oh that. She does that to everybody. Even the mailman."

"You're such a bad liar," he says, tilting his head to examine my face better.

"So, um. Do you come here often?" I ask.

"To get my nails done? All the time."

"So what happened back there? Did you single-handedly deplete their supply of black polish?"

He breathes out and looks away for a moment, looking across the parking lot as if the rows of cars will give him courage to admit what I think he's too embarrassed to say.

"I'm working. Business to business sales." He opens the portfolio in his hand to show me pages and pages of laminated sales fliers for cash register computers.

"POS systems," he says. "Mostly high-ticket items. You know, they lure you in with promises of huge commissions, but they don't tell you how hard it is to make a sale."

"Sales are hard," I say. "We used to have to upsell breadsticks with every pizza order. I was the worst at it. Who wants a side of bread with pizza? It's basically pizza dough without the good stuff on it."

"Toppings are the best part."

"Right?"

We stand in silence for a minute and I notice purple skin beneath his sunglasses. I have the urge to hug him, but my nails are still wet.

"Sorry about my brother," I say. "I tried to talk to him—"

"It's okay. Nothing I didn't deserve."

"You didn't deserve to be punched in the face. You didn't do anything."

He turns to look away. The cars on the other end of the parking lot need his attention now apparently.

"He left this morning," I say. "So you can come home now."

This makes him jolt his attention back to me. "Come home?"

"Yeah. You haven't been home in a few days. I figured you were avoiding Ian. But he's gone now so you can come back."

He just stares at me. "Okay."

I glance down at his portfolio and back at him and the tie around his neck.

"Well, congratulations on your job. Does this mean you'll get your trust fund again?"

And move out. He won't be my next-door neighbor anymore. That makes me feel all twisty inside.

"I have to prove I can hold down a steady job. So no. Not yet."

"And how long have you had this job?"

"A couple weeks."

"Oh okay. How many sales have you made in two weeks?"

He holds up his hand between us, with his thumb touching his fingertips to form a big fat zero.

"None? Dang. It's not a hundred percent commission, is it?"

The expression on his face confesses that it is. Which totally bites.

"I'm sorry," I say, wishing I could snap my fingers and we'd enter a magical world where all we'd have to do is play our music.

The manicurist comes outside and yells at me from across the parking lot.

"Hey! You coming back?"

"Yes, be right there," I call back over my shoulder.

"You better go before they ban you, too."

"Yeah, I guess so."

He nods once and turns to go, but something inside me can't let him. He hates this job. And I might have a lead for him.

"Mateo?"

He stops in place but doesn't turn around, so I run to him and go around to face him.

"I have a friend," I say tentatively. One eyebrow lifts on his gorgeous face. "Actually, he's not really a friend. More of an acquaintance."

The eyebrow lift turns into two eyebrows lurching down.

"His name is Scott…"

He raises a hand, palm facing out.

"You don't have to tell me. He's a lucky guy."

"No! Listen. He's in a cover band. And they're looking for a guitarist."

"Oh. Nice. Are you thinking about doing it?"

"Me? No. You. I can introduce you and—"

"Thanks, but no."

"No? Just like that? Like, no information, just no?"

"I can't join another band." He shakes his head like he feels defeated by the whole thing. Perhaps he's worried about it interfering with his sales job.

"It pays. Really well. They go on tour and have good

gigs at festivals and casinos. You can quit this crappy job—which I know you hate. It's legit."

I'd miss him when he goes on tour, but it would be worth it to see him happy.

"I appreciate what you're trying to do, Paloma. I do. But… I don't know. Something changed in me. That night you played your original music… it inspired me. *You* inspire me. I may not be as talented as you, but I felt a spark like I haven't felt in years. It's like I suddenly remembered why I love music."

"That's amazing, Matt. All the more reason to take this opportunity. You'll be playing instead of going door to door getting kicked out of shops with brooms."

"It's just, I told myself I'm not going to play in cover bands anymore. I'm taking myself seriously now. Writing every day. I want something big, and if I join a cover band, that would feel like selling out."

"You can still write if you're in a band."

"Every gig with The High C's was a big nightmare dealing with someone's ego. Every single time. Guys in bands are the worst. I'm sorry. But I can't do that again."

"Okay," I say. "I get it. No cover bands."

"Thanks for understanding."

"You're welcome."

"And I appreciate you telling me about the gig. That was sweet of you to think of me."

"Always."

"So… should Ian be worried about this Scott guy? Because I can save him the trip and punch the guy myself."

I poke his ribs. "Stop it. Nobody's punching anyone."

"Hey," he says, gently touching my elbow. "I'll take a fist to the face any day. You're worth it."

Awww. But also no. I am adamantly against violence.

"And Paloma? I don't know where you thought I'd gone, but I was staying with Enrique for a few days. Dog sitting while he and January went to Tijuana. They're fighting against illegal puppy mills."

"I didn't think you'd gone anywhere. I mean, I wasn't jumping to conclusions."

The corner of his mouth curls into an all-knowing grin.

"Sure you didn't, Paloma."

Dang it. He knows me so well.

Elvis may have been
the king of rock 'n' roll,
but I am the queen.

-Little Richard

Chapter Ten

MATEO

On the day of Francesca's wedding, my eye is still black and blue. January is trying to cover it with makeup.

"Hold still," she says. "You're squirmier than a fish."

"I feel ridiculous," I say.

"Think about it like stage makeup. Those guys… what's their name again?"

"Mimes?"

"No. That 70s rock band with the face paint and the platform boots." She sticks out her tongue and makes a rock and roll hand gesture.

"KISS?"

"Yes. Those guys. Makeup is cool, see?"

"Why don't you paint a black star over his eye while you're at it?" suggests Enrique, rummaging through her cosmetic bag. "It'll cover his bruise better and improve his looks."

January swats his hand. "Why don't you go check on the groom?"

Enrique chuckles. "Because it's more fun to make fun of Mateo's black eye."

We're all piled in Mom's craft room because we were kicked out of the entire second floor. Besides January and Enrique, Sebastian and Dante are here, mainly so Dante can judge me and Sebastian can capture this moment on camera. I cringe to think how unflattering Sebastian is making me out to look. He's known to put his settings at ludicrously zoomed in. I expect to find several photos of *just my eye* on his social media.

Dante's sipping a Mexican Coke from the bottle, grunting disapprovingly at me.

"You guys can go now," I say to all three of my brothers present. "January has everything under control. I don't need you gawking."

"What you need," says Dante, "is a matching black eye. What were you thinking? She's your best friend's sister."

"Ian's not my best friend anymore. We've both changed since we were kids."

"No. He's always been a goody-two-shoes boy scout,

and you've always been…" He flaps his hand up and down at me. "Well… whatever this is."

"This," I gesture at myself, "is my style."

"Unbrushed hair and sneakers? At least make an effort for your own sister's wedding."

"I'll have you know these are brand new custom embroidered Converse Chuck Taylor All Stars. I ordered them just for today."

I turn my ankle to show the words *Bride's Favorite Brother* stitched on the side of my shoe.

"How much did you pay for those, Matt?" he asks with fierce disapproval. "Dad said you need to stop spending."

"What's wrong with a new pair of shoes for your sister's wedding?" asks January. Glad to know she's on my side.

"Because he has more shoes than you," says Enrique. "And that's saying a lot."

She shakes her head. "That's impossible."

January comes from money. *Loads* of money. As a hotel heiress and former reality TV star slash socialite, she probably does have more shoes than me. But I admit, I do own a lot. So what? I like nice stuff.

"The point is, *mi amor*," says Enrique, "is that he spends money he doesn't have."

"Now hang on a minute," I protest.

January shrugs as she pats powder on my face. "My mom always says that people who think money can't buy happiness just don't know where to shop."

I nod. "I agree wholeheartedly."

"Hold still," says January.

"Don't enable him," says Dante. "Matt doesn't need any more excuses to shop."

"Nonsense," she says. "I'll take you shoe shopping, Mateo. My treat."

"No!" Enrique and Dante shout in unison.

Sebastian laughs. "I got that on video. So good."

"You better not post that," I warn. "And get outta here."

January puffs something on my face with a final flourish and presents me with a mirror. "There. You can hardly tell you had a run-in with your best friend's fist."

"Ex-best friend." I say. "Tom Cruise wanna be."

"I met Tom once," says January. "Nice guy."

"Well Ian is *not* a nice guy," I say. "Hence the *ex* part of our friendship."

Dante scoffs. "You're the one with the chip on your shoulder, *hermano*. No wonder he asked me and not you to look out for his sister when he joined the Navy."

I stand up and get in Dante's face. "Desirée is a grown woman. She doesn't need a babysitter."

"And you think it's okay to fool around with the next-door neighbor?"

"I already told you," I say through gritted teeth. "Nothing happened."

Dante, who is a verified giant, puffs up his chest and gets even closer to me. "Ian caught you sneaking out at four in the morning. Half naked."

"I like to think of it as half dressed, but I'm just an optimist."

He pokes my chest repeatedly. "Stay away from that girl."

"Woman," I correct.

"Okay, okay. Break it up guys." January inserts herself

between us, pushing us apart with two makeup brushes. "If Mateo said nothing happened, then nothing happened."

"Nothing happened," I repeat. "Just ask Anthony Hopkins."

"That's the name of the rabbit," says January. She couldn't stop laughing when I told her and Enrique the story while I was staying at their house. I figured the rest of my family would have heard by now, but I guess Dante is too stubborn to listen.

"And how do you explain the four in the morning part?" Dante crosses his arms, waiting for my answer.

I mumble under my breath.

"What's that now?" he asks, leaning his ear closer to me.

I mumble it again.

"Still can't hear you."

"Yarn bombing!" cries January, cracking up. "He went yarn bombing."

"This is too good," says Sebastian, holding up his phone.

"I'm going to throw that thing in Dad's koi pond if you don't stop recording right now," I say with a growl.

"Sheesh," he says, pocketing his phone. "Vibe check."

"I was just making sure she got home safe," I say to Dante. "Honest."

Dante uncrosses his arms and plants them on his waist with a hard exhale.

"I don't even want to know what yarn bombing is, but you better call Ian and explain yourself."

"No thanks," I say. "I gave up jerks for Lent."

"You're going to call him and apologize. Then you're

going to grovel. And then, maybe then, he'll call the entire US Navy off my back. I've had it up to here."

"Alright dudes," says January. "This whole pickle swinging contest will have to wait. We have a wedding to attend."

Just then, the door flies open and Olive bursts through.

"Has anyone seen Ignacio?"

"He's at the church with Edmund," answers Enrique. Why? Please don't tell me you fell into the cake again."

It better not have anything to do with the catering. Ignacio promised he wouldn't interfere this time. He was way too stressed at Enrique and January's wedding. That's also the day Olive tumbled into the wedding cake. Good times.

"Har har. No. It's the donkey," says Olive. "He's... sleeping."

Enrique jumps up. "Sleeping? What happened? Where's Elvis?"

My sister Francesca didn't have many demands for her wedding. She wanted a simple ceremony, and even simpler reception. But the one thing she requested was a horse drawn carriage to transport her from home to the church and back again for the party. Like a princess. She'd found a service for that, but Dad, who likes to make deals with every Mexican in Southern California, found a guy who agreed to lend his buggy out for the day. It wasn't until last night that we found out there is no horse. It's a donkey. And of course, there's no one to drive the buggy. Which is actually a souped-up fruit cart. So, at the eleventh hour, Olive and January beautified the buggy/fruit cart with paper flowers, and Elvis, who's a friend of Dante and Enrique, agreed to dress in an old-timey costume (thanks to Francesca's theatre connections) and act as her carriage driver. This ruffled Enrique's feathers, who owns an actual limo business, and caused a little drama between Elvis and him. But it's all good. Except now, with a sleeping donkey, apparently.

"Elvis stayed next to the donkey, just in case," says Olive. "He sent me in to get help."

Enrique storms out of the room and we all follow except January who says she's going upstairs to join Francesca and the other bridesmaids.

"Seriously. I can't believe Dad," grumbles Enrique all the way out. That's when Tía Lucy happens to be walking by. My Tía Lucy has impeccable timing, especially when it comes to collecting gossip.

"What did my sister's husband do now?" she says with an ornery look in her eyes. "I'm making a list."

More like writing a book.

Enrique just shakes his head and runs outside with Sebastian following, filming the whole way. I think he's going live with this.

"Tía, will you go find my dad, please?" asks Dante in a gentler tone than he ever takes with me. I don't stick around to hear how he continues to butter her up. When I get to the curb, there's Enrique pacing back and forth, Elvis with a permanent shrug in his posture, and Olive trying to jostle a donkey that's clearly out of it.

"Elvis!" cries Enrique. "You had *one* job."

"What's wrong with it?" I ask Elvis. "Sebas, what did I tell you about that phone?"

I go to grab it, but Sebastian runs away and disappears around the back of the house. The kid is in college studying law. When is he going to grow up?

"I dunno what happened," says Elvis. "I've been here the whole time. Frickin' donkey just decided to take a nap."

A second later, Dante exits the house with Dad on his tail. We have to get to the church in twenty minutes and Dad's still not dressed in his tux.

"*Que pasó?*" shouts Dad. "*Maldito burro!*"

"You really did it this time, Dad," says Enrique. "What were you thinking?"

Dad stops in front of the donkey and snaps his fingers. "*Oye! Burrito feo.* Wake up."

"I think there's something wrong with him," says Olive. "Maybe he's sick."

"Dad," I say. "Where did you get this donkey?"

"A guy," he says.

"What guy? Does he even take care of his animals?"

Dad flaps his hands up. "A guy. Doesn't matter. He give me burro for free."

Dante slaps his forehead. "Dad! Francesca's your *only* daughter and you're trying to save a buck?"

Dad points a finger back at Dante. "I came to this country with twenty dollars in my pocket. You kids don't know."

"We know, Dad," I say. "But you don't have to act like we're poor."

"Says you," he grumbles. "The way you spend…"

"Can we just figure out what we're going to do?" grunts Enrique.

"It's so weird," says Olive. "Can you remember anything, Elvis? Did the donkey eat anything unusual?"

"He nibbled on a few of those flowers," he says. "But I shooed him away as soon as I caught him ruining the landscaping."

"What flowers exactly?" asks Enrique.

Elvis points to a bush with bright green leaves resembling basil, but with stems of white and purple flowers.

"Dad," I say tentatively. "Who planted these?"

"A guy," he replies.

Of course. Dad has a guy for everything.

"Do you even know what this is?" I ask.

"It's mint, no?"

"No," I say. It is definitely *not* mint. "This is *Salvia divinorum*. It's a hallucinogen."

Enrique gives me a look. "How do you know this, Matt?"

"Yeah," says Dante. "How do you know this?"

This sets Dad off more than anything.

"I knew it," he cries. "You're on drugs."

"I'm not on drugs, Dad. "I just know some things about plants, that's all. No, not *those* kinds of plants, Dante. Don't give me that look."

"So," says Elvis. "The donkey is… high?"

"Oh no," sobs Olive. "Will he be okay?"

"He'll be fine," I say. "Just not in time for the wedding."

"Where are we going to find another donkey at the last minute?" she asks.

"Preferably a horse," replies Dante, already doing a search on his phone.

"If I leave now, I could probably be back in time with a limo," says Enrique. "Or Elvis can do it."

Elvis looks at his watch. "Eh, that's cutting it a little close. Even if we call one of the drivers to come out."

"What if we find something else to pull the wagon?" I suggest. "Like those guys in New York that ride tourists around on bikes."

"They're called pedicabs," says Olive. "We have 'em in Jersey."

Dante levels me with a hard stare. "We are not a bike riding family."

"Francesca has a bike in the garage," says Enrique.

Dad shakes his head. "Flat tire. I've been meaning to fix it."

"I think we should have Pancho Two pull it on foot like they do in Asia," says Enrique. "Make him earn his keep."

"No way," I say. "I don't want him ten feet from my baby sister."

"She's not just your baby sister," says Dante. "And I'm her favorite. Tell that to your shoe guy."

"Pancho Two can't leave the property line anyway," says Dad, slicing a finger across his throat. "Or else."

"The ankle bracelet won't electrocute him, Dad." says Enrique. "We've discussed this."

This starts a nonsensical disagreement and a quick Google search by Enrique to prove Dad wrong. They're going on and on about it, but my ears only hear the muffled noise of their voices when I catch the sight of Desirée stepping out of her house. I haven't seen her since the nail salon incident. She's a vision in a sundress that cascades down to her ankles. I can hardly breathe. My feet begin to carry me toward her like I'm being pulled by a string, but Dante slams his arm across my chest.

"Don't even think about it, Matt."

I turn to him and grin. "I have an idea that might solve our donkey problem."

Talking about music
is like dancing
about architecture.

—Steve Martin

Chapter Eleven
DESIRÉE

"You don't have to do this," Dante says. His arms are crossed and he's situated himself in between Mateo and me.

"I don't mind, really. I wanted to do something for Francesca, and this is as good an opportunity as any."

When I saw Mateo waving me over, I thought it was to let me know he made up with Ian but that would be too easy.

Apparently, the Precios have a problem with the donkey currently sleeping on the street and are hoping my Vespa can pull the little carriage. I think yes. We just need to figure out how to attach it.

"I can manage that," says Dante. "I just want to make sure you're okay with us using your Vespa."

"Totally fine," I say. "I should probably change out of my dress."

"No, don't do that," Enrique says. "Elvis can drive it. He won't put a scratch on it. Right, Elvis?"

The guy named Elvis is currently trying to jostle the donkey to move it somewhere.

"I need to take care of this guy first," he says regarding the donkey. "Unless you want to do it."

Dante waves his arms. "No way. I need to get to the church soon."

"I'll do it," says Mateo. "Drive the scooter, I mean. Not take care of the donkey."

"I really don't mind," I say. "I even have a costume I can wear that will make me look like the coachman from Cinderella."

"No," says Mateo, shaking his head. "That's asking too much. You're a wedding guest."

"And you're a groomsman," I say. "I'm sure Edmund is wondering where you guys are."

"He was worried we'd prank him," says Enrique. "Not that we would."

"We totally would," says Dante. "But not on Francesca's wedding day."

Mr. Precio, who's wearing shorts, flip flops, and a

Dodgers T-shirt, throws up his hands. "I think I can go get dressed now, okay?"

His sons shoo him off saying, "Go, hurry."

"Well?" I ask. "Are you going to let me do this or not?"

The three brothers exchange looks. It's clear they don't like the idea but what choice do they have?

"I think we need to take her up on this, guys," says Enrique. "I'll help Elvis move the burro. Dante, bring the Vespa over here and work your magic. Matt, go with Desirée and bring her up to speed with the route Francesca planned out."

"No way," says Dante. "Ian doesn't want Mateo in the house."

"Seriously?" I say.

"What do you think I'll do over there in five minutes?" says Mateo.

"We're on a time crunch," says Enrique. "You idiots can squabble later. Not you, Desirée. You're not an idiot."

"Fine," says Dante. "But you better be back in four minutes."

Dante and Mateo follow me to my house, where I hand off my Vespa keys to Dante. He rolls it over to the carriage, scowling at Mateo for as long as possible before going into his garage for whatever tools he needs.

"You promise me you'll change back into this dress for the reception?" asks Mateo when we enter my house. His eyes rake over my body from head to toe.

"You like it?"

He steps to me, tugging lightly at the strap holding my wrap-around dress together.

He hums. "Mmmhmm. Then again, maybe you

shouldn't wear it. There'll be too many guys looking at you."

"What do you suggest I wear?"

He grins, flashing his eyes down and up. "Four minutes, Paloma. Tick tock."

I squint up at him. "Are you… wearing makeup?"

"Thanks to the ornament your brother gave me. I'm surprised it's not in the shape of his fist."

I examine the makeup more closely. "You did a pretty good job covering it up. Are you sure you're not a closet drag queen?"

"Okay, you got me. I dance at La Cage on Thursday nights."

"Oooh, can I come see you sometime? I have more dollar bills than I know what to do with."

"You're thinking of a different kind of dance show, lady."

I hitch up one shoulder. "What's your stage name? Oh wait, let me guess. Miracle Maddy… oh… Madeline the Musical Maven."

"Can you please just go change?" he says impatiently.

"Fine. Madeline."

I go into my room to change into my costume while Mateo talks to me through the door. He tells me the timing and exact spot I need to drop Francesca off. The church groundskeeper has allowed the carriage onto the lawn so we can make a grand entrance for all to see. Then, after the ceremony, we're to parade the bride and groom through the neighborhood with the wedding guests processing behind on foot all the way back to the Precio house for the reception. It's all very romantic. Or it would be if it had gone as planned. Mateo tells me the whole thing. How his sister wanted a fairytale moment but his dad got a donkey cart instead of a horse and buggy. But he makes sure I know how grateful he is that I'm stepping in to help out.

I emerge from my room in costume and Mateo's jaw hits the floor.

"What… is that?"

I scan my gaze down myself. "My costume."

"It's so… bright."

"Yup," I say proudly. "Oh! I have a hat to match. Hang on."

I go get my hat and flop it on my head to complete the ensemble.

"Ta da!"

"Are you sure that's a coachman costume?"

"Not strictly speaking, but I think it works. A few years ago my friends and I thought it would be fun to dress up as Sgt. Pepper's Lonely Hearts Club Band for Halloween. I was Ringo. Glad it still fits."

He tilts his head to the side and tries to hide a smile. "It sure is something."

"Hey, just gettin' by with a little help from your friends, right?" I sing-song, fanning out my hands.

"Yeah, this might be more dangerous than the dress," he says, checking me out on all sides. "Where are your pants?"

I swat him away. "They're called hot pants."

Okay, so my friends and I dressed up as *sexy* Beatles. The band jacket is a little form fitting, and does show *some* belly button, but it covers my chest. And I think it's cute. Plus, the shimmery pink shorts are stretchy and I'm wearing tights underneath. All in all, I love this costume, and we won an award at the party we went to that night, so there.

Mateo lets out a long swoosh of air.

"Alright. I guess."

When we get to the front of the Precio house, Francesca is already outside, looking radiant. Her dress has a sweetheart neckline, but then lace continues up to the shoulders and down the sleeves. There's a super long train which is currently being held by her bridesmaids, and an elegant soft tulle cathedral veil falls from a silver clip at the top of her loose bun.

She has a natural glow to her. If she's wearing makeup, it's perfectly understated.

She's every little girl's dream bride, and suddenly I'm feeling that pang inside me. The one that reminds me I'm nowhere close to getting married.

Also, now I feel like a clown in this costume. The bridesmaids are all so graceful and lady-like.

I'm so… pink.

"Desirée!" Francesca waves joyfully when she sees me. "You're the best! Thank you soooo much."

I shrug. "I'm no Clydesdale, but I'll get you to the church on time. I hope."

Dante grunts from the other side of my Vespa. He's adjusting something with the towing bar.

"How cute you are!" chirps Francesca. "Love the outfit."

"This old thing?" I swish my hand.

Francesca waves over to her bridesmaids. Everyone, this is Desirée. Desirée, this is Beth, Bernadette, and Lydia."

Lydia bypasses the formality of shaking my hand and goes right in for a hug.

"Mad respect," she says. "This whole look? Legendary. Can I be your friend?"

"I'd like that very much," I say, laughing brightly.

Beth, who's holding onto Francesca's train, smiles sweetly at me. "I'm Beth. I'd hug you too, but, ya know, train duty."

Not gonna freak out or anything, but Beth is a famous actress. Also, I happen to know she's married to Hollywood hunk, Will Darcy. I don't usually get starstruck, but I'd make an exception for him. And if she's at the wedding, he might be, too.

"Nice to meet you," I say, trying to keep it cool. I move on to shake Bernadette's hand, but she also hugs me.

"I didn't used to be a hugger," she says. "But I'm working on it. Hope you don't mind."

"Not at all," I say. "I'm all for hugging. Or boundaries. Whichever."

"Bernadette is my cousin, says Francesca. "And of course you know my sisters in law, Olive and January."

Olive I know. She's come to some of the High C's concerts with Ignacio. But no, I've never met January. A.K.A. the mega famous hotel heiress January Madison. Or… Precio now, I suppose.

"I don't think I've had the pleasure," says January, shaking my hand.

Keep it together, Desirée. They're just people like me. Very rich, very famous people.

"Glad to finally meet you," I say. "I see you and Enrique sometimes from my house. When you visit your in-laws. Not like I'm watching from my window or anything. I live next door."

Ugh. Where is there a hole I can crawl into?

"I know," she says with a laugh. "Mateo talks about you."

"He does?"

"I do not." Mateo chimes in from behind me. I actually forgot he was there.

I turn around to see a faint blush of pink in his cheeks. Cute.

There's a sharp whistle from the side gate of the house, and Enrique comes into view. *"Vaminos,"* he calls out, clapping loudly. "The burro is safe in the gazebo."

"The gazebo!?" says Francesca. "We were going to do pictures there."

"Well now you can do pictures with the burro. We'll put a bow on him."

"Is he okay?" asks Olive.

"He's fine," Enrique reassures her. Elvis gave her a wet willy and she woke right up."

"Seriously?" asks Olive, surprised.

"No," he says. "Because that would be gross. Strangely, though, it's not unlike Elvis to do something like that."

"All set," Dante announces, tossing a wrench in his tool-box. "You want to try it out, Desirée?"

"Time is of the essence," I say.

He shows me the things he did to rig up the buggy to my Vespa and goes over some safety measures. Then he follows me as I do a loop around the block without any passengers. Right before turning back onto our street, he gets in, telling me his weight probably matches Francesca and Edmund combined. Of course that's crazy, but he's concerned about the makeshift carriage being safe for the ride back to the house after the wedding ceremony.

We're met with applause when we pull up to the curb in front of the Precio house. Francesca and her bridesmaids pose for about a thousand photos, then we're off. I try to go as slow as possible for the wedding party to follow on foot. The church isn't far, but it's still farther than I'd want to walk in heels, personally.

When we arrive at the church, the guys go inside to process down the aisle. We help Francesca out of the buggy, and the girls fluff up her dress and straighten out her train. Before the doors open for her, she looks at me over her shoulder, and thanks me again.

"You coming inside?" she asks.

"Sure thing," I say with a wink. "I'll be in the back pew in case you want to make a hasty departure."

"That's definitely not going to happen," she says, laughing.

Once she goes inside, I sneak around to the side entrance in time to see her walk down the aisle looking radiant and the happiest I've ever seen a person. All the Precio brothers are lined up as groomsmen except Memo who is officiating.

I look over at the groom, and his face says it all. If anyone were to picture two people in love, this is what they'd see. I don't usually cry at weddings, but today I'm getting a little teary-eyed. It's the most beautiful thing.

I'm so caught up in the pageantry and majestic music, I almost forget my post when the bride and groom make their way to the back as a married couple. I'm clapping like a fool, and that's when Mateo catches my eye. He and the rest of the wedding party follow Edmund and Francesca down the aisle to the greeting line, and when he sees me, a grin overtakes his gorgeous features. He's always delicious looking, but Mateo wearing a tuxedo makes it nine thousand degrees hotter in here. He drags his eyes over my figure and wags his brows—the rake! Then he cocks his head in the direction of the front entrance. Oh, yeah. I have a job to do.

I scoot out the side again, as there's a huge line to congratulate the bride and groom and their parents, etc. Before I make it around the corner outside, a hand tugs on my coattails. Mateo pulls me back, swinging me around with one hand and resting the other on my waist.

"You should stay here, or all eyes will be on you instead of the bride," he says hotly. His mouth is right up against the skin of my cheek. My peach fuzz is probably standing on end.

"Shouldn't you be in the receiving line?" I ask.

He briefly glances back over his shoulder and shrugs. "They won't miss me."

"How do you know that?"

"My sister has seven brothers. Trust me. If my family ever went to Paris for Christmas, I'd be that Home Alone kid. They hardly know I'm alive."

"That's not true," I say, suddenly feeling a little sad for him.

"You're right," he says. "They'd never spend the holidays in Paris. There are no tamales there."

I don't know why he does this—makes jokes about being the black sheep. The forgotten brother.

"Should we take a selfie before you turn back into a pumpkin?"

I shove his shoulder, mainly to create some much-needed distance between our bodies. "The coachman turns back into a goose, I think. Or maybe a lizard. I can't remember."

He pulls his phone from his pocket and extends his arm out in front of us, snapping a couple of selfies. Then he steals a quick kiss on my cheek and runs back to where his family is shaking hands with all the guests. I feel his brand on me all the way back to the reception, after I go back to my house to change into my dress, and all through the buffet dinner.

A gentleman
is someone who can
play the accordion,
but doesn't.

—Tom Waits

Chapter Twelve
DESIRÉE

The backyard at the Precio house is transformed into an elegant venue, complete with fairy lights strung throughout. Mateo is on the stage playing guitar for his uncle's cumbia band. Judging by his bored expression, he's not thrilled with the idea. Even so, his competence on the instrument transcends any genre of music.

He just shines.

Currently, I'm in line for churros with Olive on the other

end of the yard. We've been waiting in this line for almost a half hour, but I hear the fresh, made-to-order treats are worth it. I keep seeing wedding guests walking around with greasy parchment paper cones of mini churros. These are not the frozen footlong sticks you find at amusement parks. Oh no. These are doughy cinnamon sugar delicacies. These are wonky shaped pieces of heaven, hot from the fryer. So yeah, I'll gladly wait another half hour if necessary. Luckily, we're close to the front of the line.

"There are a lot of famous people here," I say to Olive. "I mean, I expected to see January, but I had no idea Francesca was so connected in Hollywood."

Earlier, Mateo had taken me around to meet some of the guests, and I made a complete fool of myself at the celebrity table. When I realized I was in the presence of *the* Stella Gardiner, stage and film royalty, I stupidly quoted a famous line from her Queen Victoria movie. In an English accent!

Then I apologized saying, "I'm sure you get that all the time."

And she graciously answered, "Yes I do, dear. But for you I'll allow it."

I didn't dare say anything to Will Darcy, even though I'm told he's not as fierce as he seems. Beth did all the talking for the both of us.

Then there are the famous YouTubers present. Edmund has a popular channel, so I should have guessed he'd have some friends in the business. Mateo didn't take me over to their table.

And finally, I hear there are some Broadway stars here, but I wouldn't recognize them from the next guy, so I probably acted normal if I'd met any of them.

"Oh yeah," says Olive. "Francesca performs at the Gardiner charity gala every year. And she makes friends everywhere, you know?"

"I absolutely do."

An elderly woman, who Mateo introduced me to earlier as his *'abuela'*, comes up to Olive and presses something in her palm, saying something in Spanish. She makes a wry glance at the churro booth and wags her brows.

"Uh…" stutters Olive in broken Spanish. *"No… necesito el dinero… The churros are… libre."*

Abuela scrunches her face and says something else, and noticing me standing next to her, takes both my hands inside hers and squeezes.

"Parece que haces feliz a mi nieto."

I nod and smile.

"She says she's happy there's ice cream," says Olive.

"Oh. I didn't see any but that sounds delicious," I say.

Olive produces a wide grin for the old woman. *"Felizitamos tambien."*

Abuela is momentarily confused, but then her eyes light up with understanding.

"¿De veras? ¿Se requiere felicitaciones a mi nieto?"

Olive says, "She wants to know what flavor ice cream is your favorite."

"Oh. Okay. Um… peanut butter, I guess."

"Cubrir mantequilla caca whatay," Olive tells the woman, so incredibly proud to be translating.

Abuela gives me the side eye and walks away.

"I guess she doesn't approve of peanuts," says Olive, opening her hand to reveal the three nickels the elderly woman placed in her hand. "What am I supposed to do with this?"

"You could tip the churro guy," I suggest.

We get to the front and ask for three orders of churros. While we wait for a fresh batch, Bernadette finds us, laughing.

"What did you guys say to Abuela? She's convinced you're both nuts."

Olive shrugs. "We were having a conversation about ice cream."

"Ice cream? Are you sure about that?"

"Yeah. She said she was feliz for nieto."

Bernadette doubles over, cracking up. "Nieto? Or Nieve? Nieto is grandson. Nieve is ice cream."

Olive's face falls. "Ooops."

"Oh my word, Olive," she says through her laughter. "I love you, prima, but I think you might have given Abuela the wrong idea about something."

We finally get our churros, piping hot and smelling of fluffy cinnamon sugar goodness. I almost burn my tongue on the first bite, but I don't even care. This is the best thing ever. Crispy on the outside, soft and doughy on the inside. Perfection.

Olive delivers Abuela's churros and comes back, gleefully munching on her own treats.

"Did she say anything?" asks Bernadette.

"No. But she did smile and roll her eyes."

The rumble of a truck stops on the street, and almost as soon as the iconic brown can be seen beyond the side gates, the band music comes to an abrupt halt, and the drummer jumps from behind his drum set, leaps off the stage screaming something over and over in Spanish, and bolts out of sight. Soon after, a UPS delivery man, complete with his brown shorts and a clipboard, comes into the yard with an envelope, which Pancho Two signs off on.

Why is this guy getting packages at the Precio house?

I guess I'm the only one who thinks this is weird, because the rest of the band members explode into peals of uncontrollable laughter, even after the delivery man leaves in his big, brown truck. Some of the family seem to be privy to the joke, and chuckles wave across the party guests.

"What's going on?" I ask.

Bernadette shakes her head. "Poor Oscar. Somehow he thinks the UPS truck is La Migra."

"La Migra?" I ask.

"Immigration enforcement," supplies Olive. "I learned that from a TV show."

"And nobody told him otherwise?"

Bernadette says, "Nope. The guys in the band think it's too funny."

"That's not funny at all," I say.

The rest of the band is packing up since they lost their drummer, and Ignacio and Enrique take the stage next to Mateo.

"Checking, check check," Ignacio says into the microphone.

Mateo sets down his guitar and smacks Ignacio in the shoulder. "It's on, you dork," he says, and even though he's not that close to the mic, we all can still hear him. Enrique leans in.

"We have a few words to say to our sister's new husband," he says sternly. "Get him up here."

The other Precio brothers climb onto the stage; Guillermo, the oldest, and Sebastian the youngest, while Dante and their other brother, Nataniel, seize Edmund from his seat by the shoulders and hoist him onto the stage. Once the brothers are all situated in an ominous half-circle around a petrified looking Edmund, they all lay their hands on him, lift him up over their heads, and start chanting over and over, *"Edmundo. Hermano. Ya eres Mexicano. Edmundo. Hermano. Ya eres Mexicano!"*

Olive squishes her churros over her heart. "Awww."

"Awww? Why awww? What's going on?" I question.

"They're finally accepting Edmund into the family," explains Bernadette. "They've been giving him a hard time since he and Francesca were in the first grade."

"Yikes. He seems to take it with grace, though," I say, recalling dinner the other night.

The wedding guests cheer and hoot while the brothers usher Edmund off the stage where Francesca is waiting with open arms. A love song from *West Side Story* plays over the speakers and they dance like they don't even notice anyone else around. It's like they're in their own world, not even noticing when Enrique and January join them on the dance floor. Olive urges Ignacio to dance, too, and soon everyone seems to be coupling up on the dance floor.

As I watch for Mateo, a tall, ridiculously handsome man seems to be walking straight toward me. I swear, he's Henry Cavill's twin brother. Daaang! I've never met him, so I wonder why he has his sight set on me, but as he gets closer, it's evident his eyes are fixed directly over my shoulder where Bernadette stands. Her bright smile shines at him like a beacon.

"Care to dance?" he asks, extending his hand out to her.

Okay, I'll just be invisible over here.

Clearly this guy only has eyes for Bernadette.

"Oh, I don't know," says Bernadette. "My boyfriend might get jealous."

"Then he's an idiot for leaving you alone," he says.

"I'm not alone. I'm with my new friend, Desirée."

Henry Cavill's doppelganger looks at me for the first time.

"Hello, Desirée," he says with a voice dripping of honey. "May I call you Desi?"

"Unnggg…" I'm at a loss for words as he takes my hand and kisses my knuckles. "I… I'll allow it."

His eyes twinkle as he smirks, the corners of his mouth peeking out behind my gangly hand. Bernadette rolls her eyes playfully.

"Enough of that." Mateo appears seemingly out of nowhere and steals my hand away. He pulls me to his side and doesn't let go. "Bernadette, control your man."

Bernadette laughs and squeezes her arms around the man in question. He squeezes her back and kisses the top of her head.

"Desirée, I'd like you to meet my boyfriend, Eugene. He's just trying to get a rise out of me so I'll dance, but jokes on him. I don't dance."

"Oh yes you do," he says. He picks her up, throws her over his shoulder like she's a sack of feathers, and steals her away. She squeals, waving goodbye to me.

"Watch out for my cousin, Desirée. He's a heartbreaker."

Oh, I already knew that.

"I'll bear that in mind," I call after her. But someone turns the music up, blasting out my words.

"Frickin' Uncle Borris," shouts Mateo over the music. "He's going to kill the speakers."

"Hmmm, the neighbors might complain," I say, jokingly. "Maybe that's why I was invited."

"All the neighbors were invited," he says. "Free food and nobody calls the cops."

Now I feel a little less special about the invitation, but I laugh it off.

"I saw a guy filling his Tupperware containers with the buffet food earlier," I say.

"That would be my Uncle Pedro. He always does that."

Some man, one of the family members, I presume, gets on the microphone and announces something in Spanish. Whatever is said, Mateo doesn't like it because he groans.

"Not karaoke! Anything but karaoke."

"What's wrong with karaoke?" I ask. "Karaoke is fun."

"Have you ever heard the sound of cats dying? How about cats dying to the underscore of narco music?"

"I can't say I've had the pleasure."

"My uncles singing Norteños off-key would bring you zero percent pleasure. Come on." He squeezes my hand and leads me away from the main part of the party. We pass the donkey at the gazebo, where they set up a photo booth. A bunch of teenage girls are petting and hugging him.

The backyard at the Precio house is impressively spacious. There's a small copse of fruit trees at the far end of the property. There are oranges, lemons, apricots, and avocado, but we stop under a cluster of cherry trees, where the pink blossoms have exploded this spring.

My own backyard is nothing but drought friendly artificial grass with ornamental American flags around the perimeter. My parents have always preferred simple landscaping, but now that the house is mine (and Ian's) I'd like to do something with it. Maybe start with a garden bed full of carrots and lettuce for Mr. Hopkins.

Mateo releases my hand but keeps close to me.

The depth of his gaze reaches down into my center, sending ribbons of warmth around my core. It's quieter here, and I can almost forget there's a party going on, as long as Mateo continues to look at me like that. The sensible part of me screams *"Run!"* But the other part of me, the one who makes bad decisions like having another slice of cake, or sleeping in when I should be looking for a better paying job, she likes Mateo's attention, the little hussy. She has absolutely no regard for future me, who is destined to lie on a bed of her own jagged, broken heart bits when she realizes Mateo's just a player. Like that Fleetwood Mac song… they only love you when they're playin'.

"You got churros without me," he says with a raspy whisper. "I hope you saved me some."

My hand curls around the paper cone of churros, even as he moves closer. I only have one left and I'm not sharing.

"You can go get your own," I say.

He shakes his head. "The line's too long."

"Too bad. You're just going to have to wait like the rest of us." I take a bite of my last churro, leaving only a small amount.

"I'm not good at waiting," he says. "When I see something I want, I take it."

Gulp.

He's too close. I can feel the air grow hotter with the proximity. I step back, but he just keeps coming until my shoe catches on the base of a cherry tree. My feet wobble beneath me, but he catches me and pins me against the trunk. The bark gently scratches on my back, but it's nothing compared to the prickly sensation all over my body. Mateo angles himself over me, supporting himself with his palm on the tree trunk above my head.

"Give me a taste, Paloma."

"Not a chance."

While I still have my wits about me, I bring the last bit of the churro to my lips and hold it there like a cigar, teasing him, crunching into the sweet, twisty dough.

Mateo's eyes darken with mischief as dark hair falls in curls over his forehead. He growls and snatches hold of my wrist, keeping me from polishing off the final crumb. My heart begins to race as I realize how dangerously close he is to me. With a devilish grin, he bites the other end of my churro. His fingers peel my hand away and he nibbles and nibbles until his cinnamon lips meet mine. He's warm and sweet and sticky, chewing, mouth against sugary mouth.

I close my eyes and enjoy the heck out of that deep fried pastry on my tongue, the crispy ridges, the fluffy doughy middle… and Mateo's lips all over mine moving like a dang dance as he chews… and chews… and chews.

This is the best freaking churro I've ever had in my life!

His lips hover for a minute, and yet every other part of his body doesn't touch me. I look up to search his face and he meets my gaze, his dark, intense eyes locking on mine with a glimmer of amusement. Without missing a beat, he swipes his tongue over his lips to lick off the excess sugar, close enough to barely graze the surface of my skin.

"Mmmm," he grumbles. "Got any more of that?"

This is too much. Is he teasing me here? What was that exactly? Not really a kiss. But not strictly platonic, either.

I shove his chest and he stumbles back. "You stole half of my churro," I say, pretending to be bothered.

Get it together, girl. I will not be one of his many women. I refuse.

Mateo shrugs his shoulders, flashing that devil-may-care smile of his. "Sharing is caring, Paloma."

The audacity of this man!

He ambles back to me and brushes his thumb over my bottom lip, swiping off the remaining cinnamon sugar. With a hot glare, his eyes fixate on mine as he brings his own thumb to his mouth and drags it down the inside of his lower lip.

"What was that, Mateo?"

"I'd say that was a pretty good churro," he says with a wink.

I crumble the parchment paper into a greasy, sugary ball, so angry at myself for enjoying the feel of Mateo's lips all over mine. I push myself off the tree and toss the paper at him.

"I've had better," I say, and I walk away to get another order of churros which I don't intend to share.

People haven't always
been there for me,
but music always has.

—Taylor Swift

Chapter Thirteen

MATEO

"Mister Precio! I can't take you anywhere."

Mom is absolutely livid, but I think a part of her wants to laugh.

"You're overreacting, woman. Nobody heard me."

"Everybody heard you! Every single soul inside that church. Heads turned. The priest looked directly at you."

Never a dull moment in this family. Make that double

when my father decides to go to church. Thank heavens we're almost home. Next Easter, I think I'll leave the country.

"Good," says Dad. "Next time he'll get better candles."

"The priest isn't in charge of buying the candles, Dad," says Nate.

"And there's nothing wrong with the candles," adds Mom. "Except for the people who don't know how to hold a candle without dripping wax all over themselves."

"The cups are *chaffa*," says Dad.

"My cup was fine," says Dante.

"Mine, too," adds Enrique. "How was yours, dear?"

January shakes her head. "I'm staying out of this one."

I'm getting a huge headache and just want to go to bed. Easter Sunday Mass is ridiculously crowded, and we have a gigantic family, so getting seats is near impossible. That's why Mom decided we'd go to the Saturday night vigil instead. Admittedly, it was beautiful. They passed out candles (with perfectly acceptable plastic cup shield thingies) to everyone and shut off all the lights. There was an orchestra and a fire pit outside for the lighting of the candles. And best of all: not crowded. But it lasted almost three hours. My butt hurts. My knees hurt. And to top it all off, Dad dripped hot wax on his hand when he tipped over the candle, causing him to curse like a Spanish sailor. Loudly. During a quiet moment of the Mass.

My poor mom looked like she wanted to sink under the pews and hide.

"*El saserdote no entiende.*" Dad waves it off like an annoying fly.

"No," says Mom. You're wrong. As usual. Father Mike *does* understand Spanish, and now I can't show my face around the Pastoral Council for at least—I don't know— until Advent."

"*No inventes,*" he scoffs.

"I burnt myself on the menorah once," says Olive. "I blew too hard and the wax went flying."

"A customer did that years ago," says Ignacio. "That's why the restaurants don't have candles on the tables anymore."

"I'm fine now," says Olive to Ignacio. "Thanks for your concern."

Ignacio pulls Olive to him. "I'm sorry, honey."

Bleh. Could these two get any sappier?

They fall back to give each other butterfly kisses (or whatever) while the rest of us continue down the sidewalk. In the distance, I see a single headlight coming our way. It's either a car with one light burnt out, or it's a two-wheeler. As it gets closer, something inside me jolts when I realize it's Desirée. All of a sudden, my headache lifts and the general ickiness I feel in my body dissolves. Just the sight of her makes me feel a thousand percent better. It's magic.

She pulls into her driveway just as we approach her house. She gets off, unstrapping a canvas grocery bag, and waves at us.

"Hi Mr. Precio. Mrs. Precio. Everybody."

My parents and siblings wave back, all greeting her in their own way. I break from the pack and run over to her.

"Save me," I whisper. "Say you need my help or something."

She regards me with a strange look but then smirks and almost shouts, "Oh Mateo. I'm so glad you're here. I sure could use some help with these groceries. It will just take a minute."

I squeeze my eyes shut. "Maybe tone it down a bit?"

"Oops."

"I'll help you," grunts Dante.

"Whatever, dude. We'll both help her," I say.

Desirée grins and lifts up the one bag by hooking her pointer finger in the loop, and hands to me. I take it, shove it into Dante's chest, and we follow her to her porch. Dante sends me a hard stare while we wait for Desirée to unlock her front door, and then we both jam into the doorframe at the same time, fighting to go in first. He wins, of course.

"You don't need to be here," he hisses. "Go home."

"I don't want to go home," I growl back.

"Can I get you two anything?" Desirée singsongs.

"No thanks," says Dante at the exact moment I say, "Tequila."

Desirée giggles. "I don't have any tequila, but I do have these old wine coolers. I don't know how long they've been in the fridge, but you're welcome to them."

"I like to live dangerously," I say, grabbing the canvas bag from Dante to set it on the kitchen counter. It weighs almost nothing.

"We're not staying," says Dante, harshly.

"Speak for yourself," I say as Desirée hands me a bottle of something fruity and carbonated. I know I'll hate it but I'm gonna suck it down anyway, just to annoy my brother.

I pop it open and take a slow, luxuriating sip. It tastes

like cherry cough syrup and I want to gag, but there's no way I'll let Dante see that.

He glowers at me with that lumberjack face of his and I stare right back, hitching a brow in a silent standoff. I can see Desirée from the corner of my eye. She's quietly watching us, biting her lip so as not to disturb the lions. Only the screech of my father's booming voice breaks the sound barrier to jolt our attention.

"Dante!" he yells from our own front yard. "Move your truck. You're blocking Nataniel's car."

"Sounds like Nate wants to get on the road, Dante," I say.

He grunts. "Let's go."

"I think I'll finish my drink first," I say cheerily.

He sends a pointed look to Desirée. "Will you be okay?"

In other words, will she be okay with me around?

"I think I'll survive," she says. "Thanks for your help. With the groceries."

Dante glances at the canvas bag on the counter, scowls at me, and squints at Desirée in a strange way.

"Yeah. You're welcome."

Relief wooshes from my lungs once the front door closes behind him.

"I thought he'd never leave," I say. I offer the wine cooler to Desirée. "Do you want to finish this?"

She grimaces. "I think my parents bought those for the fourth of July three years ago."

"I'll just recycle this then."

Desirée pours herself a glass of water while I pour the wine cooler in the kitchen sink and rinse out the bottle.

"So what's going on?" she asks, taking a sip of her water. "Why the plea for help?"

Setting my bottle on the counter, I turn and lean against it.

"I'm going crazy with all those people in the house. Especially Pancho Two. My parents, my dad, my uncles showing up unannounced. Francesca had the right idea by leaving."

"Francesca got married," she says.

"Yeah, so? If that's what it takes."

Halfway through her sip, she snorts, dribbling water on her chin.

"You?" she asks, laughing like a loon.

"What's so funny about that?"

"I just don't see you as the marrying type." She swishes her finger at me in a zigzag. "Clashes with that bad boy image, that's all."

"Bad boy image? Is that what you think I'm going for?"

"Pahleese! Long, messy hair. Tattoos for days. A girl at every gig."

"I don't have a girl at every gig."

She rolls her eyes and takes a chug of her water, finishing it in one swallow. When she's done, she places the glass in the sink.

"Three girls, then. Didn't mean to insult your libertine ways."

I don't know what she thinks of me, but I'm not here for this conversation right now. "What's in the bag, anyway?"

"Oh, you mean the one you and your burly brother had to take turns carrying because it's too heavy for my weak womanly muscles?"

Womanly muscles. I'm not even going to let myself think about Desirée's womanly anything.

"You do know whatever *'watching out for you'* Ian wants my brother to do, that's only half the reason Dante's giving me a hard time."

"Oh? And what's the other half?"

"That's just Dante. My whole life. He thinks I break everything in sight like I'm some sort of screw-up."

"I don't think he does," she says, placating me.

"He literally said to me the other day, *'You really screwed it up this time.'*"

"Well, if it makes you feel any better, Ian has me on a short leash. He's probably watching the security cameras right now."

She motions to a camera in the corner of the living room ceiling and waves. "Hi Ian."

So that's new. Her brother had the time to install a frickin' baby monitor but couldn't be bothered to take down the Christmas lights?

"Yeah, hi Ian." I also wave. With a one-finger salute.

She laughs and shoves my shoulder.

"So?" I point to her mystery satchel. "Bag?"

"Oh, just stuff for the egg hunt tomorrow." She opens the bag, taking out jelly beans and a package of plastic eggs.

"You're going to an egg hunt? Who do you know with kids?"

"It's a thing we do for the community kids. We do it every year."

"Who's we?"

"The Bunny Hop League." She says this like I should totally know what the heck a bunny hop league is."

"What's that? Is it anything like the Lollipop Guild? Because if it is, I'm gonna have to intervene."

"No," she says, unpacking the eggs and jelly beans. "The Bunny Hop League is a fun organization for rabbits to display feats of agility."

"Can you repeat that in non-nerdy terms?"

Desirée pops open a few eggs and begins to fill them with the jelly beans.

"Equestrian. For rabbits. Anthony Hopkins is top of his breed class. He's a Rhinelander Rabbit, so his hip to shoulder ratio gives him an advantage for hurdle hopping."

"Okay, Radagast the Brown, let me get this straight. Your terror of a rodent is in a bunny hopping club, and tomorrow said club will get together to hide eggs for kids. Is that right?"

"Rabbits aren't rodents. And it's not a club. It's a league. The agility competitions are a big deal with trophies and prizes. There's even a guy with a cart selling hot dogs and sodas…"

"Oh, well if there's a guy selling hot dogs."

"They're good hot dogs."

"I'll bet." I steal a handful of jelly beans and pop a few in my mouth.

"Stop that. They're for the kids."

"Okay, you convinced me."

"Convinced you of what?"

"I'll come with you tomorrow. The hot dogs were the clincher."

"I didn't invite you." She moves the bag of jelly beans out of my reach and fills another plastic egg.

"How are you going to carry all these eggs and your rabbit on that Little Tykes motor scooter of yours?"

"I can manage."

"I'll drive. And before you thank me, just know I have ulterior motives."

"Oh? And what would that be?"

"You'll find out tomorrow."

My brain:
2% phone numbers,
3% names,
5% school knowledge,
90% song lyrics.

-Unknown

Chapter Fourteen

MATEO

It's too hot and too early in the morning, and too early in the morning to be this hot. Los Angeles weather makes no sense. Or maybe it's me. Because watching Desirée skipping around the bunny agility course is making my chest warm. She's leading Mr. Hopkins through hoops and over hurdles in the floweriest dress known to mankind, and when she runs, the hem swishes and flips up, exposing her whiter than white legs. She looks like one of those blue floral teacups. That damn dress brings out her eyes and when I picked her up this morning, it felt like I was getting hit by a hurricane. Why did I think this would be a good idea?

Anthony Hopkins is going through the agility course like the little star he is. Apparently he's a fan favorite, hopping over hurdles higher than some of the earlier rabbits could. You'd think any old rabbit could clear four rungs, but no. The fat, floppy-eared one named Butterscotch could barely jump over one without knocking it off the rails.

Desirée's face lights up every time her rabbit clears a hurdle. The way her hair swooshes all over the place as she runs. Her smile and lighter-than-air giggles. Something behind my belly button swoops and dips.

Maybe it was the hot dog. Who eats hot dogs so early in the morning? Okay, it's not the crack of dawn, but it's earlier than I'm usually conscious.

Desirée leads Anthony Hopkins over the last section of the agility course, and the assembled crowd applauds. It's a step up from a golf clap, but Desirée treats the cheering like a quarterback making the winning touchdown. She throws her hands up in the air and pumps her fists. Then she scoops up Mr. Hopkins in her arms and does a victory lap. The park is small, so it's not a long lap. The announcer calls the time. I'm not paying attention to him, though, because I'm too caught up in Desirée's blue floral dress and the way her bangs part a little in the middle when the wind catches them.

"Whoo hoo!" she hoots as she makes her way to me.

"Did you see that? He didn't miss a hurdle. Who's a good bunny?" She scratches the bunny behind the ears.

"So did he win?"

"I don't know yet. There are still a couple more contenders, but Mr. Hopkins made good time. I think it's his best yet."

"Well, I'm glad he has a hobby to keep him off the streets."

"Wanna buy me a Dr. Pepper? I'm parched."

"I think the hot dog man is sick of me, but yes, I will buy you a Dr. Pepper."

"How many hot dogs did you eat?"

"Four. But they're not big like Dodger Dogs. Don't look at me like that."

"Whaaat? I'm not looking at you. I have a twitchy eye, that's all."

"Better get that checked," I say.

We head over to the hot dog stand where the guy is too preoccupied with his phone until I clear my throat. "One Dr. Pepper please."

The guy gives me a weird look as I get out my wallet.

"I want a hot dog," says Desirée cheerily.

So. Damn. Cheery. My chest is going to explode.

"I guess I'll have another, too," I say.

"Wanna make it an even dozen?" asks the guy with a sarcastic grin. Then his eyes skate over Desirée in a way I do not like at all.

"I dunno, maybe. Do you have a punch card?"

Punch-him-in-the-face card, if I had my way.

He ignores me, though, and keeps his eyes on Desirée

the whole time he's serving up our order. Even when I hand him the cash.

"Saw you out there with your rabbit," he says all smarmy, blatantly flirting. "Nice job."

"Thanks." Desirée is either completely oblivious or—no that's all. She's just too nice to think he's flirting with her.

He plops my hot dog on the cart and gently places hers into her hands.

Creepwad.

"Mustard?" I say, annoyed out of my mind. After four hot dogs, he should know to add the mustard. Or at least ask.

"Here." He slams the bottle down and jerks his chin, still gawking at Desirée.

Okay, it's self-serve, now. I squirt a good measure of mustard on my dog. I'm getting my money's worth, dammit. I might just take some for later.

"How long does it take to train your rabbit to jump like that?"

"Well, rabbits love to jump, and Mr. Hopkins is especially talented…"

"Can we go now?" I ask impatiently.

"Would you like some mustard on your hot dog?" he offers Desirée, picking up the bottle.

"Just ketchup," she says.

He reaches for the hot dog in her hand, deliberately touching her. "Allow me."

That's enough of that buddy.

"Nope. I got it. I'm really good at this," I blurt, reaching inside the cart to steal the ketchup. "I just did my own mustard, so I'm practically an expert now."

The guy shifts his eyes to me then back at Desirée. "Is he your boyfriend?"

Her eyes go wide and she blurts, "No! Not at all. Are you kidding? *Not* my boyfriend."

She's forcing a laugh now.

"Wow," I say. "The idea repels you that much? I get it."

"No, that's not what I meant."

I hand her the ketchup and scowl at the guy. "No tip this time, dude."

I walk away with my mustardy hot dog. Maybe too mustardy but I'll never admit that to anyone. A few moments later, Desirée catches up to me. She's got her hands full with a hot dog, a can of Dr. Pepper, and Mr. Hopkins' leash.

"Hey, wait up."

I take pity on her and take the leash. "Did he get your number?"

"Whatevs, Mateo. He's not my type."

"Oh yeah? What's your type?"

"Guys without an attitude."

"That rules hot dog guy out. Impossible to get good service these days."

"I know, right? He didn't even offer to show us the wine list."

"I took extra mustard."

She glances down at the monstrosity of my hot dog. It's just a yellow blob at this point.

"So, you said you had an ulterior motive for coming today?" She swipes a finger through my mustard and deposits on her hot dog. Quite the talent while carrying a can of Dr. Pepper.

"Did I say that?"

"Yes you did, sir. So fess up."

I decide I don't want to fess up. Fessing up is overrated. Definitely not for me. Because that would entail telling her I care for her feelings more than I want to get with her.

Crazy, I know.

What I'd really like to ask her is if she'd be upset if I had a little talk with Ian and tell him to back off. She's a grown woman and doesn't need a babysitter. But I'm a chicken, and after hot dog guy, I've decided I don't like the idea of men creeping all over her any more than Ian does. Or Dante, for that matter.

I hate thinking about the scumbags she comes across delivering pizzas. How many invite her in. Or worse. Try to force her in.

"I… I wanted to tell you…" What comes out of my mouth next is either inspired or completely asinine. Either way, it's spur of the moment and certainly not planned. But all I can think of is taking Desirée away from her pizza delivery job. Keep her close where I can see her. And away from the prying eyes of my brother, her brother, and those frickin' security cameras at her house.

"I'm listening," she says, taking a sip of Dr. Pepper.

I'm a fool and an idiot and a selfish rapscallion for this. But that's me, I guess.

"I wanted to tell you I'm interested in meeting your friends. For the guitarist position."

Her face lights up. It's a beautiful sight. I'd do anything to see it.

"Really? Are you serious?"

"Yeah. I hate my job. I can't wait to get out of my parent's house. A tour sounds perfect right now."

"You won't regret it. And just because you go on tour doesn't mean you can't work on your own stuff. I believe in you."

"Then you're the only one."

She hugs me, hands full still. I'm wrapped in her arms with a hot dog and a cold Dr. Pepper against my back. I wish she'd never let go, even though I know I'm an ass for making this decision based solely on taking her with me on tour. I won't tell her that right now, though. Timing is everything. And for the next few seconds on the clock, all I care about is the way her body fits against mine so perfectly. Like a cello filling its maestro with the sound of hope through warm, living tones and broad vibrato.

In other words, I am of unsound mind and should have my head examined.

She's in a great mood all the way home, and so am I… until we notice the enormous motorhome parked in her driveway. That could only mean one thing.

Disappointment drips from Desirée's lips as she says, "My parents are back."

Let's take a moment
to thank earphones
for helping us ignore
stupid people all around us.

-Unknown

Chapter Fifteen
DESIRÉE

Mateo parks his car on the street between both our houses.

"Have I ever mentioned your dad reminds me of Robert DeNiro?"

"Like, Goodfellas Robert DeNiro, or Godfather Robert DeNiro?"

"*Meet the Parents* Robert DeNiro."

I look thoughtfully at my parent's motorhome. "I don't see it. But I know where you're coming from."

"Come on. Your dad is a retired military man, his son is a military man, and he probably expects you to marry a military man."

"Is it the thousand and one American flags that give it away?" I joke.

"Do you want me to go in there with you?" he asks. I know he doesn't want to, but I appreciate the gesture anyhow.

"No. I can handle Mr. Hopkins' crate on my own. You go ahead and celebrate Easter with your folks."

"Hmmm. I don't know what's worse. My parents or yours."

"I'll call you later to work out a time to meet with my friend Scott."

"Who?"

"The guy with the cover band?"

"Oh. Right."

We climb out of the car, Mateo helping me remove Mr. Hopkins from the back seat. Just as we shut the doors, my dad barrels outside to greet us.

His arms are outstretched, but I know he's putting on a show. The question is, for whose benefit?

"Let me see my beautiful girl," he says. "Give your old dad a hug."

I set Mr. Hopkins on the grass and tuck under Dad's arms. He practically crushes me.

"Hi, Daddy," I squeak under the pressure of his grip.

He glares over to Mateo, who's trying to sneak home.

"Mateo Precio," Dad calls out. "Well, well, well. Don't you look all grown up. Get over here."

Mateo throws me a look and I hitch one shoulder as if to say, *'sorry, but you might as well come say hello to my overbearing father.'*

Mateo ambles over and Dad shakes his hand with one hard squeeze. I can barely tell the grimace on Mateo's face, but I know he's hiding the pain.

"Wow, that's quite a handshake, Mr. Grant," he says, flexing his fingers.

"You can tell a lot about a man by his handshake. I can see yours hasn't changed much since you were a kid."

"Dad!"

Mateo shakes his head at me. "It's fine."

"Speaking of handshakes, pumpkin. There's someone I'd like you to meet."

He motions for me to follow him into the house.

"Nice to see you again," says Mateo, backing away.

"You're coming in, too, aren't you? We have some catching up to do."

As he turns his back to go into the house, I hear him say under his breath, "Since you've made yourself so comfortable in my house lately."

"My house?"

Even though Mom and Dad signed the deed over to me and Ian when they decided to live the RV life, I'm beginning to see that it was just a formality.

"Um, I should probably check on my parents," Mateo says, hooking his thumb over his shoulder.

"I won't take no for an answer, young man."

What is my dad up to?

Mateo silently mouths the words *"Robert DeNiro"* behind my dad's back as we follow him into the house. I toss him a sympathetic look.

When we get inside, there's my mother holding a charcuterie board. Where did she even get that? From inside the motorhome?

"Oh hello, dear," she says. "My hands are full. How about a kiss?"

She puckers up and offers me her cheek, so I go in for an air kiss. *Muah muah.* We're not even French.

Mateo's right behind me with his hands in the front pockets of his jeans, probably recovering from that handshake. That's when I notice his eyes fixed on something behind Mom. I follow the direction of his gaze, and land on a blond guy with a short-clipped haircut, broad shoulders, and a salmon-colored polo shirt. He rises from the sofa when he sees us and stiffly approaches like he's got a stick up his spine. But he's got a nice smile—white, sparkly teeth and all. I can feel the heat of Mateo's discomfort behind me.

"Desirée, darling," says Dad, nudging me into the living room. "This is Chet."

Mateo snorts a stifled laugh but Dad plows through.

"He's Vice Admiral Ward's boy. You remember the Ward family don't you?"

"I think I met them at the officer's ball," I say. It's a lie, of course. I tune out completely at those things.

Chet's smile widens, but even I can tell this *'impromptu'* meeting is making him uncomfortable.

"He's making captain soon," says Mom. "Isn't that nice?"

"It's nice to meet you, Chet," I say. Mateo clears his throat. "This is our next-door neighbor, Mateo."

"Sup," says Mateo, doing a chin jerk.

Chet looks like he doesn't know what to do with his hands. Does he offer a handshake? Does he salute? Such a conundrum. He settles for a head nod and a cordial greeting.

"Nice to meet you both."

"Oh, Mateo," says Mom. "I didn't see you there. Salami?"

She holds out the charcuterie.

Mateo holds in a chuckle. "No thank you. I've had a lot of meat today."

Five hot dogs. That I know of.

"Why don't we sit down? I'm sure Chet would like to get to know you youngsters. I was thinking, wouldn't it be nice if you kids hit the town?"

Ugh. This is so typical of my parents. All my life, they've tried to set me up with other humans my age as if being ten, or a teenager, or a young adult is enough in common to be friends forever. And now I know why dad insisted Mateo come inside. To flaunt clean cut G.I. Joe in his face. To let him know he'll never live up to their expectations.

"Mom, Dad, can I talk to you in the study please?"

I don't even wait for them to answer, stomping off into Dad's old study on the other side of the house. I've been meaning to turn it into a knitting and sewing room, but I haven't had the chance to convince my brother yet.

I feel a little bad leaving Mateo in the living room with

Military Ken Doll, but I need to set things straight right now or I'll lose my crap.

As soon as I know we're all present, I spin around to my confused parents.

"What are you guys up to? Is this your idea of a set up?"

"Such a warm greeting, Desirée," says Mom. "Can't we come see our daughter on Easter without the third degree?"

"Come on. I haven't seen you for three Easters in a row. Why this one? Why now?"

"We missed you," she replies diplomatically. "Besides, we're going to Mazatlán next and thought we'd pop in on the way."

"And Chet just happened to hitch a ride?"

"Don't be silly," says Dad. "His father found out we were going to be in town at the same time and asked me to offer some hospitality to the boy. He's back from an eighteen- month deployment around the South China Sea."

"That's swell, Dad."

"And I thought, well, your mother and I thought… you might get along. He'll be stationed in San Diego. Just a day trip for you."

"I'm sure he's very nice, but I can make my own friends."

I'm willing to bet this Chet guy isn't any more thrilled than I am. I don't mind hanging out, but ya gotta admit, this is awkward to the thousandth degree. Plus, I know my parents. They have something up their sleeves.

"It wouldn't hurt you to go on one date, Desirée," says Mom. Aaaand there it is. "We took great pains to invite him over. Imagine how it looked when you weren't even home.

And to find you've been out... who knows where with that neighbor boy."

"That neighbor boy gave me a ride to the rabbit agility tournament. By the way, Mr. Hopkins won first place."

"And that's another thing," says Dad. "We don't like you riding around on that scooter. It's not safe. We're buying you a car."

"I can buy my own car, Dad."

"Then what's stopping you?"

"I like my Vespa. When I get married and give you a hundred grandkids, I'll get a more sensible vehicle."

"Why do you think we brought Chet over?" says Dad. "He drives a Volvo. Safe. Reliable."

I try not to let my eyeballs roll right out of my head.

"Honey," says Mom. "We'd like to see you settle down. Is that so wrong?"

I sigh, feeling like a jerk. "No Mom. I'm sorry. It's not. I just want you to trust me to do things in my own time."

"As long as you marry a military man," adds Dad.

Nice. Soooo subtle.

Then he adds under his breath, "At least you wouldn't have your Christmas lights up in April."

"Oh great. Does Chet know this or are you going to spring it on him on the wedding day? How many goats was I worth, by the way?"

"You don't have to be so dramatic," says Mom.

"Who me? I'd just like to know if he prefers gin and tonic or an old fashioned when he comes home from work. Pipe or cigar? And how about a foot rub?"

"All right, Desirée, that's quite enough," says Mom. "Can we go back to our guest now?"

"Guests, Mom. Plural."

"Yes, yes, of course that's what I meant."

We go back into the living room and my heart skips a beat at the sight of Mateo on the couch holding Mr. Hopkins on his lap. What the blazes is wrong with me?

Poor Chet seems incredibly uncomfortable. I can only imagine what kinds of things he and Mateo talked about for the last couple of minutes. Probably sat in stone silence engaged in a staring contest.

Chet springs to his feet as soon as he sees us. Seriously, if his posture was any better, he'd be a flagpole.

Mateo gets up too, in his own casual way. He's still cradling Mr. Hopkins. I know it's a rabbit and not a human baby, but my ovaries are throwing a samba parade, shaking their sequined and feathered tushies to the soundtrack of Rio.

"Soooo…" says Mom. "Why don't we all sit down? We picked up some Prosecco at Whole Foods. Chet, would you like a glass?"

"No alcohol for me, ma'am. I need to stay sharp."

So, no gin and tonic for him when we're married.

"Good call," says my father. "I respect a man who's dedicated to his career."

"Thank you, sir."

"Now, Mateo. What exactly do you do for work?"

Mateo's eyes slice to me for a way out of this. He doesn't want to be here even less than I do. I consider embellishing his sales job, playing it up for him since I know he won't. But there's a ruckus going on outside in the Precio yard, and it's just loud enough not to ignore.

From where I sit, I can only see the top of Mrs. Precio's

head, and her arms flying up every few seconds. She seems to be running back and forth, shouting something in Spanish.

My own mother hisses out a breath. "What on earth is that woman up to now?"

She says this as if she's totally bothered by the shenanigans of the next-door neighbors on a daily basis. She's been here a whole thirty seconds and already complaining.

Mateo and I scurry to the window to see what's going on.

There in the backyard, Mrs. Precio is charging back and forth with an empty green box in her hand, rattling off colorful expletives in Spanish. At least they seem like expletives.

"Oh boy," says Mateo.

"What's happening?" I ask.

"Somebody got into her Girl Scout cookie stash."

"Oh that's bad," I say. That woman has been stashing her Thin Mints for months.

"What is it?" asks Mom, stretching her neck up from her seat on the sofa. "What's bad?"

"I better go," says Mateo. "There is a reckoning afoot."

"Don't leave me," I whisper. "I'll be forced to hang out with plastic Ryan Gosling."

He passes Mr. Hopkins into my arms. "I think you'll survive." He winks at me and then waves to my parents. "Mr. Grant, Mrs. Grant… it was nice to see you again." Clearing his throat, he gives Chet a dude nod. "Chet."

Chet half stands, then sits back down when my father signals for him to stay put.

Mateo heads to the front door and I follow him, only to

hear my mother call out, "What is going on outside? I demand to know."

"Nothing, Mom."

I catch Mateo just before he steps off the front porch. "Hey."

He pauses and glances at me sidelong.

"Tell your mom she can hide her cookies in my freezer any time she wants."

The corner of his mouth ticks up. "She'll probably take you up on that."

I wait until he's out of sight and the shouts of his mom hunting for the Girl Scout cookie caper are nothing but muffled sounds behind the walls of their house. Then I go inside and plaster on a smile I don't feel.

These go to 11.

-Christopher Guest

Chapter Sixteen

MATEO

Desirée's friend Scott owns a guitar repair shop in West L.A., but right next door, an elderly hippie couple runs the weirdest ukulele store I've ever seen. Granted, I haven't been in many ukulele stores, but I'm sure this one takes the cake.

They sell nothing but ukuleles, which isn't strange, but the shabby chic decor mixed with Hawaiian tikis of various sizes is a sight to behold. I've counted no less than eight velvet couches, hammocks swinging from the ceiling, a chair shaped like lips, fur covered stools, and orange shaggy rugs that could have been transported straight from 1975.

Apparently, Desirée comes here every Thursday night for the weekly jam session. Bring your own ukulele, patchouli provided.

I don't play ukulele, but Desirée insisted I bring one of hers and told me I'd probably learn pretty quickly.

There's a cloud of smoke that smells curiously of skunk, but I'm told it's just incense. Some guy in a fedora pointed out the incense burner earlier, in case I needed further proof. There are lava lamps everywhere, and beaded curtains along the walls.

All in all, the evening is one big kumbaya circle, and Desirée was right about the ukulele being easy to pick up. Easier than guitar, anyway.

She's so at ease here, happily strumming along to "Tequila Sunrise" and "Close to You" by The Carpenters. Then again, she can fit in anywhere. She'd fit in at Carnegie Hall, or the Hollywood Bowl, or in some boho tea house on open mic night. That's Desirée for you. So incredibly talented, yet so humble. Everyone here seems to love her, and of course she's on a first name basis with them all, even asking about their families, or how that one thing or the other turned out for them.

In the middle of "This Land is Your Land", which I thought I'd never have to sing after the fifth grade, I ask, "How do you know this guy Scott?"

I'm not jealous. She can know guys named Scott all day long.

"He comes to the ukulele jams sometimes. But when I called him, he said he's swamped with repairs, so he couldn't make it. He's expecting us once this is over.

"And you don't know what kind of tribute band this is?" I ask. "Because I draw the line at disco."

"What's wrong with disco?" she asks with that adorable throaty giggle of hers.

"Nothing wrong with disco. I love disco. It's the bell bottom jumpsuits that get me. The make my butt look big."

"Oh stop that. Your butt looks great." Her eyes grow wide, and she back pedals, stuttering. "I mean… I haven't really noticed your butt… so I guess it's not big. Otherwise I'd notice. Just because of the size."

A flush of pink blossoms in her cheeks, contrasting beautifully with the blue of her eyes. She scrunches her nose and buries her face in the curve of her ukulele.

"Hey." Hooking my thumb under her chin, I lift her face to meet my gaze. "I'd be disappointed if you didn't notice my butt."

She bites her bottom lip and chuckles. "Um, okaaay."

Madres! The ache I've been carrying in my chest spreads south. She has no idea the effect she has on me. Everything about her is killing me softly. The way she smiles, her raspy giggle, her incredible musical talent. And those eyes. It's impossible how blue they are, as if they've been artificially dyed like candy.

"For the record," I say deeply. "I think *you'd* look amazing in a bell bottom jumpsuit."

She visibly gulps and twists her lips to the side.

"Well, I don't think it's a disco group," she says. Scott's a rock and roll guy. I think it's a Led Zeppelin cover band or something like that."

"Led Zeppelin's cool. I can do that."

The song comes to an end and the whole room erupts in applause. These people are serious about their ukulele jams. And folky all-American anthems, apparently.

The gray-haired lady who owns the shop stands up, rosy cheeked and glassy-eyed. "That concludes our jam for this week. Thank you for joining us, beautiful strummers. And remember, if you love life, life will love you back."

"That was quite the climatic finale," I say.

"We end with that song every week," Desirée says, packing up her instrument. "It's kind of our alma mater. You'll memorize it if you want to keep coming."

"I memorized it in choir. Then I blocked it from my memory."

"I didn't know you were in choir. What's this Mateo lore I keep discovering?"

"Oh, I was a complete choir nerd. Cardigan and everything."

Her face lights up, like she's just progressed to the next level of the *Get to Know Mateo* video game.

"Wow. Show choir?"

"No. We didn't have that at St. Cecilia's, thank God."

"But you would have been so into it if they did. Admit it."

I clear my throat. This whole thing. Sharing stuff about myself—beyond the music, beyond the immediate physical layer—is more than I've ever revealed to any woman.

"Scott's probably waiting," I say.

She gives me a mock pout and goes to say goodbye to a

few of the other strummers. They're all bummed she has to go so early, apparently.

"I usually stay for cheese and hummus," she says, slinging her ukulele case over her shoulder.

"I hate to keep you from your post-jam snacks."

"It's fine. Mom's charcuterie will hold me over in cheese for a week."

We go outside, heading over to the repair shop. Her parents left Los Angeles yesterday, but I sense their presence is still hanging over Desirée's head.

"So, how long will they be gone this time?" I ask, treading lightly.

She scrunches her shoulders to her ears. "Who knows? Christmas, maybe. But I have a feeling Mazatlán won't be their thing, so maybe sooner."

She told me they were planning to explore Baja California's beaches where there's a whole community of American and Canadian RVers. Some of the friends they made on their adventures somehow convinced them to meet them there. I doubt they'll survive past Rosarito.

We reach Scott's Guitar Repair, triggering a hanging jingle bell as we open the door. It's a guitar graveyard in here. Dozens of instruments line the floor in various arrays of disrepair. There's a counter serving as a front desk with a sign that says, "Be groovy or leave."

"Hello?" Desirée calls out. "Scott?"

A crash comes from the back room, and seconds later, a tall forty-something man emerges wearing a sleeveless leopard print T-shirt. His ruddy face is further accentuated by the long, blond rocker wig he's wearing. It's so obviously a wig, it's almost yellow.

When he sees us, he breaks out into Neil Diamond's "Desirée".

"Desirée, oh Desirée!" he sings, coming around the counter with his arms outstretched.

"Hi Scott," she says, so sweetly. "This is my friend Mateo I was telling you about."

Scott makes a sharp turn to face me, looks me up and down, and nods in approval.

"I like what I see," he says in a Cockney accent. "We can work with this… *if* I like what I hear."

"Oh," says Desirée, a little surprised. "Have you always been British, Scott, or am I just not that observant?"

Scott places a palm on both of our shoulders, creating a huddle.

"Between you and me and the big blue sea, love… I'm getting into character. You can call me David for the foreseeable future."

"Okay," she chirps. "I like your hair."

He flips it over his shoulder. "You ever heard of method actors? I'm a method musician. Immersing myself in the persona. I *am* David."

"Bowie?" I question. Because that would be super cool. I'd be up for playing in a Bowie tribute band.

"St. Hubbins," he says with a serious look. "One of the greatest rockers to ever live."

I'm trying to recall who David St. Hubbins is, or was, when we're interrupted by the jingle of the door.

A short guy with long, dark hair, bangs, and a bushy mustache bursts in and sticks out his tongue between his pinky and forefinger.

"Rock and roll," he shouts, also with a Cockney accent.

Scott answers back with his own version of the rocker hand sign. "Rock n roll, mate."

Desirée makes a hang ten sign. "Yeah, rock and roll. Woot woot!"

I tip up my chin, definitely not repeating any hand signs or declarations of rock and roll devotion. I mean, I love rock as much as the next guy. That doesn't mean I have to announce it everywhere I go.

The two guys stare at me for a moment, bobbing their heads as though waiting for me to join their spandex club. Spoiler alert: not gonna happen.

"Is this the chap?" asks the newcomer.

"This is the chap," says Scott.

"I'm certainly not the chap," says Desirée with a cute giggle.

Scott extends his arm. "Mateo, meet Derek Smalls, our esteemed bassist."

"Hey up," says Derek, offering me his hand.

"Hey," I say, about to shake his hand, but he makes a fist. So we're doing fist-bumps then.

Desirée also fist-bumps him. "Nice to meet you."

"Let's have a butchers," he says to me, twirling a finger.

"A… what?"

"He wants you to spin around," says Scott.

Oh…kay.

These guys are a little odd, but I tell myself to trust the process. Maybe they just want to make sure I look the part they're trying to fill.

"So," I say while turning in place. "Desirée didn't say what kind of music you play. Actually, she didn't seem to know much."

"Rock n roll, mate," says Scott and Derek at the same time. I half expect them to do air guitars and climb into a time traveling telephone booth.

"Yeah, but. Like, do you do 70s covers? 80s covers? You kind of have that Van Halen hair going on."

Scott wraps his arm over my shoulder and tugs me, practically into his armpit… His face is so close, I can feel his breath on my cheek.

"You are going to love this. Oh by the way, where's your guitar?"

"I'll get it," says Desirée cheerily.

I left my Gibson Les Paul in the car, keeping that baby safe. I love that guitar. Flame top blueberry burst. The color of Desirée's eyes. Plus, I didn't want to draw attention by bringing a big hard case inside the ukulele shop.

I watch as Desirée walks out the door, mesmerized by the bounce of that dark chocolate hair, swaying back and forth like a metronome.

Focus, Mateo.

I blink away the haze. "So, as you were saying?"

"Ah yes," says Scott. "This is epic."

"I believe you."

"Ready?"

"The anticipation is killing me," I deadpan.

He lets go of my shoulder and goes to stand shoulder to shoulder with Derek. He lifts his hands to spread them over his head like he's reading a marquee. Derek mirrors him, wagging his bushy brows.

"The name of our band is…"

The door jingles as Desirée enters with my guitar. I help her with it right away, setting it gently on the floor. She's strong enough, but I shouldn't have let her act as my roadie.

"Thank you, Paloma."

"You're welcome. I didn't want you to miss a thing."

I whisper in her ear. "Believe me, there was nothing to miss."

We look expectantly at Scott and Derek, who still have their palms splayed over their heads. They look back at us awkwardly.

"Um… the name of your band?"

"Yes," says Scott. "Are you ready?"

"I'm more than ready," I say, losing patience.

"I like that," he hoots.

"Rock and roll," says Derek.

If this goes on much longer, I'll walk right out of here. But I promised Desirée I'd give it a shot. And it wouldn't be fair to make her look bad in front of her friend. I think.

"Rock and Roll is the name of your band?" I ask. At this point, I wouldn't be surprised. They've been saying it enough.

Scott flops his hands to his sides, huffing. "No! Smell the Glove. Smell the Glove is our name."

"Smell… the Glove?" What kind of name is that?

Desirée glances at me, then back at them. "Wait a minute. Isn't that from that movie? Turn it up to eleven… what's it called?"

Ooooohhhhh. That's where I've heard of Smell the Glove. It's the name of a fake album by that fake band.

"*This is Spinal Tap*," I say.

She snaps her fingers. "That's the one."

"So, it's a Spinal Tap tribute band?" I ask.

"Yeah, mate. And if you can play like Desirée says you can, I have a feeling we'll be calling you Nigel from now on."

"Um, I think I left my pick in the car. Desirée, can you help me look for it?" I jerk my head toward the exit.

"We have plenty of picks, mate," says Scott.

"Uh, thanks, but I really like this particular pick. It's my lucky pick. I'll just be a minute."

I clamp hands with Desirée and bolt out the door. When we're a few shops down the sidewalk, I say, "How close a friend is this Scott guy? Because he's certifiably nuts."

"He's a little out there," she says. "But he's a good guy, I promise."

"Is there something going on with you two? He's undressing you with his eyes."

"Don't be silly. You think every guy is undressing me with his eyes."

"That's because they are."

She crosses her arms. "I think you should go back in there and give them a chance. It's a gig. It may not be glamorous but at least it's better than your door-to-door sales job."

"I never said I was looking for something glamorous. And I already said I'd consider a cover band. But Spinal Tap? I dunno, kid."

"But you love Spinal Tap."

"Yeah, because it's a funny movie. I'm not interested in being seen as a joke."

She sighs and looks out into the distance. "Okay. It's your call. I'll go tell the guys."

Her shoulders slump as she walks back to the repair

shop. Now I feel like crap. No universe exists where I want to be the man who disappoints Desirée. Not even a little bit. And I might regret what I do next, but I told myself I'd do everything I can to get her out of the fenced in cage she lives in. Even if it's a pretty, white picket fence.

"Desirée. Wait."

Singing is the shower
is all fun and games
until you get shampoo
in your mouth,
then it just becomes
a soup opera.

-Unknown

Chapter Seventeen

DESIRÉE

Some women go gaga over men in suits, specifically the slow folding of dress shirt cuffs, revealing gratuitous muscles that would give Popeye a run for his spinach. These women basically go bananas over some good shirt-sleeve porn, which is understandable. I like a forearm reveal as much as the next gal.

But may I suggest something a thousand times sexier than some stuffy suit wearing guy letting loose after a long day in the office?

Stuffy suit guy has had his moment in the sun.

Ladies, I present to you… competence forearms. That's right. Forearms that flex and swell from the effort of physical work. Forearms with defined muscles, intricately engaged by the execution of precise, and flexible movements. Skilled, proficient movements, which activate veins, sinews, and corded muscles.

Among these non-suit-wearing types, no other can match the mastery and artistry of a guitarist's arm. The speed and dexterity when finger picking or constructing bar chords. The command and proficiency he has over the instrument, hands gliding over the fretboard, fingers flexing, creating elegant, long shapes all the way up to the elbow. Tanned skin covered in ink, with a light dusting of dark hair. Thin scraps of leather randomly tied onto his wrist. And the black and silver rings adorning his fingers—how cold and hard they'd feel pressed against my—

"Desirée? Are you okay?"

"Huh?" I blink away my daydream. "Yeah. I'm great."

Just peachy.

Mateo blinks at me with his blue guitar on his lap, the aforementioned forearm hanging over the curve of the body. There's still a low hum coming from the guitar amp, live and hot from his brilliant, soulful shredding.

Scott and Derek gape at him, mouths hanging open, practically salivating. They were only looking for a guy who could play the song list for their Smell the Glove band, but Mateo's flashy arpeggios and pitch bends were just a little bit extra, and probably his way of showing off.

I don't see the guys complaining.

"Wow, mate," says Scott. "I think I speak for the rest of the band to say you're in. Derek, what do you think?"

"I say he's in," says Derek (whose real name is Rusty, we found out).

Scott… or David now, I guess… extends his hand to Mateo. "Welcome to Smell the Glove, Nigel."

I clap my hands over my chest. "Yay. You're Nigel now."

"Hang on now," says Mateo. "We need to discuss the terms first."

Scott and his friend give each other a confused look.

"Sure," says Scott. "I mean, there's not much to it. I already went over the pay and the proposed tour schedule. We rehearse Sunday afternoons and Wednesday nights unless we're on the road. Derek's wife makes the costumes. I can email you all the deets."

"And what about Desirée?"

Scott glances back and forth between me and Mateo. "Uh… I think we've got the costumes covered."

"No. Desirée joins the band or I walk."

"Mateo, what are you doing?" I hiss under my breath, even though the other guys can totally hear me.

"Mate, there are no ladies in Spinal Tap, therefore, there are no ladies in Smell the Glove. Besides, we don't have the budget."

"I'm sure you can fit her in somehow. She can play any instrument. Like… I don't know, keyboards while you guys are doing a costume change or something."

"Look, mate. We have five spots in the band and only enough money to split five ways."

"She can have my pay."

"What? Mateo, no."

"She can have your pay? Like you're only in this for the fame and glory but not the money?"

"I guess you could say that."

Derek bobs his head with approval. "That's so rock and roll."

"Definitely rock and roll," agrees Scott. "She could play the tambourine."

"Tambourine?" I cry. "I'm not taking Mateo's pay."

"I was just telling David last week," says Derek, "I said David, do you know what this band needs? A tambourine. Honest to goodness that's what I said. In'nit right, David?"

"True story. A tambourine would be ace."

"Can you guys excuse us for a minute?" I give Mateo a look that says get over here or die and exit to the front of the store. He follows a moment later, having set down his guitar first.

"What the heck are you doing, Mateo? These guys are making you an offer and you're making ultimatums."

"I'm negotiating a contract. That's a lot different."

"I don't care what you call it. You're being ridiculous."

"Listen, Paloma. Do you want me to take this job?"

"Of course."

"Then these are my conditions. I don't want to go without you."

There's red hot desire in his face every time he looks at me, but his words are another story. All these years, I've been convinced he never gave me a second thought. But lately, something's shifted. I wish he'd come right out and say it. Instead, he finds little excuses to be near me. To touch me. To let our lips touch.

And now he says he doesn't want to go without me?

"Why, Matt? Tell me why you want me to go with you."

His response is a study in cool indifference. "Why not?"

"Um, I don't know. Maybe because it's crazy."

And also because I swore I'd never be in a band with him ever again.

"Don't you want to play gigs again?"

"The tambourine?" I deadpan.

"I guarantee once they hear you play, they'll decide they need extra keys."

"It's an all-guy band," I say, stating the obvious.

"You can wear a fake beard and hide behind the exploding drummer."

"Eh, nope. And also, I can't take your cut. I won't do it."

"I already spoke to Ignacio. My trust fund deposits are coming back through as soon as I sign with these guys. I won't need the money and I want you to have it."

"But... why?"

He hooks his forefinger under my chin, tipping it up. "Because. That's why. Unless you're happy where you are —behind that white picket fence, living life how your parents want you to. Marrying some khaki-wearing doofus your dad brings around, owner of a sensible haircut and a four-door Volvo."

"Ha! Well, I might not marry anyone, so there."

"So don't. You do you. I don't care. But I'm not going to leave you behind, so if the answer is no, then fine."

He turns to return to the back of the shop, but I tug on his shirt.

"What about my job?" I ask.

Mateo's dark chocolate eyes sweep over my face with a glint of levity.

"Your pizza expertise will be in high demand when the tour is over."

"Oh! And what about Mr. Hopkins?"

"You can bring him with you."

Ideas are running through my head. "Or maybe Tootsie can take him. She loves Mr. Hopkins."

"So is that a yes?"

This is crazy. Oh my gosh, this is so, so crazy.

"Are you sure Ignacio's okay with this?"

"Desirée," he warns. As if he wouldn't stand here for hours while I work this through my brain. He'd wait for days if it turned out in his favor.

"Okay okay. But only if you promise to keep writing your music."

He forces out a shallow exhale. "I promise."

"I'll need video proof. I mean it mister. You are going to spend your free time creating music."

"Seriously?"

"And, after you've given Smell the Glove a proper chance, if you absolutely hate it, you can't quit unless you have something else lined up." I point my finger at his face for good measure. "And… give them plenty of notice."

"Man, you're bossy."

I twist my finger to drive home another point but he's grinning at me and, I can't stand how cute he looks right now. So I settle on using that finger to bop his nose.

"Boop," I chirp. "And you don't forget it."

Somehow I think he's taken that notion to heart, because he's as docile as a golden retriever when we return to Scott and Rusty to finalize the details. He even takes me to dinner afterwards to celebrate, letting me decide where I want to eat.

And the next day, when I get home from work, I find him on my roof, taking down my Christmas lights.

Music makes one
feel so romantic
- at least it always
gets on one's nerves
- which is the same thing nowadays.

-Oscar Wilde

Chapter Eighteen
DESIRÉE

I could get used to sitting by Mateo's side in his Stingray. Sure beats a Volvo. And I gotta tell ya, I'm mesmerized by the way he handles the car—his right hand commanding the stick shift while his left foot jolts down on the clutch. The way he maneuvers the turns and lane changes, his strong, inked arms bulging and flexing. Gah! I never thought I'd be one of those muscle car girls, but here we are.

Rehearsal for Smell the Glove went over today because Rusty/Derek brought the costumes for us to try on. Mateo almost lost it when he saw the stretchy spandex pants he's supposed to wear. He refused to come out of the bathroom which we used as a fitting area. It took a lot of coaxing and bribery to draw him out of there to show us how it fit, and oh my word! Those things are TIGHT! Really tight. My eyeballs will never be the same.

It was all business as usual for Rusty/Derek's wife as she got in close and personal to check for alterations. She seemed pleased for the most part but had issues with his hair.

"Could you perhaps cut your bangs?" she'd said.

The answer was a definitive no.

So now he'll have to wear a wig, which is silly because his hair is already long.

"Maybe we can find some kind of fake bangs," I say as we pull into our neighborhood. "The rest of your hair is the right length."

His jaw ticks as he shifts down. "I'm already starting to regret this."

I resist the urge to reach over and stroke his face to ease his tension. But that would be too forward of me, I think. So I resort to my tried and true method of cheering people up. Singing.

"Let's play the name game!" I say.

"Let's not and say we didn't."

"Mateo, bay-oh, bo-bay-oh. Banana-fana fo-fay-oh. Fee-fi-mo-may-oh. Mat-ay-o!"

"There's no way I can get you to stop, is there?"

"Nope. Desi, Desi, bo-besi—"

"Oh look, we're home!"

Drats.

He parks on the street between our houses and cuts the engine just as his family reaches their yard from their usual Sunday walk from church.

"Oh no," says Mateo. "Mom's gonna kill me."

"That reminds me. Did she ever find out who ate her Girl Scout cookies?"

He pops the trunk and we both get out of the car.

"Pancho Two," he says angrily, pulling his guitar out. "And I think Nate got into them as well."

His mom comes over to us and plants her hands on her hips.

"You're late."

"I'm sorry Mom," he says, kissing her cheek. This seems to soften her up like butter. "How was church?"

"It was amazing! Too bad you missed it. Jesus himself was there."

"Did you tell him I said hi?"

"You can tell him yourself," she huffs. Then she turns to me and shoots me an enormous grin. "Hello Desirée."

"Hi Mrs. Precio. I'm sorry to hear about your Girl Scout cookies."

She lets out a weary exhale. "It is a travesty. But I ordered more on eBay."

"That's good. I didn't know you could get them like that."

"Yep. The wonders of the internet. Do you happen to have a box freezer?"

"No, but I can make room in my regular freezer for you."

She comes over and pinches my cheeks. "You're so sweet. Don't take too long, niños. Dad made his famous bratchurros."

She scuddles into the house with a spring in her step.

"What are bratchurros?" I ask.

"Trust me," says Mateo. "You don't want to know."

No sooner do we step into his house, does he set his guitar down, takes me by the hand and says, "You wanna get out of here?"

I will go anywhere with you, Mateo Precio, as long as you never let go of my hand.

"Not in the mood for bratchurros?" I tease.

He scrunches his nose. "How about sushi?"

"Did someone say sushi?" His brother Nate jump scares us both.

"Don't sneak up on us like that. Cookie thief. And tell Mom we're going out."

"I had *one* sleeve of Thin Mints. One!"

"Bye!" Mateo squeezes my hand and we're back inside his car before anyone can come after us. He skids away like a maniac.

"So," I say. "Do you have a favorite Japanese restaurant?"

A smile spreads across his features. Even in profile, it's magnificent.

"Actually, I have an idea."

***

Forty minutes later, we're at the service entrance of the City Zoo and Botanical Gardens with bags of Japanese take-out in our arms. Mateo leads me to an opening in the fence that doesn't look like it's supposed to be there.

"Um, are you sure this is legal?" I ask, hesitating at the gate.

"I have a friend who works here," he says, sliding through the opening. "He's the one who gave me the green light."

"Can't the animals get out through here?"

"The animals are in their enclosures. In any case, we're not going to that side of the park."

He holds out his hand. "Come on."

Ugh. I can't resist an opportunity to hold his hand. It's like an addiction. So, I give in to his charms and slide inside with him.

The service area isn't remarkable, but who'd expect it to be? There are warehouse type buildings and crates stacked everywhere. The smell is anything but appetizing.

"How lovely," I joke.

With his hand still wrapped around mine, he guides me swiftly past the buildings, and around a corner to a wooden gate. Once we cross it, we're in a tropical forest, with trees and plants lining a serpentine paved path. The sun is about to set, so the pathway is on the dark side, but still the golden light of magic hour filters through the canopy of leaves overhead.

He hurriedly takes me toward his destination, until the pathway opens up to a lush oasis. We cross a red moon bridge, and slow down to a stroll through a garden of weeping higan trees and artfully pruned hedges. It is so serene here. The gentle essence of the trees swaying in the wind coupled with the birdsong of local occupants calms me like nothing I've experienced before.

Or, it could be the effect of a certain warm hand wrapped around mine.

He stops for a moment to look at me. *Really* look at me. His eyes are so dark and beautiful I can hardly take it.

"This is my favorite place," he says.

And because this is all too much, I tease, "Hmmm. I'll bet you bring all the ladies here."

But he doesn't rise to my teasing, and only blinks softly, saying, "I've never brought anyone here before. I never wanted to share it with anyone. Until now."

Oh my heavens. It's a good thing he's holding my hand, or I'd fall right over.

We go over to a Japanese pagoda, where he sits down, laying out our dinner. He uses the plastic bags as placemats and we dig into the chicken teriyaki, caterpillar rolls, crunch rolls, and tempura vegetables. He smothers his portion in everything spicy he can find.

"You really love your wasabi," I say, piling pickled ginger on my crunch roll.

He shovels a huge bite into his mouth. "The best."

"Doesn't that singe the hairs right out of your nose?"

"In the best possible way."

The food is so good, we practically inhale it. I thought we'd ordered too much but I majorly underestimated how much Mateo could eat. In fact, he's polishing up the last of the teriyaki while I lean back on the palms of my hands with a full belly. I puff it out a little extra for the fun of it.

"Look, I'm pregnant."

His eyes darken profoundly. It's like someone pulled on

a string to shift the window shutters in his eyes to the blackest setting. He drags his gaze over me, washing me with a heated look as though blanketing my body in a waterfall of want, and I'm soaking wet.

He moistens his lips, pinning me with a stare so penetrating, it makes my chest ache.

Then my brain sends off an S.O.S. signal. Alarm bells go off. A blinking red light alerts my hormones to just cool it already. I can't believe I almost fell for Mateo's signature smolder.

I deflate my belly and try to assume a normal position. Or at least as close to normal as I can manage and toss my crumpled up chopstick wrapper at him. It bounces off his chest and lands in his miso soup.

Oops.

"You're going to pay for that," he says, fighting a chuckle.

"Oh. I thought you were done."

"I am now."

"If you eat one more bite, I'll have to roll you out of here."

"Doubtful."

"Then think about it like you're saving room for dessert."

I deposit the containers and food trash in the plastic bags, making sure there isn't a crumb left behind.

"What's for dessert?" he asks, wagging his brows. Such a player.

"I don't know. What are those bratchurros like? Are they like churros only bigger?"

I suddenly realize the error in bringing up the subject of

churros and heat spreads across my face like brushfire. Mateo's lips curl just a fraction of an inch. He's thinking about that churro kiss, too. But he has mercy on me, taking the plastic bag of trash out of my hand and setting it down at our feet.

"We'll take that with us when we go. Want to sit on the grass for a while?"

"Uh, sure."

We find a small clearing and Mateo surprises me by taking off his hoodie. The T-shirt underneath rides up, exposing his abs and I'm treated to a peek at tan, smooth skin with a dusting of dark hair forming nicely into a tidy trail. Like an army of fuzzy ants.

He spreads the hoodie on the grass and motions for me to sit on it. He takes the spot next to me, but there's not much room on the hoodie so our thighs are pressed up against each other.

He leans back on his elbows and I now can't see his face anymore. Or his abs. Probably for the best.

"A bratchurro is a big German sausage dipped in churro batter, and deep fried," he finally answers. "It is the most disgusting thing you'll ever put in your mouth. But my dad thinks he's a culinary genius and keeps making them. None of us have the heart to tell him they're terrible."

I turn to my side and bend my arm to cradle my head so I can face Mateo. He looks up to the sky and inhales deeply. It's dark now, and this place has turned into a nighttime paradise. The stars aren't very visible in Los Angeles, but the few we can see are twinkling down on us.

"Does he put cinnamon sugar on them?"

His gaze dips to my lips.

"No," he says huskily. "No cinnamon sugar."

"Oh. I guess that's a good thing."

"Is it?" he asks. "You don't like… cinnamon sugar?"

Okay, that's it. He's poking the elephant, and I need to clear the air before we go any farther.

"Are we ever going to talk about the churro incident?" I blurt. "Because I don't know what that was."

He gulps and rears his chin back into his neck. "The churro incident? Is that what you're calling it?"

"You tell me."

"Uh, I'd call it a churro *sharing*."

Pfffft. Typical. "So that's all it was? Not your sneaky attempt at a kiss?"

He snorts uncomfortably. Bet he's regretting that wasabi right about now.

"Believe me. If I were to kiss you, you'd know it."

"So do you make a habit of stealing bites of food by way of smothering someone's lips with your mouth?"

His brows lurch down. "No."

"Okay then. So please explain."

"I guess I feel comfortable with you. More comfortable than I do with anyone. I'm sorry if you felt violated."

My elbow is starting to go numb from the weight of my head, so I scoot down to lie on my back. The moon is a thin sliver tonight, and there are no clouds, allowing the stars their moment.

I sigh. "I didn't feel violated. Just confused."

Mateo joins me, falling onto his back. His arm is warm against mine, and yet I shiver from the contact. He watches the stars with me for a long while, breathing in tandem with me.

After a long silence, he asks, "What if that *was* a kiss? Would you have wanted it?"

I don't hesitate with my answer. "No."

"Oh. Okay then."

What is that crack I hear in his voice? Is he… disappointed? Part of me dares to hope he is, and now I feel compelled to explain. Even though finding the words is hard.

"I'm taking a break from men," I say, aware that it sounds really stupid out loud. "I mean, I'm taking some time to find happiness on my own. I feel like, with the guys I've dated, they never could see me for who I am. They don't see my value. They don't see the whole person. They say all the right things and they're so nice and attentive—but it's just so they can get in your pants. And the next morning, they're just gone."

I pause to catch my breath. "I don't need that kind of bologna in my life. It's for the birds."

Mateo's silent—his gaze still fixed on the stars, but I know he's hanging on my every word. He's giving me the floor, quietly listening so I can continue uninterrupted. I've never told anyone this, and it feels a little raw. A little naked. But I go on while I have the courage.

"The few times someone stuck around for more than a week, I never felt pretty enough. Either they'd say things like how soft and squishy my body is, or they'd call me cute and quirky. One guy said I was his pixie dream girl. But I'm not a girl. Or a pixie. I'm a woman. I remember taking a picture of myself one day. And that's when I could see it. The emptiness in my eyes."

Mateo turns his head to look at me. There's no judgment in his expression. Only an open, inviting face.

I force a little giggle to lighten the mood.

"So I told him to take a hike. *Say-on-ara* sucker."

He stares at me a while, unblinking. Allowing me to process all the things I just regurgitated at him. He curls his body toward mine and reaches a hand to my face, gently grazing his fingers under my bangs, and down the side of my cheek.

His voice is raspy when he finally speaks.

"Who made you feel so little? Like you aren't the most amazing woman in the world?"

His eyes search mine. They glimmer in the moonlight.

Shrugging one shoulder I say, "That's just life."

"Seriously. I want names."

I laugh. "Okay, sure Detective Clouseau. What would you do with that sort of information?"

"I would find them and burn their houses to the ground. Preferably with them inside," he says darkly.

"Ooh. Such a dangerous side."

"You have no idea," he growls.

"Is that why this is your favorite place? So you can dump the bodies?"

I point over to a cluster of greenery. "That looks as good a place as any."

He glances over. "Those are fiddlehead ferns. They're edible, you know. Kind of a cross between asparagus and green beans."

"I'm full, thanks."

"Those pink flowers over there are camellias."

I noticed those earlier, admiring them while we ate. "They're gorgeous."

"They are. And easy to grow."

"How do you know so much about flowers? From investigating where to bury your victims?"

He ignores me and goes on.

"Japanese gardens are designed to achieve balance and proportion. They have to be well tended, but at the same time, look natural. Like as though they're sculpted by wind and water."

"Wow. That all sounds so very Zen."

"Are you making fun of me?" He pinches my side to tickle me. I shriek and swat his hand away.

"No. I mean it. I wish I could plant a garden without killing it. But I have a black thumb."

"I'm sure that's not true. What kind of flowers do you like?"

"I never really thought about it much. I like those pink ones you pointed out."

"The camellias."

"Yes. Oh, I just remembered. I love peonies. I stayed at the Ritz with my parents once and there was this fancy table with a vase overflowing with peonies. I could die in a room full of them."

"Peonies are nice. But they don't grow well in Southern California. Earth Angels look almost identical. They're crazy fragrant. And they have these cupped blooms with shades of warm cream and blush. They'd go well with your camellias."

"And my fiddlehead ferns. Say that ten times fast. Fiddlehead ferns. Fiddlehead ferns. Fiddlehead ferns."

"Fiddlehead ferns," he repeats, and we laugh until we're out of breath. I feel so safe here with him. Although I'm eighty percent sure we're trespassing.

Minutes pass in contented silence, and when a chill hits the air, I shiver, and Mateo wraps me against his warm body. It makes me a little sad... since I swore off men and all.

"It's a beautiful night," I say into the sky.

"It is," he agrees, sighing.

"Noche bonito," I try, even though my Spanish is terrible. Worse than Olive's.

"Hermosa Noche," he says, correcting me. Then searches my eyes. "Muy hermosa."

Gulp.

If anyone's going to make me reconsider my 'no guys' rule, it's him.

The cad.

And honestly I think he's full of it. And I want to know the truth.

When I drum up the courage, I finally ask, "What if I did want it? The churro kiss. What if I'd said yes? Would you have kissed me?"

He seems to consider this deeply, but then says definitively, "No I wouldn't. "

Ouch.

He just shrugs.

"Are you going to tell me why?"

He removes one arm away from me and coolly tucks it under his head.

"Well, frankly, my dear you're too controlling, and I don't look good in polo shirts."

"Stop!" I smack him. "Be serious, I just vomited a big truth all over you. Now it's your turn."

"You want me to vomit a big truth all over you?"

"Yes, vomit away."

He turns his eyes from the stars and gives me a solemn look."

"Okay. Do you want the truth? The truth is I'm not a good man. I've done a lot of bad things. And… I can't be trusted."

I let the words swirl around me for a moment, trying to decide if he's still messing with me.

"You know I was just joking about the dead bodies," I say.

He exhales a long, deep breath, like the ocean breeze depends on it.

"My little brother, Sebastian, is six years younger than me," he says. "He was kind of a whoops baby. I think that's probably why they spoiled him.

Anyway, one day, when I was about twelve, Saint Cecilia's was having their annual carnival and I was hanging out with my friends, going on rides, causing trouble. It was the highlight of my year, that carnival.

But my parents had to volunteer at one of the game booths for an hour, so they asked me to look out for Sebastian. One hour. One stupid hour.

All he wanted to do was win a cake at the cakewalk. I was so bored watching him go around and around, never winning, then going around again and again.

And my friends were bugging me.

I thought to myself, I could just go on the Zipper once. I

would ride the Zipper with my friends one time and then I'd come back.

I gave Sebastian some tickets and planted him right there at the cakewalk. Around and around in circles, to that stupid music and maybe he'd eventually win a cake.

When I came back, he was gone. I searched all over the whole carnival. I couldn't find him. I was panicked. Finally, my parents caught up with me and I had to explain what happened. He was missing for what seemed like hours and all I could think about was how selfish I'd been. He was only six years old. I was twelve. I should've known better."

"So what happened to him? Where was he?"

"Somebody found him inside the claw machine. He was a skinny little kid, so he climbed in there through the slot that deposits the winning prize. I guess he just crawled in there to pick a toy he had his eye on. But then he got stuck. My head got caught in a chair when I was younger, so I know what it feels like."

"How did they get him out?"

"The same way he got in. To this day he's afraid of small spaces. Ever since then, none of my family trusts me with anything."

"Mateo, you were twelve years old. You can't blame yourself for something that happened years ago."

"My point is, I always mess things up. I'm a jinx."

"That doesn't mean anything. You were a kid."

"I'm not a responsible person."

"Now that's just stinkin' thinkin' mister."

"Don't you get it? I can't do relationships. I'm not good at it. I am not equipped to provide for anyone. Protect anyone. I'd only hurt them in the end. Just like those guys whose houses I'm going to burn down."

"I don't believe you're like those guys at all. You're sweet."

"You've got to be kidding me. Sweet?"

"You are. Stop trying to deny it. You took down my Christmas lights."

"I was sick of looking at them."

"You're a secret sticky bun. Mushy on the inside."

"I'm telling you; I'm messed up. I've never even had a girlfriend."

I fake a gasp. "No way!"

"Cross my heart. Not one girlfriend."

"Oh, then wow. You really *are* a loser."

"I tried telling you."

"I guess you'll have to dry your tears on the boobs of all those women who hang on you at concerts."

"It's not as sexy as it seems, you know."

"Just wait til they see you in spandex. Tell me, was that a cod piece in there?"

His eyes crinkle with amusement, like he's got a dirty comeback but he's not sure if he should cross that line.

In for a penny. That's what I always say.

Our stimulating and super intelligent conversation is interrupted by a metallic clicking sound followed by a *pop pop pop.*

Mateo darts his eyes around. "Oh crap."

"Crap? Why crap?"

Then there's a hiss and a *tick tick tick.* Mateo jumps up, pulls me by the hand, scoops up his hoodie and shouts, "Run!"

"We don't even make it three feet before the sprinkler system activates and sprays the lawn from all directions. We scramble towards the path, but Mateo stops abruptly and says, "The food trash!"

He runs back through the sprinklers getting completely drenched and snaps up the plastic take-out bags, then runs back to me. Our clothes are soaked through by the time we cross the moon bridge. We're out of breath and exhilarated as we reach his car.

With a floppy wet slap, I slam myself against the car door, laughing as Mateo joins me, breathing heavy, dripping wet. His hands are on my hips, the hard planes of his body pressing my back against the car. Water droplets running down his face, he hovers his lips over mine, panting and smiling and sighing.

Kiss me, you Philistine.

But in the distance, we hear a booming voice shout, "Who's there?"

Wide eyed and giggling, we vault into his Stingray, making little puddles on the beautiful upholstery, and hot rod it out of there faster than an auctioneer can hum Flight of the Bumblebee.

People never ask
people doing serious music,
'Do you ever think about
doing funny music?'

−Al Yankovic

Chapter Nineteen

MATEO

I am the worst kind of human. Here I am at a freaking convent, hands deep in the dirt, planting petunias. Essentially serving my penance for being the idiotic jerk that I am.

And all I can think about is how I'd rather be burying these same hands in Desiree's soft, lush hair. Dark like wet earth, but with the scent of a Snickers bar. It's so Desirée. Sweet and gooey. A little nutty. With a nougat center.

What I wouldn't give for a taste.

Yeah. I'm definitely going straight to H-E double-toothpicks.

My unholy thoughts must be directly connected to a cell tower, because my phone immediately vibrates in my back pocket. I dig my gloved hands deeper into the soil to ignore it, but the A.I. voice in my earbuds alerts me of the caller.

"Incoming call from Ian Grant. Would you like to answer it?"

"No!" I bark. Then I feel guilty for taking it out on the A.I. because it's not her fault I have unresolved issues with my former best friend and his beautiful little sister. This is messed up ten ways til next Monday.

A minute later, another notification alerts me to a new voicemail. Hmmm. Wonder who that could be.

"Siri, turn up the music," I say. Then add, "Please."

In the End by Linkin Park screams in my ears, fueling my angst. I continue to work long into late morning, the sounds of my rage playlist blasting so loud in my ears I don't hear the footsteps approaching.

It isn't until the shadow of Sister Monica's windswept frock hovers over me that I notice I'm not alone.

Ordering Siri to cut the music, I get on my feet and take off my gloves. I've been avoiding this conversation for weeks now, but with the band finally ready, and the first tour date fast approaching, I have to tell her I'm leaving for a while.

"Are ye thirsty, lad?" she asks with that wry expression of hers.

When I was in high school, I was convinced it meant she'd wished she had a ruler to slap me with. But now, it seems that same eyebrow raise paired with that closed-lipped crooked smile means she's at least curious about me. And at most, has taken a liking to me.

I hate to admit the feeling is mutual.

"Thanks, but I'm almost done here. Do you want me to give you a rundown of all the new plants?"

"That would be quite lovely. Yes."

I wipe a sheen of sweat from my brow with my sleeve and take the earbuds out, snapping them in their magnetic case. They could use a charge, and somehow it feels a tiny bit rude to have them stuffed in my ears while talking to Sister Monica.

Pointing to the most recent installment, I explain the variety of plant, and how much sun and water it needs. I've designed the landscaping according to the amount of shade and rainfall it might get, coupled with the rudimentary knowledge I have of where the sprinkler system reaches— or at least as much information I could squeeze out of Lloyd.

"You've done a fine job, Maddy," says Sister Monica. "May the good Lord look kindly upon ye."

I look heavenward, silently wincing at my earlier thoughts and wondering if the man upstairs would be moved by Sister Monica's vote of confidence.

"Would ye like to come in for lunch? The tacos smell divine, and I have it on good authority the cooks made guacamole today. Somebody donated a shy ton of avoca- dos. You should probably take some home to yer wee brothers, too."

That would be fitting because it feels like there's an avocado pit lodged in my throat. Several weeks ago, I would have been overjoyed to leave this place and never look back. But now, I actually enjoy my time here. And, although the morning Mass and breakfast with nuns will never feel second nature, working in the gardens is the most cathartic thing I could have asked for.

At first, it helped to take out my aggressions on the weeds, punishing the hard clay dirt with a shovel, and tearing my muscles apart by moving around mislaid bricks and stones. But as time went by, and the soil softened by relentless tilling, fertilizing, and nourishing, I began to feel that balance—sort of like the Japanese garden, only more me. And also more sacred…. since we're standing on holy land and all. Sister Monica told me that herself when she quipped about adding holy water to the sprinkler system.

"Is there something wrong, lad?"

Figures Sister Monica could read faces. I'm still not one hundred percent sure she can't read minds.

"That obvious, huh?"

"I have taught six Precio brothers. And although I did not have the pleasure of having your delightful sister in my class, I think I can tell when something's troublin' one of ye."

I suck in a deep breath, deciding it's better to just rip off the bandaid.

"I… can't come back here. At least for a while."

"Oh?"

"You see, I got a job. In a band. And we're going on tour. We'll be on the road for weeks at a time."

A smile blooms over Sister Monica's features. "Why that's marvelous."

"It is?"

"Don't you think it is? One should never hide one's light

under a bushel. It is your duty and obligation to share your God-given musical talent with His people."

"You're not upset?"

"Why would I be upset?"

"Well, I... what about the community service? My penance?"

She blinks at me.

"What on God's green earth are ye going on about lad? Community service? Penance?"

"Isn't that why I'm here? To pay for my... transgression?"

"What gave ye that notion? You're here because ye want to be dear boy."

"No. I mean... and not that I don't like it here *now*. But after what happened on St. Patrick's Day... you called my parent's house looking for me. To get me to come here." I make a sweeping motion at all the work I've done in the garden.

"Young man," she says. "I called ye here that day so that you could break bread with us. Because I was worried about ye."

"Worried? About me?"

"Aye. When ye came into my class, ye were a right bugger. But ye did the work. Barely. And when ye graduated, I felt it in my heart that I'd failed ye. Aye, ye passed me class, but the human spirit is more valuable than quadratic equations."

Okay, I'm not one to cry, but I'm fighting back this burning sensation in my throat with every ounce of strength I possess.

"What about what happened at O'Malley's pub?" I ask.

"Ach. I forgave ye before we even hit the ground."

Forgiveness? Mercy? Self-control? If I didn't know better, I'd think I was learning a thing or two from this nun.

"I never expected ye to do all the work ye've done in the garden. But ye kept coming back. Every week with a new load of dirt and flowers. Here I was thinking ye were returning because you liked to dig and such. So we let ye be."

"I do like gardening, actually."

Funny how it took me jumping to conclusions to realize how much.

My back pocket buzzes once more, this time with the short bursts of a text notification. I don't even have to check it to know it's Ian.

"Well, for what it's worth, the sisters love having ye here. And we appreciate all ye've done."

"Well, I don't think I ever apologized," I say. "So, I guess this is me apologizing. I'm sorry. For everything. For flattening you to the floor at the pub. And always giving you a hard time in high school."

Like that time me and my friends superglued troll dolls to her desk.

Maybe I'll confess that another time.

"Ach. I think you apologized enough." She gestures to all of the flowers and shrubs I planted. "And I think you've apologized so much, you're good for another ten stage dives."

I laugh. "My stage diving days are over."

"Now why don't you come inside and have some tacos. Unless you don't like tacos."

"I'm Mexican. I never turn down tacos."

Even though the tacos here leave a lot to be desired.

She waves for me to accompany her to the dining hall, but I gesture to my tools.

"I need to put these away," I say. "But I'll be right there."

She nods, eyes sparkling with what looks like a hint of pride, and then she turns to go, her robes flapping behind her in the breeze.

Before I hurry into the business of picking up my tools and locking up the shed, I sink onto the cool ground, just listening to the rustle of leaves, the birds chirping in stereo, and the distant hum of the city behind these walls. I'll miss this place.

I breathe in the soft air for the last time here at the convent, and with new determination to be a better human, I reach into my back pocket for my phone and read the last text. Just as I predicted, it's from Ian.

The only words are:

Ian: call me?

Without listening to his voicemail message, I smash my finger on Ian's contact image (a picture of Tom Cruise) and hit the call button.

Rock 'n' roll will never die.
There'll always be some
arrogant little brat
who wants to make music
with a guitar.

–Dave Edmunds

Chapter Twenty
DESIRÉE

"Give me the Wiki and don't you dare leave anything out. And if you won't admit your Latin lover boy is a total superfreak, you're dead to me."

"Will you stop with that? He's not my lover boy."

Calling Tootsie from backstage in the middle of a set may not be the wisest idea I've had. But I at least hoped a short phone conversation would urge her to ration her words. But here we are, and her line of questioning is one-track minded as usual. She's relentless, I'll give her that.

"There is no possible way you've been in close quarters with that spicy meatball for three weeks and not Slytherin the Hufflepuff."

"Sometimes I wonder if you woke up one day and decided to invent your own language," I say.

"Girl, I am telling you, I need this. The midlands are in a serious drought. I have to live vicariously through you."

"I'm sorry to disappoint you but there's nothing going on."

"You have to give me something. Anything. How about… there weren't enough hotel rooms, so you had to bunk up together. And oops, you find out Daddy's not a pajama guy."

"I'm not discussing this with you."

"He doesn't strike me as a pajama guy," she says thoughtfully.

"Can we please stop talking about him?"

"Then why the frickity frack did you call?"

"To check up on Mr. Hopkins."

"Oh, he's fine."

"Fine? That's all I get?"

"What am I supposed to say? He chews lettuce all day, which is more action than you're getting."

Seriously. Next time I'll just text her.

"Listen, I can't talk for long. Can we focus?"

"You're missing a good opportunity here. I've seen the way that man looks at you. Rawr!"

The song before my next entrance is winding down and I need to get off the phone.

"Crap. I have to go on stage soon. Kiss Mr. Hopkins for me?"

"Don't call me back until you can tell me what's under those spandex."

"Goodbye Tootsie."

Well, that was an unproductive phone call.

I hang up and slip into my black, hooded druid robe. When Mateo insisted I join Smell the Glove on tour, I honestly didn't think I'd have a lot of stage time. But surprisingly, Scott and the guys have given me lots to do. I play keyboard during breaks and interludes, and also when the band makes their grand entrance. It's all very dramatic, with a fog machine, laser lights, and Scott on a backstage microphone right before they walk on saying, "Ladies and Gentlemen… This. Is. SPINAL TAAAAAAAP!"

Then the crowd cheers like crazy and the guys go on one by one, ending with Scott with his arms in the air.

I also play tambourine on a few songs, for my role of David St. Hubbins' girlfriend. I was given a choppy blonde rocker wig, leather pants, and permission to sass it up while Mateo pretends to hate my guts. We have a whole bit.

For this next song, I cover up my glitzy self with the black robe and do a little interpretive dance with a Styrofoam model of Stonehenge. The audience totally knows it's me, even with the hood on. That's part of the gag. They love it.

I make my entrance with the mini Stonehenge and do my dance. I wave it over my head to the music, spinning and weaving back and forth between Scott, Rusty, and Mateo. Or, as I've been instructed to call them, David, Derek, and Nigel. Scott even insists we all stay in character off stage—for the whole tour, even though Mateo's British accent could use some work.

I do a little comedy thing where I bonk Mateo on the head with the foam Stonehenge, and he tries to kick me but fails. I love this part of the show. Anytime I get to interact with Mateo is my favorite.

Also, I feel a weight has been lifted from my chest ever since Mateo had a long talk with Ian. Even Mateo seems to have changed somewhat. He smiles more now. Also… I'd like to take a moment to appreciate how he totally rocks the guyliner.

He's still not thrilled about the spandex pants, but I have to admit I love the perky rear view.

In fact, after the show, as the guys are lined up for their encore, I momentarily lose a few brain cells.

I don't know what comes over me. Maybe Tootsie's getting into my head.

My hand moves of its own volition. I watch in horror as my pointer finger curls into Mateo's spandex, hooks into the waistband, pulls, and snaps the elastic on his backside.

"Ouch," he cries, spinning around fiercely ready to retaliate, but freezes, like he's surprised it's me and not one of the crew. The annoyance in his face melts into molten steel, and his eyes turn dark and hooded.

With the heat of Hades glowing all over his body, he lazily crowds into me, and growls huskily into my ear, "Do that again Paloma, and I'll put you over my knee."

Zing Pow.

A million pinpricks shoot up my legs and explode out of my belly button with a *woosh*. That must be the feeling of common sense leaving my body. I'm so lightheaded, I wobble on my spike heeled boots.

His mouth spreads into a wicked grin. He knows the effect he has on me, the jerk. He knows and takes me right up to the cliff where I might fall for him completely, but at the last possible moment, he changes the rules. Pulls back. And never crosses that line.

I shouldn't get so worked up over it, really. He's only acting like a gentleman. Well, *mostly* like a gentleman. I told him about my celibacy journey and he's completely respecting that. Even though sometimes, like right now, he says or does something that makes my female organs stage a coup.

They're very organized with matching T-shirts and everything.

And then my heart cracks a little to experience his silent affection and altruism.

For instance, that mistake Scott made when booking the rooms since I came on board last minute. (Yes, Tootsie was right about that. Of course I'll never admit it.) But instead of making me bunk with one of the guys, Mateo gave up his own room for me. He told me he took the couch in Rusty's room. But one night, as I was wandering the hotel when I couldn't sleep, I found him curled up with a blanket on a pool lounge chair.

I didn't confront him about it.

But tonight, after the show, I'll tell him how I feel. No more longing glances. No more little excuses to touch. And especially, no more leaving me standing in a puddle of need with the heat of his breath on my neck as he turns to go back on stage.

Grrrr. Intolerable man!

When the concert is over and the band is signing programs and posing for pictures, the guys get the usual attention. Mostly from women. Sometimes middle-aged couples or entire families. But tonight, a slightly inebriated man approaches me for a selfie. His breath is so rank, I might get drunk off the second-hand fumes. After a picture or five, he hangs around me, sticking to me like glue. At first, he's kind of funny, so I don't let it bother me.

Mateo catches my eye and chuckles. "Oh how the turns have tabled," he says, standing on the other side of our drummer, Mick (who won't tell me his real name).

Mateo, of course, is responding to the little digs I make when groupies hang all over him and hand him sharpies to autograph their chests. He turns a shade of fuchsia when I tease him about it.

Presently, Drunk Dude's belly keeps brushing my arm, and when I take a polite step back, he advances the few inches I'd gained, chatting nonsensically.

"I just had an idea," he says. "How about you and me go get a drink?"

"Um, I think I'm good," I say. "Maybe you should call it a night, too. Sleep it off."

I pat him on the shoulder and turn away, but he manhandles my upper arm.

"We can sleep it off together."

I try to free my arm, but his clammy paws grip it tighter.

"I'm going to have to ask you to let go now, sir."

His eyes glass over, looking at me with melancholy desperation, and I sense there's something more to his story. Like he recently got dumped or something.

"I'm sorry," he says, but still doesn't let go of me.

Oh gosh. What if he's a psychopath who thinks I look like his dead wife and is going to find my hotel room only to kidnap me and make me wear her clothes?

"She asked you to let go." Mateo's by my side, shielding me with his body, getting right into this guy's face. He's taller, but the drunk man has more girth. Plus, there's the alcohol factor which gives uneducated men a heck of a lot of confidence.

Drunk Dude puffs up his chest. "I saw you. Turn it up to eleven. Funny stuff."

This disarms Mateo momentarily, but he doesn't back down one bit.

"Kindly take your hands off my friend. Then I'm going to call you a cab and send you home."

Awww. Only Mateo can threaten a guy and show compassion at the same time.

The guy hiccups. "I'm not going home. I'm going to the bar."

He yanks my arm to pull me along, but Mateo slams his hand in the guy's chest, making him rock back.

"I'm not going to ask again," he hisses through gritted teeth.

By this time, we've gained the attention of the rest of the band and a few stragglers waiting for autographs.

Scott comes around to get between me and Drunk Dude, while Rusty, Mick, and our keyboard player, Ken, form a half circle behind Mateo. I feel Scott peeling the man's hand from my arm.

"Okay, okay," Drunk Dude says, holding up his palms in surrender. "We're all just here to have some fun, right?"

"I think you've had your share of fun, Mate," says Scott in that silly Cockney accent.

Drunk Dude turns his watery gaze to Scott, wobbling in place, closed-lip smile and all. For a second, I think he might pass out right in front of us, the way he shuffles his feet, teetering top heavy and unbalanced, sloppily mumbling something nobody can understand.

And it happens so fast, I don't have time to register that he's lunging my way to cop a feel until he's almost on top of me. All I see is the blur of Mateo's arm crossing across my vision and landing a swift fist squarely on Drunk Dude's nose.

There's a collective gasp as the man tips like a tree and lands on the floor with a plunk.

"Is he dead?" asks Rusty.

The man begins to snore.

"Nope," replies Scott. "Now… who fancies a pizza?"

My taste in music ranges from
"you need to listen to this" to
"I know, please don't judge me

—Unknown

Chapter Twenty-One

MATEO

"Earth to Mat-feo."

I'm in a tunnel.

"Dude!"

Everything is muted.

"I broke one of your guitar strings."

I jerk my head up, blinking. "What?"

Enrique, Nate, and Francesca sit across the table from me laughing.

"I told you that would work," says Francesca. The other two groan and pass her a dollar each. She doesn't have her purse at the dinner table, so she hands the money to Edmund.

"What are you guys doing?" I grumble.

"You were in la la land for fifteen minutes," says Enrique.

"Never underestimate the power of threatening someone's instrument to get them out of a trance," says Francesca smugly. "You guys are amateurs."

"I wasn't in a trance," I say in protest.

Just deep in thought.

"Then what was Nacho just talking about?" says Nate.

"What the heck do I care what Nacho was yammering about?"

Ignacio stands up, clearing some empty plates, throws me the evil eye, and brandishes a fork in my direction.

"I will stab you."

"He was telling us his news," says Francesca.

Oh, right. All I remember was him clearing his throat and saying "I have an announcement."

Then I completely tuned him out.

I just can't think straight lately. At least Smell the Glove has a week break from our tour schedule so I can come to my parent's house and reevaluate my life.

I actually thought things were changing for me. I have work I more or less love, I've been making strides with Ian's friendship, and the most beautiful woman in the world believed in me.

Now I realize I'm deluded.

That guy that hit on Desirée after our Tulsa concert. I

tried to reason with him. Instead, I broke his nose. After all this time, trying to turn over a new leaf. Working to be a better man, someone who Desirée can rely on. And I can't even control my temper.

The look in her eyes.

Disappointment.

Fear.

I've never felt such shame in my life.

What if I hurt her? My fist barely missed her face when I swung for the guy. If I can't protect her against myself, how can I protect her from anyone or anything else?

Someone next to me says, "Oh hi Desirée!"

When I snap my eyes up, all my siblings and their spouses bust up.

"Made you look," says Sebastian.

"You are an immature child," I say.

"Where is Desirée, anyway?" asks Mom. "Didn't she want to come to dinner?"

"She's sick of looking at Matt's ugly face," says Nate.

"Nataniel Aquinas Precio!" cries Mom.

Ooh! You know Mom's angry when she uses your full name. Funny thing is, Nate's not wrong. Desirée probably is sick of my ugly face.

"Do you want to tell him your good news, or should I?" Francesca asks Ignacio.

"I don't feel like repeating myself," says Ignacio, piling plates on his arm. "Tía Lucy, are you finished?"

I glance over to Tía Lucy, and accidentally snag eyes with Pancho Two, who's at that end of the table. He's giving me the death glare. I hate that man. He should be grateful Dad took him in after all he's done to our family.

Embezzled money from the restaurant. Stole stock to sell it on the black market. Endangered Nacho's life by doing shady business with a surfer gang. And the crime du jour, eating all Mom's Girl Scout cookies.

But that slimeball is anything but grateful. He's disrespectful, doesn't clean up his messes, and I don't trust him.

"As I was saying," continues Francesca, Nacho's opening a new restaurant in Laguna Beach."

"Wow, congratulations," I say, truly meaning it. "Laguna Beach. That's far."

"I'll finally have some good food on my lunch break," says Nate. He owns an insurance agency in Laguna Beach, so he must be stoked.

"You'd eat out of a trash can. You're like Ratatouille's brother in that cartoon," Ignacio says, taking the plates into the kitchen.

"When are you going back on the road?" asks Dad. "Any place exciting? Like Barcelona?"

"It's just a domestic tour, Dad," I say.

"So when do you leave us?" asks Mom.

"We're heading to Denver next week. From there, we're mostly doing small venues."

"Are you playing the casinos?" chimes in Tía Lucy. "Vegas is where it's at."

"Um, no we're not playing Vegas," I say. "We'll be in Laughlin next month, though."

Tío Enrique's ears perk up. "Laughlin? I love it. *El sol. El calor.* And you know the water… *es muy frio.* Es so good."

"We should go!" says Mom. "Family trip."

Oh please, no!

"We'll go see Mateo perform. Rent some jet skis, eat at the buffet. Lucy can play her penny slots."

"Pass," says Nate.

"They got rid of the penny slots," says Enrique.

"*No me digas!*" cries Tía Lucy. "*Desgraciados.*"

"You guys really don't have to go to Laughlin to see me play," I say. "We're doing the Huntington Surf Fest in September. You can come to that."

"Too many crowds," gripes Mom.

"And the parking," adds Dad.

Mom nods. "Oh yes. Oof, the parking."

"You'd rather drive five hours to the middle of the desert than circle around for twenty minutes for a parking space?" I'm trying to wrap my head around my parent's logic, but once again, it eludes me.

"Sebastian," says Mom. "Find us a deal on Expedia."

Sebastian has his phone out and is already tapping away with his thumbs. "On it."

"No, try Priceline instead," says Dad.

"I'm setting up alerts as we speak," says Sebastian.

Mom pats Dad on the shoulder. "Trust the process, dear."

"I can make some calls," says January. "We don't have a hotel in Laughlin, but like my father-in-law always says, 'I know a guy'."

Dad winks and nods. He approves.

I decide to get up from the table before my parents make more crazy plans that include piling my whole family in a hotel room. Because even though they have money, Dad is always looking to save a buck.

I collect some plates and head to the kitchen. Ignacio's in there, filling the leftovers in food storage containers.

"I'll wash the dishes," I say, setting the faucet to scalding hot. It feels good. Something about plunging my hands under the running water and getting soap suds up my arms is therapeutic.

Ignacio slaps me on the back. "Thanks man."

Then Olive comes in with more dishes and I turn my attention out the window to avoid their PDA show.

Summer is in full force, so even at eight o'clock, there's still some light.

I created a mini oasis in the front yard so Mom can sit out there to watch the neighbors walk their dogs. She likes to pet them all as they go by. Lola, with her wagging tail is the front yard equivalent of a Walmart greeter. They've become quite popular.

There's a small table where Mom can set her drink while she works on her crafts or reads a book. I planted several colors of Hydrangeas and added potted Geraniums around the Adirondack chairs, which I'll figure out later where to plant them permanently.

Right now, a couple of yellow finches are fluttering from the telephone pole to the bird feeder. They fill their beaks with food, hop around the flower beds, and take off again.

Sebastian bumps up next to me, dropping more plates in the sink. He just messed up my piles.

"Hey! I have a system here."

"If your system is letting the water run while you daydream out the window, may I remind you we're in a drought."

"Smartass."

Just then, something catches my eye out the window. That VW van I saw when I got back from yarn bombing with Desirée is passing our house at a snail's pace. Both guys in the front seats glare directly at me. It's dark, so I can't make out their faces very well, but I don't like the way this feels.

"Do you know who's van that is?" I ask Sebastian. Maybe Desirée's right and it's just a neighbor. And they're going super slow because there might be kids playing in the streets?

Sebastian squints out the window and shrugs.

"I didn't see anything."

"Have you noticed a van lately? A VW bus parked in the neighborhood?"

"I'm gone nine months out of the year," he says. "I don't know what cars the neighbors drive."

I shut off the water and run outside to investigate. But by the time I make it to the front yard, the van is nowhere in sight. I stare down the street, hoping it will make a U-turn and come back. But the street is fairly quiet, and the van doesn't make another appearance.

I'm about to go inside, when I notice Desirée pulling her trash bins to the curb. She doesn't need help, but I run over there anyway.

"Let me get that for you," I say, taking hold of the handle.

"Mateo. Oh. You're alive."

"Yeah. Why? Have you heard otherwise?"

"No. I just assumed, since you're a ghost."

I don't have a response to that. I just blink at her with my hand next to hers on the trash can handle.

She shakes her head. "I got this. You can go get my recycle bin."

I do as she says and beat her to her curb with the blue bin. She's only one person, and doesn't produce much trash, so the recycle bin weighs nothing. But I need to feel macho tonight, so I go back and help her with the other one.

"Thanks," she says. "I have a box of feathers I might need help with later if you're not busy."

"Hmmm. Box of feathers. I don't know if I can handle that."

She forces a laugh, and we both stand here on the street in awkward silence. I've been trying to give her some space ever since the night I punched that guy. I feel her slowly slipping away. We're in forced proximity together on tour, but it's more like we're coworkers sharing the same office space. Once we're off stage, I eat alone, and we don't talk much.

"Did you see that VW bus go by?" I ask, breaking the excruciating silence.

She looks around as if it will appear out of thin air. "No. I didn't see any cars go by."

"It went that way," I say, pointing down the street.

"Come to think of it," she says, "I did see them the other night. Mr. Hopkins got out of the house, and I chased him all the way to Lilly Belle road. The van was parked about five hundred feet away. And there were two guys."

"Two guys? Did you see what they looked like?"

"Yeah. One of them waved at me."

"Waved at you?" I can feel my blood boil. If they touch one hair on her head, I will end them.

"Relax, they were just waxing their boards."

"They were waxing their surfboards. Parked on the street. In the middle of the night?"

"I never said it was the middle of the night. It was more like… eleven."

"And that doesn't strike you as odd?"

"Mateo, not everyone is a bad guy lurking around to do bad guy things."

She doesn't flat out say it, but I know she doesn't look at me the same way since she witnessed my violent streak. She went so far as to feel sorry for the drunk bastard because he *"seemed so sad."* If she only knew his intentions like I did, she'd sing another tune.

I guess it takes one to know one.

"Next time your rabbit gets out, or you have to go outside for something, call me first."

She scoffs and looks out into the distance, avoiding my eyes.

"You want me to call you." She doesn't phrase it like a question. More like a thought she's having and she's trying to decide if it's worth her while.

"Yes," I say. "I do."

"Well, Mateo, I could say the same thing to you."

"I don't follow."

She blows out a heavy breath and turns toward her house. "Never mind."

I'm not about to chase her down. I'm too pathetic to think of it. But as soon as she reaches her front door, she spins on her heel and stomps back with her forefinger pointing at me like a missile. I'm one hundred percent certain she's about to chew my head off. She huffs, and puffs out her cheeks, and growls in frustration. It's like she has all these words jumbled in her mouth, but they got shuffled around like Scrabble tiles.

"Uuuugh!" she grumbles, curls both hands into fists at her sides, and storms off again.

"Don't leave your house after ten PM," I call after her.

She slams her door.

Give me books, French wine,
fruit, fine weather
and a little music
played out of doors
by somebody I do not know.

—John Keats

Chapter Twenty-Two
DESIRÉE

Laughlin is hotter than the devil's breath after a chili-eating contest. Still, I'd rather be outside than in the dimly lit, smoke-filled casino. My hair hates me right now because of it.

Smell the Glove is booked through the weekend in the small nightclub attached to the hotel. Our show last night was filled to capacity, and the audience seemed to have a good time. Mateo's family came. That was… fun.

Mr. and Mrs. Precio were in the audience, cheering us on. I think that embarrassed Mateo, and that was basically the highlight of my evening. Joining them were Mateo's aunt, Lucy, who proudly told me she has never been married, and one of her divorcee friends, Ursula. I don't think those two ladies have slept since they've been here.

There's also Mateo's rowdy uncle Enrique (not to be confused with his brother Enrique) who danced with Ursula for five seconds before he got handsy and she kneed him in the you-know-what.

Sebastian is also here. But he's not allowed in the casino and couldn't see us play our set.

The men set up two EZ-up tents at five o'clock this morning on the beach and rented a jet ski. I was told if you don't snag a good spot super early, you're out of luck. Mr. Precio and Tío Enrique guarded the spots while the rest of us slept in.

The Precios invited the whole band to join them on the beach today, but the guys wanted to go into town and shop.

So here I am in a modest tankini, trying to keep cool under the shade of the tent. When Mateo comes ambling along the sand with his windswept hair, wearing nothing but board shorts, I'm filled with profound regret for leaving my room in the first place. He is so beautiful, it hurts. Acres of inked, tan skin blanketing artfully sculpted muscles glow in the mid-morning sun. His broad shoulders curve gracefully into the slope of a clavicle so breathtaking, my fingers twitch to touch him there. And the abs. Oh my heavens. The abs. Let's just say if he ever decided to take up bluegrass music, he'd be the best washboard player that ever was.

I moisten my lips as he approaches, feeling a distinctly different heat than from the sun. He's wearing sunglasses, so I don't see how his eyes snag on me as he passes my chair, but the corner of his lips quirk devilishly. That's all the acknowledgement I get before he wanders over to the other tent, taking a beer from the cooler, and lowering himself into a beach chair.

Okay. I see how it is. The Adonis has claimed his throne. All you mere mortals (mainly me) keep to yourselves and try not to get a sunburn.

"Are you hungry, dear?" Mrs. Precio's bright voice shakes me out of the hypnotism Mateo performed on me just by existing.

"Actually," I say. "I am a little peckish."

I had a bagel for breakfast from the coffee cart because the wait was too long for the buffet. Come to think of it, I'm starved.

"Help yourself to the snacklebox," she says, pointing to a yellow case I had thought was for fishing. She opens it up, unfolding tray after delicious tray of snacks in little compartments. There are crackers and cheese, yogurt covered pretzels, an assortment of nuts, dried fruit, baby carrots, and mini sweet peppers.

"Thank you. Yum." I take a handful of cheese and pretzels, and slink back into my chair.

"Such a fun idea," I say. "Did you have this in your hotel room?"

"I went on a grocery run this morning, but we brought our box from home."

"I hope we can finish it all," I say. In this heat, it will go to waste otherwise.

"Oh we will, trust me. When Sebastian and his father get back from jet skiing, they'll devour half of it. And if these sleepyheads ever wake up, they'll need something for their hangovers."

She inclines her head to Lucy and Ursula, fast asleep in low back beach chairs. I understand they sat at the slots all night terrorizing the cocktail waitresses for free piña coladas. They wandered down to the beach an hour ago and have been out ever since.

"I suppose we should let them sleep," I say.

Mrs. Precio hums in agreement then glances over at Mateo.

"You know, these cashews are making me thirsty. Would you be a dear and bring me a peach margarita? They're in the cooler over there."

Of course she means the cooler by Mateo. The one he's currently using for a footrest.

"Okay," I say, getting up. "Is it in a bottle, or…?"

"You can't bring glass to the beach, so we poured it into individual travel bottles. Like the kind you put shampoo in. Don't worry, it's food safe."

I go over to the other tent and stand directly in front of Mateo. He doesn't budge. Just scrolls on his phone.

I clear my throat. He glances up to me and shifts one eyebrow.

"I would like to get something out of that cooler, please." I say.

He turns his heavenly dark eyes down to the cooler and then back to me. I wish he'd put his sunglasses back on.

"Go right ahead."

I squint my whole face at him.

"Will you kindly move your feet?"

He smiles wickedly, blinding me with those shiny teeth.

"What's the magic word, Paloma?"

"Your feet are covered in sand and you're getting it all over the cooler."

"The lid's closed."

Grrrr. Why is he being so difficult?

"Fine." I bend down, curl my hands under his ankles and lift his legs up. His skin is warm under my fingers, and the leg hair soft. I feel a charge zap up my arms.

And I'm just standing here, my feet on other side of the cooler, holding his ankles like I'm a human hammock. He's enjoying this too much. Unfortunately, so am I.

After a blazing hot staring contest, he has mercy on me and bends his knees. He even opens the lid of the cooler and digs inside the ice for the margarita.

"Would you like one?" he asks, and I swear there is actual honey dripping from his words. I can't read him. One minute he's aloof, the next minute, he's ornery, and the next five minutes, he's an enormous flirt.

"Just water," I say. I need to stay hydrated around this man because he's making my body steam out all my liquids.

When he hands me a bottled water, his fingers graze mine, and he holds them there for a few seconds longer than necessary.

A sharp whistle and succession of claps sound behind me. Tío Enrique's coming onto the beach from the shoreline, shouting something in Spanish. Then he switches to English.

"Who's up next? Let's go!"

He claps incessantly and continues to whistle like he's rounding up a herd of sheep.

"Mateo. *Ándale.*"

"Maybe later," says Mateo.

"Oh come on," says Tío Enrique. "*Es muy* fun."

Tío Enrique appointed himself the guy who organizes all the jet ski rides. He takes count of how many times someone goes out into the water, helps them launch off, waits at the shoreline, and times how long they take. Since I've been here, it's been a rotation of Sebastian, Mr. Precio, Tío Enrique, Sebastian riding with Mr. Precio, Tío Enrique with Sebastian, and my personal favorite, Tío Enrique straddling behind Mr. Precio. Mrs. Precio went out once by herself.

"What about Desirée?" suggests Mrs. Precio. "She hasn't had a turn."

"Oh, I don't think so," I say. "I've never gone out before."

"Mateo will take you," she says. "Go on."

I look at Mateo, hitching up a shoulder in quiet supplication. For what, I'm not sure. He licks his lips, raking his gaze all the way down to my feet and back up again.

After a long pause, he says, "No. I had a beer."

Tío Enrique scoffs. "Only one beer? *No pasa nada.*"

Mrs. Precio springs up from her chair. "I'll take her."

"But what about your margarita?" I say, still holding the little plastic bottle.

"I'll have it when we get back."

She hobbles through the sand, waving me to follow. Mateo lifts his eyes to me and takes back the drinks. His face is an expressionless stone.

At the shoreline, Mr. Precio and Sebastian are waiting to pass off the life jackets. I take Sebastian's because it's the smaller one, and he helps to strap it on me.

I'm a little bit frightened when we hop on the jet ski. I know they're technically safe, and not unlike my Vespa, but the water is unpredictable. Also, I've seen some wipe out videos on YouTube and that put the fear of God in me.

Mrs. Precio has me sitting in front, so I control the gas. I decide I want to start slow, so when Tío Enrique pushes us out, I don't rev the engine yet. Getting a feel for it first.

"We're going backwards," says Mrs. Precio. "You have to gun it."

Behind us, the men are screaming from the shore to hit the gas. Sure enough, the waves are rocking us to shore. I didn't think rivers had waves, but it's a big river, and there are boats causing ripples and wind blowing the water in soft waves into the sand.

With the kill key attached to my wrist, I push the throttle… very slowly. There are so many boats and other jet skis going by, I'm afraid to head into traffic.

"Go faster. You have to go faster."

I push the throttle again and then stop.

"Go go go! We're taking in water," cries Mrs. Precio. "We have to move to let it spill out the back."

Okay, okay. I can do this.

Twisting the gas again, I take us out to the middle of the river. Every time we accelerate, I feel like we're going to fall off backwards. This is not like a Vespa, which stays level to the ground. Solid, firm ground. This thing rears back like a bucking horse every time we go over a wave. I think I have the hang of it, though, so I venture out a little more, still going fairly slow.

"You need to go faster, dear," Mrs. Precio says in my ear. "Trust me, it's safer to go fast."

"Ack! I'm afraid!"

I hesitate, going with trepidation. Mrs. Precio is getting a little frustrated behind me and is probably regretting taking me out on the water. A boat passes by, creating a large wake.

"Turn into it," she screams, "Drive into the wave!"

With wobbly hands, I pull the throttle and turn the handlebar toward the wave. But I'm not fast enough, and in a half a second, we're rocking to the side. Mrs. Precio's screaming. I try to compensate for my weight, but the wake is too wooshy. In one swoop, we tip over, plunging underwater.

All I can think of while we're under is if Mrs. Precio is okay. Did she bonk her head on the jet ski? Did she swallow water? Who knows how far she flew?

I surface in a panic and find the jet ski upside down.

"Mrs. Precio? Where are you?"

Reorienting myself, I see her on the other side of the jet ski, paddling to get to it so she can hang on. Thank goodness for life vests.

She's gasping for air. Oh no! What if she dies? I killed Mrs. Precio!

Doing a doggie paddle, I try to get to her. I don't know what I'm going to do since I can barely swim myself, but I will save her no matter what.

That's when I notice she's not choking on river water or

having trouble breathing. She's laughing. A delirious, help-less fit of laughter.

"Mrs. Precio?"

Between cackles, she says, "You are so bad at this."

"I'm sorry. I suck. Oh no, the jet ski. I ruined it."

"We need to hurry and tip it over."

She pushes on it but it doesn't budge. Then she laughs again.

Then, two jet skis circle around us, carrying three men. One of the men jumps in the water and flips our jet ski right side up like it's nothing.

"Are you alright ma'am?" he asks Mrs. Precio.

She just nods at him.

"We'll help you get to shore. I'll take care of your water-craft to make sure it's not flooded. Tony will take you to safety."

Tony reaches out a burly arm and helps Mrs. Precio to mount his jet ski. Her face gets doughy and ruddy, and there's a grin on her face spread out ear to ear. This Tony guy is a certi-fiable silver fox. Bulging muscles peeking out of the life vest, salt and pepper hair clipped short, and he has a kind smile.

The third man, riding alone, is considerably younger. My age, probably. He is not wearing a life vest, likely due to a swift lunge into action to rescue us. I look up at him mounted on the jet ski. He's bathed in sunlight, and towers above me like a golden demigod. A crisp breeze, which sweeps off the river, wisps his sun-kissed honey locks across his forehead. His striking blue eyes are framed by generous, dark eyelashes, set on a perfectly symmetrical face. And elegant, long muscles etched in clay make up his strong arms and toned back. His skin has the tan of a young man who spends his whole life in the sun, but it's smooth like butter without the effects of UV damage.

In short, a veritable dreamboat.

"Can you climb on, miss?" he says to me, twisting his torso from a seated position on the jet ski.

"I think so."

I honestly don't think so. The seat seems so high above my head. How am I supposed to get up there?

"There's a step in the rear, under the stern. Grab onto the platform and pull yourself up."

"I don't know if I'm strong enough," I say, feeling really stupid.

"It's like getting out of a pool," he says. "Take your time."

Take my time. I've already wasted five minutes of this guy's time. I know these men aren't lifeguards, or whatever you call official river rescuers, because they're in civilian bathing suits. They came out to help us out of the kindness of their hearts. Other people would still be on shore taking videos on their phones. Actually, that's probably what Sebastian's doing right now.

It takes a few minutes of foot water aerobics to find the step he's talking about, but I finally do. I hoist myself up with a hefty grunt, stepping upright on the rear platform. But my heels stick out over the edge, and I'm not great at balancing myself. So, flapping my arms like I'm trying to fly, I teeter backwards and flop back into the water with a spectacular splash.

When I resurface, the guy isn't laughing at me as he should. He simply encourages me to try again.

This time, I climb up onto my knees, then slide on the seat behind him.

I don't know where to put my hands. What if I fall off again when he gets going?

"You can hang onto my waist," he says, as if reading my mind. "Or however you're comfortable."

Oh sir. I am anything but comfortable.

I rest my hands lightly on his waist, but then think better of it and circle my arms all the way around his torso. My chest is pressed against his back—which is obstructed by this extremely bulky vest, darn it. But judging by the skin-on -skin contact that is my arms holding on to his waist, I can imagine his back feels very nice, too.

Do not rest your cheek on his back, Desirée. Do not do it.

The ride back is short-lived, since I hadn't taken us out very far in the first place. When we get to shore, Mrs. Precio is disembarking the jet ski with the silver fox. Mr. Precio wades out to take her the rest of the way, shaking his head.

My rescuer slows to a halt as close as he can get to the beach.

"Thank you for helping us," I say. "Sorry about taking up so much of your time."

"It's no trouble at all," he says. "Be careful out there."

I reluctantly peel my arms off him—which is probably a great relief to him—and scoot back on the seat. Two seconds later, Mateo's standing in the shallow water, right next to the jet ski, with his hands extended. He doesn't utter a word, but he does not look happy one bit. His hands fly to my waist, and with one swift movement, he propels me off the jet ski and throws me over his shoulder, carrying me to shore.

"I think I can walk," I say, swinging upside down. I can smack his butt easily from this position if I want to.

He plops me down on the sand, scowls at me, and drags me back to the tents by the hand.

"Don't ever do that again," he grunts.

"Sorry?"

Is he upset I almost killed his mom? Because, judging by the look on her face, she's more than fine. In fact, she's already gotten into the margaritas.

"You could have gotten hurt."

Oh. He's mad that I put *myself* in danger?

I laugh. "I'm okay. See? All in one piece."

"It's not funny."

He paces back and forth in front of me, tugging at his hair. Sand flings from his feet. Then he exhales long and hard and pins me with those dark chocolate eyes.

"My heart stopped when I saw you fall. And there was nothing I could do about it."

"Your heart or the fall?" I ask.

"Both."

Later that day, I've gone back to my room, showered and changed. I have about an hour before sound check, so I head downstairs to find something moderately healthy to eat. There's a food court, but none of the offerings sound good to me. Deciding instead to get a croissant from the coffee kiosk, I use my shirt to shield myself from the cigarette smoke and cut through the casino. I'm almost there, when who do I see coming out of the gift shop?

Mister jet ski rescuer guy. He's still wearing his board shorts but has since put on a T-shirt and flip flops.

Wondering if it would be weirder to greet him or scoot by unnoticed, I hike my collar all the way to my eyes.

But he goes out of his way to come over to say hi. I don't even know how he recognized me. Must be the wild look in my eyes.

"You look well," he says awkwardly.

"Yes. I'm much better now. No more sand in my hair. Thanks for rescuing me by the way."

"I was glad I happened to be at the beach when it happened. Ten minutes later, I might have taken my jet ski up the river."

"Oh, good timing on my part, then," I say jokingly.

"Your… boyfriend seemed worried."

"My boyfriend?"

"The guy who…"

"Threw me over his shoulder? No. He's not my boyfriend."

Mateo's too busy avoiding me lately to even be in the running for my boyfriend. Not that I want one.

"Oh, okay." He seems confused, but I'm not about to bore him with the weird dynamic of my relationship with Mateo. Or, lack of relationship, as it were.

"I was just buying a pack of gum," he blurts, hooking his thumb over his shoulder.

"Nice. I like gum."

A witty conversationalist I am not. I'll blame it on sunstroke.

"Do you want a piece?"

"Oh, no thank you. I'm about to eat."

"Really? Because I am too. Do you want to get something to eat together? There's a place in town with great burgers and onion ring towers."

"Ah, that sounds yummy. But I have sound check in less than an hour. I just have time for a snack."

"Sound check?"

"Yeah. I'm with the Spinal Tap tribute band? We have a show later. I'm sorry."

"Wow. You're in a band? That's really cool. But I understand you're busy, so…" He nods nervously, glancing at his feet. I feel kind of rotten. This guy pretty much saved my life. I very well could have gotten swept up by the current and ended up in Mexico.

"Listen, why don't you come tonight? It's free as long as you're drinking. And if you don't drink you can have soda or something. They don't have onion ring towers, but I think they might have peanuts."

A twinkle shimmers in his eyes. "I think I might just do that."

"Okay. See you then." I spin and take a few steps toward the coffee kiosk.

"Oh, wait," he says. I stop and turn back around. His expression is full of wonder. "I don't know your name."

"It's Desirée."

He shakes my hand, almost swallowing it in his.

"Kieran."

When a piece gets difficult,
make faces.

-Artur Gchnabel

Chapter Twenty-Three

MATEO

He's here. That guy from the beach. And he doesn't take his eyes off Desirée the entire show.

After, when the small crowd of concertgoers came to meet us to get photos with the band, *he* came up, and Desirée introduced him to the band as Kieran.

Kieran. What an unfortunate name. Like the sound a cat makes while dislodging a furball.

She disappeared backstage to change into her street

clothes, as she does every time. She hates walking through the casino dressed like she's doling out good times to gamblers.

I keep my eyes on the cat child while I put away my guitars, glaring a *get-out* signal at him as I wind up my cables.

"Did you hear about the monsoon coming in?" asks our drummer, Mick. He also pretends he has a British accent, but his is not so bad. "It's so weird. It's summer, we're in the desert, it's hotter than bollocks, but it's raining. Like… hot rain."

"Hot rain. That would make a cool band name," Scott says, trying it out on his tongue. "Hot. Rain."

"Like Purple Rain… but hot," adds Rusty.

Oh boy. I feel for this man's wife.

Realizing I took my eyes off Kieran for three seconds, I look back out into the dimly lit nightclub. He's moved.

Searching every corner, I catch sight of him again, and Desirée is with him. She's wearing a deep blue dress with lots of frills. She takes my breath away.

Kieran has this awestruck look on his face, like she's every star in the night sky and she's shining just for him. He says something that makes her laugh, and she lays a hand on his arm in response. My eyes narrow at that one spot.

"Oy! Nigel." Scott whistles at me. "We need you Mate."

I don't dare turn around. "I'm busy."

"You've been winding that same guitar cable for ten minutes."

Kieran points at something on Desirée's face. She swipes

her hand over her cheek to get whatever it is. He laughs and tries to show her she'd missed it. Then a rock sinks in my stomach as he leans down, intimately close, and brushes his thumb along her jaw, taking his sweet time. She watches his eyes bashfully. His face is too close to hers. Inches away, like he needs to crowd over her to see what he's doing.

I hate him.

Then he backs off a millimeter and shows off whatever is on his thumb before wiping it on his jeans. Desirée giggles. I can't hear her from here, but I have the sound of her laughter memorized. I know her embarrassed laugh. Her joyful laugh. Her moderately amused laugh. And also her fake laugh.

At best, he just got an embarrassed laugh from her.

Scott slides up next to me and whispers in my ear.

"Hey, mate. This big-time agent came to see us tonight. Said he's here with his family but popped in when he heard the music. He loved it. He wants to meet the whole band and maybe talk about booking us in bigger venues. Getting us into festivals."

"Really?" My spirits lift momentarily. This is just the excuse I need to get rid of jet ski boy. Stripping off my itchy wig, I take a step off the stage. "I'll go get Desirée."

"No, no man. The bloke's backstage and he doesn't want to wait. We'll fill Desirée in later."

"But…"

He reaches down to me and turns my shoulder. "Hurry, I don't want to screw this up."

Ah crap on a stick.

"And use your accent this time, mate."

"If I try to speak in an English accent, it will scare the guy off."

I steal one more glance at Desirée, sending a wish to the universe that she'll tell her new friend to buzz off and come back to me. She belongs with me.

A minute later, she's gone.

Hours pass by. It's late. And Desirée is still not back. I know this because I've been standing outside her hotel room like the pathetic fool I am. My own room is down the hall, but I never went back there after the concert because I didn't want to miss her.

I suppose I could just call. But that would be even more pathetic. I figure once I hear her coming around the corner, I can just happen to walk by from my room to the casino. Then I could invite her to talk, and I'd confess to my assholery, and drum up the courage to tell her how I feel.

She's become everything to me these last few months. My whole world. She is air and sunlight and sleep. She's music and life. I'm an empty shell without her.

I want to be the one who brings meaning to her days. Who she looks for in her dreams. Whose name she calls as she wakes. I want to give her every joy. Shower her with patience and understanding. Listen to her talk and sing and praise her for her unparalleled talent.

I want to be the one she laughs with, cries with, shares her crazy ideas with.

Since I've been waiting for her, here outside her door, I've jotted some thoughts down in my notes app. Every few minutes, I revisit them, sculpting the sentences into groups, then stanzas. Before I know it, I have the beginnings of a song. A little while later, melodies and chord progressions form in my head. I record myself humming into my phone, then adding some of the new lyrics to it. My fingers itch to underscore this with my guitar. But I don't want to leave the hallway.

It's rough and doesn't have much of a shape, but there's a rush inside me, like I'm caught up in a waterfall. Once, when I was a kid, my parents took me on a boat ride in Niagara Falls. We came so close to the powerful water crashing down into the lake, I got soaked through from the spray—even wearing the hooded ponchos they provide with the ticket. I felt overcome with awe, and a little frightened by the mighty fury of the falls. The mist was so forceful, my lungs constricted, and I felt my soul leap to my throat.

That's how I feel now. There's something weighty about this song. Bigger than me. More than my chest can hold. Reading over the words, I know why. Desirée is my muse.

"Mateo? What are you doing here?"

So lost in my creative work, I hadn't realized I'd sunk onto the floor, leaning against Desirée's door. And I hadn't heard her approach. So now I look like a creep.

Okay I *am* a creep.

"I… I wanted to talk to you."

"So call like a normal person. Why are you still in your Nigel costume? I thought you hated those spandex."

"I do. But not as much as I hate the idea of you out with that Killian guy."

"Kieran."

"It's three in the morning, Desirée."

"So what? I don't have to check in with you, Matt. Newsflash. I'm a grown woman."

"I'm aware of that. I just worry."

"Guess what? You don't have to."

"You hardly know that guy."

"So you're jealous? Is that it? You don't want anything to do with me. You're aloof half the time, the other half you act like a caveman. And when you're not throwing me over your shoulder, you hide into your own world where nobody can follow. One might say I hardly know *you*!"

"You know me better than any human on this earth. Including my mother, and that's saying a lot. And I know *you*. Admit it."

She sighs wearily. Her eyes are welling up.

"I truly wish I did. Please excuse me."

She wedges her way between me and the door and swipes her key card.

"Paloma. Please. Can we talk?"

"Mateo, I don't know what you want me to say. I like hanging out with you. You're really fun when you want to be. But it's like you can only go so far before you shut me out. And I'm so, so tired of waiting."

"So you decide to spend the night with him. After that whole speech about giving up men."

"I did not spend the night with Kieran."

I look right into her eyes. Their beauty drives a knife into my heart.

"If you say you didn't, then I believe you."

She's incapable of lying. Still, it doesn't lessen the pain. Life has a funny way of kicking you down right when you might be on to something special. The high I felt, forming lyrics and melody. I couldn't wait to show it to Desirée. But I'm not meant for a happy ending. I've known this my entire adult life. The sooner I can reconcile myself with that, the better.

I pocket my phone, turn, and walk down the hall. Not toward my room, which is the other direction. Toward the exit. I can feel Desirée's eyes on my retreating back until I'm several doors down, then I hear a click, and the latch to lock herself in.

Smell the Glove's contract allowed us rooms on the first floor, just in case we had heavy equipment to store in our rooms. We don't actually. We unloaded the tour van right through the backdoor of the nightclub. But we're not about to turn down first floor rooms. The elevators take forever in this hotel. And they stink.

So, with no elevator to take, it doesn't take me long to find my way to the pool area. It's supposed to resemble a Hawaiian oasis, with tropical trees, bamboo shoots, and grass umbrellas. It's deserted this time of night. I'm surprised it's not gated to keep out the riffraff.

I chuckle at the thought. The riffraff used to be me.

Lowering myself on a chair, I bury my face in my hands. A silent prayer falls from my lips—not asking for anything. Not a *"why God?"* complaint from feeling sorry for myself. It's a prayer of gratitude. I honestly have a lot to be thankful for, and it's about time I recognize that.

I have a moderately cool family. They drive me up the wall sometimes, but I think I got it pretty good. I have a dream job. So what if I have to dress up in a ridiculous costume? Any guy would give up a kidney to be able to play music for a living. And I have Desirée—even if she'll never be anything but a friend and neighbor. I'm incredibly lucky to know her. And if one day we drift apart, I'll consider myself fortunate that she breezed through my life, even for a little while.

"Hey! Are you crazy? It's raining."

I look up to see Desirée's nose and lips peeking out of her window that only opens a crack. When we checked in, we all decided she would get the room with the pool view. We thought she'd like it, but in retrospect, a hundred screaming kids splashing in a pool isn't a great soundtrack when you want to sleep in past eleven in the morning.

"What are you doing out there, you nut?"

Oh yeah. It's raining. I hardly noticed.

When I don't answer her, she disappears behind the curtain. Probably giving up on me. Or calling security. Or worse—my mom.

But a minute later, she's outside under the awning, trying to stay dry.

"Mateo, come inside. You might get struck by lightning."

She's at least thirty feet away, and yet I can see the weariness on her features.

"I didn't mean to creep you out," I call out over the tapping of the rain.

"What?"

Standing up, I repeat louder, "I said… I didn't mean to creep you out!"

"Oh."

Someone opens their window on the second floor and cries, "You're creeping *me* out. Be quiet down there."

"Sorry!" I say to whoever it is.

I thought that kind of thing only happened in movies set in New York when the guy is loudly declaring his love in the streets. In the rain. Or with a boombox.

I don't have a boombox. And we're not in New York. But I realize something I knew deep inside all along. I love Desirée. I've always loved her in some capacity. As a sister, as a neighbor, as a friend. But now this ache inside of me has grown so enormous, I can't hide from it.

I love her.

So let it be a cliché. I don't care if every hotel occupant opens their window to tell me to shut up.

My gaze falls over Desirée. Her arms are wrapped around herself even though it's warm out. And even though she's under the awning, the rain hitting the ground splashes her, getting her legs wet.

"I was waiting outside your door," I yell at the top of my lungs. "I was there because I didn't want to miss you."

"You should have called," she calls back.

"I should have. But I wanted to tell you in person… that I'm in love with you."

There it is. That movie moment. It feels good to say those words. It feels great. So great I need to say them again and again.

"I love you, Desirée Grant. I love you so much it hurts."

The voice from the second-floor yells down, "He said he loves you. Now kiss him already so we can all get some sleep."

With that, the window slams shut, and I'm left anchored by Desirée's gaze, my heart out in the open. Getting drenched in a monsoon.

After what seems like a hundred excruciating minutes, she leaves the safety of the awning, jogging towards me, her flip flops slapping on the wet concrete.

About five feet from me, she comes to an abrupt halt and shakes her head, like if she doesn't say what she wants to say, she'll fall apart.

"I was with your mom. And Tía Lucy, and Ursula. Yes, I *was* going to join Kieran for a cheeseburger after the show, but the restaurant was closed. And I thought to myself, this is a sign. He seems like a nice guy and everything but it just felt wrong. And then I ran into your mom, and we got to playing video roulette, and I thought you might come find us eventually. But you didn't."

She lifts her arms out like an airplane and flops them to her sides. "And my feelings got hurt."

"You were waiting."

"I told you I was waiting. I always do. I've been waiting my whole life."

"You were waiting."

"Yes. Why are you repeating that?"

Overcome, I close the distance between us. "You were waiting. Waiting for me to man up."

"No," she says, her voice softening to a whisper. "I was waiting for you to let me love you."

Crack. That's the sound of the walls around my heart splitting open like a dam. The floodgates have been breached and there's no closing them back again.

"You love me?"

"Yes."

"But why?"

"Because I just do. Because you're… you. Because you make me feel like I can do anything."

I fly to her, crashing my mouth to hers. Drinking her in. I cradle her head in my hands, threading my fingers into her thick, soft hair. The rain falls down with more force, drenching us completely, cleansing the rest of the ugly day away, giving us a fresh start. It's ridiculous, us standing out here, but I kiss her and kiss her until I feel my chest will explode.

"You deserve better," I say, with quick kisses on her lips, her jaw, her eyelids. "So much better. But I can't live if you're with anyone but me. I would die. So I'm going to be better. I swear I'll be the man you deserve."

She reaches up and covers my face with her hands, searching my eyes. Owning them.

And she says simply, "You already are."

"I've been burning for you so long, I can't remember when it began. The need to be near you. It was a compulsion. An addiction. But then it turned into something else. Gradually. So gradually, it's hard to imagine it's ever been anything but love." I kiss her softly. "I love you. I love you so much, Paloma, I can hardly breathe."

Her eyes twinkle, scanning my face as if needing to memorize my features.

Then a little smirk tugs at her lips, and she says, "Shut up and rock me, Amadeus."

My lips swallow hers over and over, devouring every last drop of her delicious taste. She clings to me, fisting my wet, sleeveless shirt so hard I might need a new one for tomorrow's gig.

Her body is soft and pliant against mine. Her mouth,

greedy and wanton. It's as though we're pouring years of longing and pent-up desire into this kiss.

We're fused together, her body liquifying under my touch. So fluid. So compliant. The stroke of my mouth sends a tiny shiver over her. The rise and fall of her breath in response to my fingers along her back, her neck, her shoulders.

I explore the feel and taste of her, nipping at her bottom lip, the delicious sensation bolting down to my belly.

My heart thunders in my chest,

She is perfection.

The breathy sounds she makes, her tiny moans, repeating my name as she quivers and sighs—all of it shatters me into a million pieces.

I've penetrated the doors of heaven, as unworthy as I am. This angel, inviting me in, mystifies me, and I feel as if I might break down and weep at her feet.

Nothing is more beautiful
than a guitar,
except, possibly two.

-Frederic Chopin

Chapter Twenty-Four
DESIRÉE

He pulls back and we rest our foreheads against each other, nose to nose, breathing heavily. Eyes heavy and unfocused.

"I feel like I'm making up for lost time," he says, breaking away from me to gaze at me in wonder. I can hardly believe this is happening.

He slides his thumb across my jaw, then he decides to kiss me there. Featherlight kisses skittering across my chin, to the other side of my face, where he showers hot, worshipful touches of his delectable lips all over my skin.

He dips his head and devours my neck as his strong fingers curl into my scalp. Then he moves to the sensitive area behind my ear before changing course to claim my lips again.

Heat pulses through my veins, pinpricks of pleasure cascade over my body. I'm alight with electricity—which is probably a good way to get struck by lightning in the middle of a rainstorm.

Panting from his all-consuming touch, I say, "We should probably go dry off."

My breath comes out ragged. Accidentally suggestive.

He lowers his voice to a rumble. "Are you trying to get me into your room? Because I'm not that easy."

Trying to compose myself, I poke his belly. "In your dreams, spandex boy. Your guyliner is running down your face."

He's only momentarily bothered.

"It would have been helpful if you'd told me that earlier." Then he regards me with a lazy half-smile. "Am I giving off Captain Jack Sparrow vibes?"

"More like Marilyn Manson."

He laughs. A deep, free laugh in the back of his throat. Then he draws me into his arms to shield me from the rain and kisses the top of my head. I'm already soaking wet but it's endearing, how he feels the instinct to protect me from every single thing in the world.

I tuck under his arm as we walk back inside the hotel. I don't want to let go of him long enough for us to dry off. But we can't stay dripping on the carpet forever.

When we arrive at my door, he cups his hands under my cheeks and kisses me tenderly. Unlike the savage intensity from a minute ago, this kiss is slow. Savoring. Sweet.

My toes curl with delight.

His stubble grazes over the skin around my lips, it bristles and tickles me at the same time.

After a while, I feel his arms slide around my waist, drawing me flush against him. We stumble, my back hits the door, and the warm growl coming from low in his chest lets me know he is pleased. Very, very pleased.

"Do… do you want to come in?" I ask breathily.

"Yes," he murmurs with a tone so deep, it's the frequency of a bass guitar. I might just blow a subwoofer. "But I won't," he adds, achingly slow.

"That's probably for the best," I agree. "This… thing. It's still very new."

I pause to take in his features. He really is the perfect specimen of male beauty."

"Whatever this *thing* is," I add, suddenly feeling a little bashful. I don't want to be one of those girls who has to put a label on a relationship after one kiss. Except this is Mateo. I wouldn't be able to survive a one-and-done romance.

He tips my chin up with his thumb. "This *thing* is you and me. We're a duet. But I need you to know something. I'm all in. No hiding or sneaking around. I want everyone to know I'm yours and you're mine. And I mean *everyone*."

"Everyone, meaning my brother," I say tentatively, not wanting to break this magic bubble.

"Especially your brother."

Tears of joy burn in the corner of my eyes. I must look like a drowned rat.

"Okay," I say, swallowing this raw emotion. "I'll call him tomorrow."

"We'll call him together," he says. Then he brushes his fingers over my lashes.

"Why are you crying?"

"I don't know. You name it." More tears come but I'm laughing now. "Relief. Happiness. Surprise."

He kisses me gently, then kisses my tears, pressing his lips over each eye.

"Do you want to know what I did while I was standing out here like a stalker?"

I laugh. "Yes, I do."

"I wrote a song."

"You did? I love that for you." It makes me happy to know he's writing again. "Tell me about it."

"It's an alt-rock ballad, kind of poetic 90s grunge. It talks about the beauty of life and nature. How we're so small in the universe. It's about consciousness and sensitivity and doubt. Fear and awe. But it's just a work in progress right now."

"I can't wait to hear it. What's it called?"

"I'm trying to decide between "The Mundane Misadventures of a Fragile Ego," or "Love Stinks, but So Do I.""

"Hmmm. Tough choice, but I think I like the second one better."

"Yeah, me too."

As promised, Mateo holds my hand as we FaceTime with

my brother. Ian's expression is impassive as we talk, letting us finish before he responds.

He doesn't say much, only nods and looks to his left as if turning over the idea in his head.

Then he simply says, "Okay," and asks to speak with Mateo alone.

After an hour goes by, I'm worried Ian found a way to reach through the phone to strangle Mateo on the spot.

But my fears are put to rest when Mateo returns with that devil-may-care smile on his face. He tells me Ian recognizes I'm a grown woman who can make her own life decisions. That he's happy as long as I am. And that if Mateo hurts me in any way, shape, or form, he'll relieve him of his ability to reproduce.

I'm okay with those terms.

Mateo's parents are the next to know—and are not surprised at all. Then the guys in the band. Their general reaction is "It's about bloody time."

For the next month, we continue our tour, and it turns out, dating a bandmate is not as awkward as one might think. In fact, it's pure bliss. The interactions on stage are even more charged, and after the shows, we steal every moment we can together.

Mateo is funny and attentive and loves on me like there's no tomorrow.

I don't think my heart can get any fuller.

I'm happier than I've ever been in my life.

Until one day, the world comes crumbling down around me.

You might be a redneck if
you think a chain saw
is a musical instrument.

—Jeff Foxworthy

Chapter Twenty-Five
DESIRÉE

"Hey!" Aren't you that girl from the band?"

I look up from the hard, cold bench in the holding cell to see a girl that looks like a Barbie—if the Barbie had been buried in the backyard by the dog, dug up again, got her hair caught in an oscillating fan, and has been tied to the grill of a car ever since. She's staring right at me, with mascara-smudged eyes and a smug sense of confidence. A tad too comfortable casually leaning against the cinder block walls for a gal who just got arrested.

Tipping a chin in my direction, she says, "What are ya in for?"

I recognize her. Candy. She used to come to the High C's concerts, hanging on all the guys. Honestly, I thought I was invisible to her, and I'm surprised she recognizes me. Especially since I'm covered in 80's makeup and wearing my Smell the Glove costume.

"Probably the same thing you're in for," I say. "By mistake."

"We set a car on fire," she says, matter-of-factly. "But I'm the only of my friends that got caught."

Okay then. Definitely not the same reason I'm here. Also, not very wise to admit guilt out loud in the police station. Just my opinion.

But what do I know?

The whole night is a blur of smoke, screams, and the flashing lights of cop cars. But I think it's important to try and organize the evening's events in my memory—if only to rationalize the reality of it—me, locked up in the city jail with Pyro Barbie and a girl in the corner sporting a purple mohawk.

The first sign of trouble was when I noticed the two surfer guys from my neighborhood. Not really a standout thing to see surfers at a Surf Fest, but alarm bells went off when I saw them mulling about with Pancho Two. Yes, the criminal that's supposed to be on house arrest at the Precio house was in Huntington Beach. And, I'm pretty sure he's not into surfing.

I told Mateo right away, but we were about to go on

stage. We never took our eyes off them. Luckily, we only had a three-song set, since we were one of several bands booked for the night.

But as soon as the last note rang out on Mateo's guitar, he ran after Pancho Two and the surfers. Here's the thing about Mateo. He's not subtle. He'd make a horrible spy. I could have told him—parting your way through a sea of concertgoers shouting *"Hold it right there"* is not an effective tactic.

By this time, it was dark. The surf competitions were finished, and downtown Huntington had turned into party central. The next band had taken the stage—a thrasher rock/ska combo, and people were already feeling rowdy. It was a madhouse.

Needless to say, we lost Pancho Two and his goonies in the crowd. Mateo was livid, getting his brother, Ignacio on the phone.

That's when he told me about how Ignacio was kidnapped last year by a surfer gang called Point Break Posse. They were strong-arming him into laundering money through his restaurant. And the fun part of the story is… the leader of the gang is Pancho Two's nephew.

I think it would have been a good idea to fill me in on that little detail a while ago. But Mateo insisted he hadn't put two and two together until after we got back from Laughlin and Pancho Two was acting weirder than usual, staying up long after everyone else was asleep.

But the VW never came down our street after that. Not that we know of. So he passed it off as paranoia.

Gah this is too much for my brain. I have a splitting headache.

"We came down to see Red Maiden," says Candy, drifting over to sit next to me. But she thinks better of it and hovers over me instead. "My girlfriends and I follow them everywhere they play. They get the best hotel rooms, if you know what I mean."

"How nice for you."

"I know, right? The guys really like us. But imagine my surprise when I saw Mateo from The High C's in a new band! I couldn't believe it. I mean, I could recognize that ass anywhere, but I couldn't believe it."

"Yep," I say. "It's really something else, isn't it?"

"Oh, I'm sorry. You probably didn't know Mateo back then. He probably doesn't like to talk about that old band he was in. I hear he left under bad circumstances."

So she doesn't recognize me from The High C's after all.

"He does his best to avoid the subject," I reply.

"Anyway. Your band? Really rockin'. Do you write the songs as a group or is it just that lead guy?"

Oh dear lord. I *could* tell her we're a cover band for a fake heavy metal rockumentary from the 80s, but where's the fun in that?

"I wrote the songs actually," I say. "I came up with the lyrics the last time I was in jail."

"It's my third time inside," says the purple mohawk girl.

"Oh?" I say, nodding nervously because how does one respond to that? *"How nice you found a career you love?"*

I wonder if this will go on my permanent record—once they find out I'm innocent. *If* they find out I'm innocent. Oh my gosh, my dad's gonna kill me.

It was all a misunderstanding. The incident.

Mateo had already called the police. All we had to do was wait. But then all hell broke loose. A riot had broken out on Main Street. People went wild, smashing shop windows, looting. And, like Candy over here, setting cars on fire. All of downtown looked like a war zone. It was surreal.

Mateo took my hand and we ran, trying to get to safety. But then he saw the Posse again. They had bottle rockets, throwing them all over the place. Mateo told me to stay put right before he chased after them. But stay put where? No place was safe. People ran by me on the sidewalk like lunatics, practically knocking me over. Glass beer bottles broke at my feet as I tried to circumvent the destruction at every turn. When I tucked into a shop entrance, somebody smashed the window next to me, setting off a blaring alarm.

And that's when I saw the Posse barrel across the street with Mateo on their heels. They disappeared inside a store with the windows blacked out. It had a *'coming soon'* sign on it.

Mateo bolted into the store after them, and a minute later, there was smoke and fire. Then the surfers took off down the street. I didn't see Mateo come out.

I don't know what came over me. A huge spike of adrenaline, maybe. It's not smart to run into a burning building without protection. Especially when you're not a trained firefighter. But I didn't think. I ran. I ran down that street, dodging looters and crazy people dancing in the middle of the road.

The fire hadn't gotten out of hand when I got there, but I couldn't open the front door. Something was wedged in there. All I could think of was Mateo inside, probably unconscious or dead, and his beautiful body burnt to a crisp.

So I did what everybody else was doing. I found a stone—one of many forming an ornamental circle around a tree—and threw it through the shop window.

When I got inside, Mateo wasn't there.

And that's when the cops came.

Now I'm in this holding cell with a Chatty Candy of very loose virtue, and Emo Joan Jett, the side hustle queen.

I used my one phone call to contact Ian. His reply came back calm, cool, and collected, like one would expect from a Navy fighter pilot.

"I'll take care of it," he said. And that was that. Seven hours ago.

It's close to five in the morning, I'm deliriously tired, it's freezing in here, and the blankets smell like urine.

And I don't even know if Mateo is safe.

"Desirée Grant?"

Two armed guards flank the cell gate while a third punches a code in the keypad.

"You're getting out. Come with me."

I'd dance for joy, but I'm too worn out for that. As the guard takes me out of the cell, the purple mohawk girl gives me what looks like a Scout's honor salute and says, "See you next time."

Well, at least I made a friend today.

Trust me, you can dance.

-Tequila

Chapter Twenty-Six

MATEO

"Step away from the computer and no one gets hurt."

I ignore my brother Dante and continue my search for a ticket to South Carolina. I'm hard pressed to find a direct flight. A layover of any length will try my patience and that will end with my name on the No Fly List.

"*Hermano*, it's only been a week. She'll be home soon."

Not soon enough.

I scroll and scroll until I finally find a direct flight. My finger hovers over the trackpad, poised to hit the buy now button. But Dante's enormous paw effortlessly grabs my wrist lifting my arm far away from the laptop.

"Hey, watch the goods. My hands are my livelihood."

"I'm not going to snap your wrist, *feo*. But I *will* confiscate your computer if you try to buy a twenty-five-hundred-dollar plane ticket."

"I've been saving. A lot. So, I can afford one tiny airline ticket."

Yes, I like nice things. And I have more guitars than the average person. And now, because Dante helped me move it all, he thinks I have a spending problem. And it doesn't help that Desirée teased me about it. Calling me a shopaholic. Personally, I think the term is ludicrous, but in any case, I've made an effort to be more mindful of my spending these past few months. I no longer find pleasure in physical things anyway. In fact, I donated a lot of my possessions. It will make it all the easier when I move out.

"Mateo, I'm warning you."

"She hasn't called."

"She called you three days ago, and you know how hard that was."

Yes, I know. She lost her phone and had to borrow one to call me. But don't they have mobile phone stores in Myrtle Beach, South Carolina? It's perplexing. She said she needed some time to decompress at her parents' house. That's fine. I'll give her anything. Time. Space. A frickin' Zen garden on the moon. But I need to be there for when she's ready.

Now, I've just got to find an Airbnb with an open-ended stay…

Just then January bursts into the house. "We got here as soon as we could."

She comes over to give me a hug from behind. "Those doggos weren't going to rescue themselves, otherwise we'd have been here sooner."

January and Enrique have been in Tijuana for the past two weeks working with PETA and the Mexican authorities to take down illegal puppy mills.

"You didn't have to come," I say, patting the arm she has around my neck. "There's nothing you guys can do. Unless you have a private jet in that Versace bag of yours."

"It's not Versace, it's a custom Hermès. And I don't have a jet, but I can get you one."

"You really need to stop enabling him, January," says Dante.

She shrugs loftily.

"Where's Enrique?" he asks.

"Oh, he's outside with the dogs."

"Dogs?"

She smirks mischievously. "Well, there were so many cute puppers. And since PETA was taking care of most of them, I had to at least help with five."

"Five!?" cries Dante. "What are you going to do with five dogs?"

"I thought I'd give you guys first dibs. Mateo, you look like you need a furry friend to cheer you up."

Dante stomps over to the front door and screams outside.

"Hey! Kiki. Get in here."

Enrique says something back, but I can't make it out. Then Dante grumbles something under his breath and trudges outside.

A minute later, Dante returns with a puppy in each arm, followed by Enrique with three more dogs on leashes.

January squeals and snaps a picture of them with her phone.

"Ladies all over the internet are going to drool when they see this," she says. "Two burly men with puppies? Content gold."

"Don't you dare post that," says Dante.

She takes another picture and quickly puts away the phone. Dante growls at that, which catches the attention of the golden puppy who lifts his little head and licks Dante's nose.

He practically shoves the other puppy in my face. "Here. Take this."

I gotta admit, this puppy is pretty darn cute. She's tri-colored with black, brown, and white fur.

And she has striking blue eyes.

January sneakily takes a picture of me holding the pup.

"So, tell us what happened," says Enrique. "All I know is Pancho Two was doing some shady business with the Point Break Posse and now he's in jail."

"Forever, hopefully," I say.

"Ignacio said it was insurance fraud? How did he manage that while on house arrest?"

"Secret meetings with the Posse in the middle of the night," says Dante. "Messages sent back and forth with his sister, Churro's mom. He used her credit and clean record to start a fake boutique in Downtown Huntington. Forged inventory documents, filled the place with junk, and had the Posse set it on fire."

"How do you know all this?" asks January.

"Oh, he folded like a tortilla," says Dante. "Blubbering like an idiot, trying to pin it all on his sister like he was the victim."

"Wow, that guy is super slimy," she says.

My hand involuntarily runs across the puppy's back. She's so soft. Desirée would love her. "I'm glad he's gone," I say.

"I heard you got in a death match with Roach and Churro," Enrique says.

Roach and Churro are two of the members of the surf gang. I later learned there were more of them causing trouble in Huntington Beach that night, but I wasn't aware at the time.

"It wasn't a death match. I followed them into one of the storefronts and got ambushed."

One of the other Posse members I didn't know about, was waiting inside with a wooden box which he threw at my head, and then ran out the back door into the alley. Naturally, I chased after him, but my forehead was bleeding and he had a head start. Meanwhile, Roach and Churro set fire to the place and bolted.

I searched for Desirée for hours, or at least as long as I could before the police shut the entire street down. I called her, texted her. I was worried sick. Much later, after Ignacio picked me up and brought me home, Ian called me to say he was on his way to get Desirée out of jail.

She'd been arrested.

I almost threw up on the spot.

"I should have gone to get her myself," I say, full of self-loathing.

"You had a mild concussion," says Dante. "You were in no shape to drive. And who do you think has more clout with the authorities? You? Or Desirée's influential Navy family?"

He's not wrong. Mr. Grant has friends in high places. He even met the president, once.

"I gave her name when I made my statement to the Sheriff," I say.

January comes over to pet the puppy I'm holding but pets my head instead. "I'm sure your testimony helped prove her innocence, sweetie. Oooh, what conditioner do you use?"

My mind is going a million miles a minute. "I have to get to South Carolina."

January gets out her phone and is already clicking on the screen as she strolls toward the back patio. "I'm going to make some inquiries for you."

"No you're not!" shouts Dante. But January is already gone.

"Desirée doesn't blame you," Dante says in a softer tone. "You do know that... right?"

"*She* doesn't," I say, knowing how Desirée's forgiveness knows no bounds. I raise my eyes to glare at my brother. "But *you* do."

He's taken aback. I've never seen such confusion and dismay on his face at the same time.

"Me?"

"Yes, you. You made it exceedingly clear you wanted me

to stay away from Desirée, like you were her personal bodyguard. Even Ian isn't that protective."

"I was protecting *you*. I know how sappy you get."

"I don't get sappy," I say defensively.

"You do," says Enrique, now on the couch with the three dogs sleeping on top of him. "Remember that Memorial Day block party?"

Dante nods dramatically. "Oh yeah. That was bad."

"What Memorial Day block party?" I ask.

"A few years ago, when Desirée invited that guy she was dating," says Enrique. "You cried like a whiny schoolgirl about Desirée this and Desirée that, and how she stabbed you in the heart, blah blah blah. We had to take you upstairs."

"I don't remember this," I say.

"Yeah, you were pretty hammered," Dante says laughing. "You didn't hold any of your feelings back."

I'm searching my memory, but it comes back blank. This must be why I have an aversion to Jack Daniels. And block parties at my parents' house.

"Nevertheless," I say. "It doesn't change the fact that you guys think I'm a screw up. Your little brother who can't be trusted with anything or anyone."

Wow. It feels good to get that off my chest.

"Where the heck is this coming from?" asks Dante. The puppy he's holding is snoring, so he sets him down on the couch with Enrique.

"Thanks a lot, dude," Enrique grumbles.

Dante ignores him and turns to me, crossing his arms. "I have never said I don't trust you. None of us has."

I snort dismissively. "Oh come on. Ever since Sebastian got stuck in the claw machine. All your little jabs and saying things like, *"Don't let Mateo drive the car, he might lose it."* Or, *"Keep the ball away from Matt, he'll kick it in the wrong goal."*

"We're your older brothers. Of course we're going to tease you and give you a hard time. That's what brothers do. We're just joking."

"Sebas was missing for hours and hours. Mom was hysterical."

Enrique laughs. "Hours and hours? Dude. It was five minutes. Tops. And Mom's always hysterical. She'll have a conniption fit if someone leaves a sock on the floor."

"She's worried someone might slip on it like a banana peel," Dante says with a straight face.

"But she told me Sebas has a fear of small spaces," I retort. "It's from being trapped in the claw machine. I know it."

"Sebas is claustrophobic because the dummy hid inside his locker from a girl when he was in fifth grade. Nobody found him until lunch time."

"What? How have I never heard about this? And how did he fit in the locker?"

"He was a skinny kid," says Dante. "And I don't know what hole you were living in, but Sebastian slept in the backyard for a week. With no covers. Even *I* knew that, and I had already moved out."

"That does kind of sound familiar," I say.

"You were a teenager," says Enrique. "Probably hiding out in your room or lord knows what else. I was at Berkeley. But I should have been there more for you and Sebas."

Hold up just a minute. It's going to take me a while to

process this. I feel like I've stepped into the multiverse where another version of myself is living a slightly different reality. How do I know they're not just joshing me?

"I'm having a hard time believing you right now." I pause a moment to clear my head. "But let's put a pin in it. I'm super tired."

Probably due to the collective fourteen hours of sleep I've had over the course of a week.

Maybe this is a self-fulfilling prophecy. I've gone my entire life expecting the other shoe to drop whenever things were going well for me. There's always a voice in the back of my mind poking at me saying this is a temporary success. *"Enjoy being happy now sucker, because there's calamity around the corner."* Inevitably, I either self-sabotage the good stuff, or I ruin it with worry. It's like I'm telling myself *"You don't deserve this, let's burn it to the ground."*

I really suck at manifesting—which is not the best thing to admit if you want to get better at it.

"The question is," says Enrique from the couch, dogs splayed out all over his body. "What are you going to do now?"

Taking inventory of my life, and the strides I've made recently, a quickening fires inside my chest. I refuse to self-sabotage this time. The wind is changing and I'm going to own it.

"I bought a house," I blurt.

Dante blinks at me. Stunned. As brawny as he is, I'm convinced you could knock him over with a light breeze.

"You what?"

"I had a sit down with our financial guy, and some of my stock went berserk. So I bought real estate."

Enrique says lazily, "That's great. You'll have a place to put all these dogs."

"What financial guy?" asks Dante. "Tom Goldman?"

Enrique cracks up. "Fitting name for a money guy."

"Yeah," I say. "The guy taking care of Ignacio's payments to us for our share of the restaurants."

Dante and Enrique exchange a look. Clearly they haven't been paying attention.

"Fifty percent of my payments have been withheld ever since we entered into this arrangement with Ignacio," I explain. "How did you not know this?"

"All the plans are individualized," says Enrique. "I have a different agreement than you and Dante, and everyone else."

"Well, I sat down with him a couple months ago. We sold a few stocks and agreed real estate was a solid plan. So I found a place in Oklahoma..."

Dante's jaw drops. "You're moving? To *Oklahoma*?"

"No. It's an investment property. A fourplex. I already have tenants, revenue coming in, I've been reinvesting the profits... and I'm looking into a few houses in LA. For myself."

Dante still has a look of astonishment on his face. "Wow, little brother. That's... really smart."

Enrique has a less dramatic reaction as Dante. He just gives me a thumbs up and says, "Way to go."

I think he's feeling residual drowsiness from the sleeping dogs on his chest.

January parades back in the room in her usual January way—camera ready and fabulously bold.

"I found a private jet for you. Should I go ahead and confirm it?"

I chuckle. My crazy sister-in-law. She's too good to me. And now I'm thinking I need to live up to my promise to be that better man. For Desirée. But also for me.

"Actually, thank you. I truly appreciate it. But I have a new plan."

It would be interesting
if Elvis were reincarnated
as an Elvis impersonator.

-Demetri Martin

Chapter Twenty-Seven
DESIRÉE

There's no place like home. I'm not talking about a house, although I have missed my own bed. Two weeks with my parents would make me homesick even if I lived in a shack.

But I'm grateful for them, for giving me a place to gather my thoughts without the noise and chaos of everyday busyness. I didn't mean to leave Mateo hanging, but I needed it. For me.

I needed to reevaluate the trajectory of my life. What to do next. What does my future look like?

How Mateo fits into all that.

I've come to the realization that life on the road with a gig in a new town every week is not for me. I had a great time, especially the last couple of months. But I'm worn out. I'd rather stay at home with my bunny and knit. Record music in my home studio. Take the time to allow the creativity to flow.

I'll have to quit the band.

And I don't know how Mateo's going to take it. For that reason, I've been avoiding the uncomfortable task of telling him.

I thank the rideshare driver when he drops me off at home. For the first time in weeks, I can breathe again. It feels good to be back.

Taking a quick glance at the Precio house, I take inventory of the cars. Mateo's Stingray is parked in the driveway. Why am I so nervous to go over there and deliver my news? It's not that I'm breaking up with him. It just feels like I am. He'll continue on tour, and I'll be that woman back home. Pining for him.

Of course, I refuse to pine. I've got stuff to do.

Sighing, I trudge up the walkway that leads to my front door, when I finally lift my eyes to truly look at my house.

There's a new bed of flowers lining the front facade. They look like those pink camellias from the botanical garden. Turning around to take in my yard, I realize the patchy yellowish grass has been replaced by lush, green sod. And a sapling cherry tree takes up residence right in the middle of it.

I drop my bag off on my front porch and run around the side of my house where I see an archway of peonies over the side gate. No. Not peonies. These must be the earth angel roses Mateo was talking about. They're stunning, with creamy white petals that look like they're blushing from too many adoring compliments.

Venturing into my backyard, I'm struck with an explosion of color. It's like every single flowering plant in California came here to party.

"Mateo," I whisper in wonder. "You son of a gun."

There's even an herb garden.

Overwhelmed by a rush of emotion, I bound into a full-fledged sprint to get to the Precio house. With the extra land between our houses, I'm out of breath by the time I knock on the door.

Mrs. Precio answers with a warm smile, like she's been expecting me. She's carrying a puppy I haven't seen before, with black, brown, and white fur.

"Hello, my dear," she says calmly as if I'm not about to internally combust if I don't see Mateo immediately. "How was your flight?"

"Um, fine. Thank you." I crane my neck, lifting myself on my tippy toes to get a glimpse of the inside of her house. But she just stands in the doorway, not inviting me in.

"Is… Mateo available?"

"I'm sorry niña, no he's not."

Crestfallen, I catch my breath. "Oh."

I'm really trying not to read too much into that. Maybe he's in the shower. Or taking a nap.

The puppy in her arms yawns and hangs her head sideways, eyeing me. What a cute little floofball.

"I didn't know you got a new dog," I say.

"She's Mateo's."

Mateo got a dog? What will he do when the touring resumes?

"Well," I say, shrinking back, ready to go back home, "Will you tell Mateo I stopped by?"

I veer towards my house, coercing my legs to move.

"If you want to see him, you need to go to the convent."

I make an about-face so quick, I've caused a ripple in the universe.

"Did you say… convent?"

When I arrive at the address Mrs. Precio gave me, there's a line, hundreds of people deep, curling around the grounds. As I drive my Vespa closer to the main cluster of buildings, more people are gathered, milling about, talking, laughing, and sitting on the grass eating. It seems like an enormous church picnic. Until I get a better look at the picnickers.

Some have a faraway look in their eyes. Others with weather-worn skin. Most of them have layers of old clothing on or carry large backpacks. The men either have scruff or full beards, and several of the women are bone thin. I realize with stark awareness, that these people are not gathered as families or as a social group. They're here to be fed.

I park my Vespa and take in the whole scene.

My eyes follow the serpentine line which zigzags on the lawns like for a ride at an amusement park. It curves past a row of large, shady trees, and at the end of it stands a long white tent, where buffet tables are set up, covered in white linen.

If I didn't know any better, I'd think this was a wedding.

And that's when I see him.

Mateo behind one of the buffet tables, serving up tacos alongside his brothers. Ignacio rushes back and forth, barking orders for more carne asada and tortillas. Mr. Precio is on the grill, barking back at Ignacio. Dante carries a big tray of beans, dropping it into a steaming hot chafing dish while Enrique holds onto the lid. There's a bright smile on Francesca's face as she serves spoonfuls of rice on people's plates. At the end of the line, I see January and Olive passing out small dessert cups that might be flan. Nate is here, wearing an apron over his fashionable dress clothes.

Edmund and Sebastian are helping Memo pass out blankets.

The whole family is here, with the exception of Mrs. Precio who's on puppy duty back home.

When Mateo sees me, he freezes, eyes fixed on me like a statue.

My heart catches in my throat at the sight of him. He's never looked more handsome.

Ignacio nudges him, calmly removes the serving tongs from Mateo's hand, and whispers something in his ear with a chin tip my way. Mateo blinks, drops the paper plate, and jolts into motion. He throws himself into a sprint around the buffet tables, thundering toward me without a sign of stopping, until his body collapses into mine, and he sweeps me into a dizzying spin.

My feet barely touch the ground and he's kissing me,

trembling, saying my name over and over. Arms circled around me in an ardent, impassioned embrace. He exhales into my neck like he's been holding his breath for weeks, saying, "Thank God you're home."

His hands go to my face, my hair, eyes darting over me in disbelief that I'm real. More desperate kisses on my lips, my cheeks, between my eyebrows.

"You came."

"I came."

He pulls me in for another hug, holding onto me, speaking into my hair.

"I missed you. I was going to fly to South Carolina, but my brothers chained me to the floor. Figuratively."

"The flowers," I say. "They're beautiful. I have no words."

"You don't need words," he says, cupping my face in his hands. "Just knowing you're okay is enough."

"I'm an ex-con now," I say. "A hardened criminal. I might get a tattoo."

"Oh you should definitely get a tattoo. My name in old English across your chest so everyone will know you're my girl."

"Possessive much?"

"Yes. You know you love it."

He's right. I do.

"Maybe you're the one who should get the tattoo."

His deep, brown eyes twinkle in the sunlight and a smirk tugs at the corner of his lip.

"I already have, Paloma."

He stretches down the collar of his shirt, revealing dark, shaded ink in the shape of a dove in flight, its wings spread out freely with abandon above his heart. The detail is astonishing.

"It's beautiful," I say. "I love it."

"I love *you*," he says, gingerly springing his collar back into place. "And I'm so sorry you went through what you did. I wish it had been me instead."

A figure appears at our side in a brown frock and clears her throat. It's Sister Monica. I almost didn't recognize her without the shamrock T-shirt. But that Irish lilt is undeniable.

"Now I know ye aren't neckin' kids, but keep in mind, this is a place of prayer."

Mateo laughs. "Sister, I'd like you to meet Desirée."

"Ach, so you're the lass that caught our Maddy's eye." Then she leans in and whispers, "Keep him in line for us, will ye?"

"I'll do my best."

She sighs and takes in her surroundings. "Quite the event coordinator, isn't he?"

I glance at Mateo. He's blushing a little. Interesting.

"Wait. You organized this?"

"He did indeed," says Sister Monica. "He wasn't impressed with the cook's tacos, so he talked his brother into coming over. Show our cook a thing or two."

"The tacos weren't *that* bad," says Mateo. "I only asked Ignacio to help out in the kitchen once or twice. He likes doing that kind of thing."

"Yes, God bless him," says Sister Monica. "But then Mateo saw us making our peanut butter and jelly…"

"They make sandwiches for the rescue missions and shelters," Mateo explains.

"Aye, we do. And what do ye think Maddy said to me?"

I take a guess. "That he wanted to make them tacos instead of peanut butter and jelly sandwiches?"

"And he donated every last pinto bean from his own pocket."

"Wow," I say. "Color me impressed."

"I didn't do it to impress anyone," says Mateo.

Sister Monica exhales wistfully. "I'm sure I'm not the only one who'll miss you tending the garden on Tuesdays."

"I'll still come around to check on your plants. If Lloyd lets me. And my siblings want to make this a monthly thing if that's alright."

"I think that can be arranged," she says with a wink. "Now. I hear there's chocolate flan."

"Ignacio made it just for you."

She takes my hand, places it in Mateo's and squeezes. And with a sly smile, she strolls away.

Mateo gives me a tour of the grounds, pointing out all the new flowers and shrubs he planted. He tells me about the groundskeeper, Lloyd, who he often skips out on work with to play dominoes in the tool shed.

He shows me some new additions to the gardens—ceramic gnomes donated by Olive. Mateo isn't quite sure where they all are or how many but is convinced she hid a few and someday, he'll get a jump scare when he comes across one.

After a while, he asks me, "Did you accomplish what you set out to do? While you were with your parents?"

"I don't know if I accomplished anything really. But I feel a little more in control. And I see things clearer now."

"Good. Because I never want to be apart from you again. Not like that."

I suppose this is my opening. When he goes back on tour, I won't be with him this time.

"Mateo," I begin. "About the band…"

"Smell the Glove disbanded."

"What? Why?"

"Lots of reasons. Rusty missed his wife. And Scott's no spring chicken. He's tired of living out of a suitcase for weeks at a time."

"But you all love what you do."

"I know. That's why we're going into the studio in a few weeks to cut a single. Scott's always wanted to be a studio musician and a manager, and Mick had several offers lined up. It just worked out. I'm sorry. I know you wanted the touring thing to work out."

"I don't care about touring. I actually kind of hate it."

"Really?"

"That's one of the things I was thinking about while I was in South Carolina. It's fun and all. It's just not for me."

"So you're not upset?"

"Of course not."

"That's a relief. Because I have something else I want to run by you."

"I'm listening."

"I want to do this together. You and me. Your original music and mine. We'll put it out there in the world and see what happens."

I give him an open smile. "Okay."

"Okay? Just like that? I don't have to twist your arm?"

"Nope."

"I would have had to twist your arm a few months ago."

I shrug one shoulder. "Jail changes a person."

Mateo's lopsided smirk makes an appearance, and he snakes his arms around my waist. "Does it now? Any chance I can convince you to be my partner in crime? Eighty years to life?"

I raise myself up on my tip toes and kiss him.

"Let's just stick to musical metaphors from now on. And no corny ones."

"Like… let's play beautiful music together?"

"Barf."

"Ring my bell?"

I make a buzzer sound.

"If music be the fruit of love, play on."

"You're getting warmer, but zero points for creativity."

I take his hand and start walking back to the front lawns before Sister Monica comes looking for us.

"Marry me."

I snort. "That's not even a musi— What are you doing?"

He lowers himself to one knee, still holding my hand. "Marry me."

"Mateo, get up. You're ruining your jeans."

"Not until you give me an answer."

"Are you crazy? We've been dating for two months."

"You're it for me, Paloma. Why do you think I avoided it for so long? Because I knew. I knew I'd fall hard. I've known for a long time. It's always been you."

The familiar sting of tears tickles my nose. I sniffle. "Now what am I supposed to say to that?"

"Say yes."

"You'll have to sit down with my brother," I say.

"I'm counting on it."

"And my parents."

"Dreading that."

I bite my lower lip, hardly believing this is happening.

"And Mister Hopkins gets the final say."

"He can have a conference with Zeta."

"Who's Zeta?"

"My dog. She likes to hop, by the way. I think she'll like the agility contests."

"Oh, well, in that case."

"So it's a yes?"

Rolling my eyes, I send him a flat grin. "How can a lady say no when you're so convincing?"

He jumps up, throws his arms around my waist, and spins me around.

"Geronimo!"

I laugh. "What did you just say?"

"Never mind. Just kiss me, baby."

And I do.

Epilogue
DESIRÉE

Strengthening the knot of the scarf I wrapped over Mateo's eyes, I say, "No peeking."

He rumbles with approval. "No promises, baby. But are you sure you want to do this in the kitchen?"

"The kitchen is fine," I say. "Now shut up and sit still."

"Ooh, bossy. Are you going to bind my hands behind my back? Because I never thought I'd be into this kind of thing, but I'm really digging this new side of you."

I smack his knee. "I'm not going to tie you to the chair, you big wolf. You'll need your hands for this."

"She called me big."

I raise my eyes to the ceiling. "I married a man-child."

He reaches for my hips and drags me down onto his lap.

"What do I need my hands for?" His hands start to wander and they feel so nice cradling me, protecting me, I momentarily lose track of why I blindfolded him in the first place. His fingers dip under my shirt, tracing hot circles at the base of my back, then up and down my spine.

This man knows no mercy.

He reaches behind my neck and pulls me down for a kiss. His lips are playful and passionate. Relentless.

"Maybe I *will* cuff your wrists back if you don't stop distracting me."

He growls. "It's settled. I'm going to buy you a leather catsuit."

"Like I'd wear such a thing," I say flatly.

Or fit into it in a few months.

"Oh, you'd wear it." Then he lowers his voice an octave. "For me."

"You are unbelievable. I'm just glad I decided not to put this on video. I'd be mortified if our parents saw it."

"Why would our parents see it? Wait a minute." He pauses his roaming hands. "Are you trying to prank me into eating weird crap and guess what you put in my mouth? Because my brothers already tried that and lost."

"I don't even want to know the details of that story," I say. "Now let me get up so we can do this."

He licks his lips. "Bring it on, woman."

Peeling myself off his lap, I get the wand I hid in a drawer and gently place it in his hands.

"You have to guess what this is," I say.

He frowns. "It's not food?"

"I never said it was food. Sheesh."

"What is it, then?" He sniffs it. "Hmm, that's a familiar smell. Can't quite place it."

Oh my word.

He turns it over in his hands then takes the lid off and sniffs it again making a face.

"Don't take the lid off."

I realize too late that I should have taped it shut.

"Is it a kazoo?" he asks, bringing into his mouth.

"No!" I'm not quick enough, barely able to breathe with silent laughter as I weakly pull on his wrist. "Since when do kazoos have lids?"

He sticks out his tongue in disgust. "It's wet. Bleh."

I can't even.

"I washed the outside, but I forgot to wash the inside."

He sniffs it again. "Okay, there's some kind of reed. Like an oboe. But it's small like a kazoo…"

Tears are streaming down my face. "I didn't think you'd take the lid off. Stop trying to put it in your mouth."

He's like a small child. Or a puppy.

"Well what did you expect?"

I'm dying, doubled over in a fit of giggles. "Clearly not that you'd try to lick it."

"Why not? It's a kaz-oboe."

"Because I peed on it." My whole face is hot and red, and there's a howl choked so far up my throat, I can hardly get the words out.

"You whaaat? Eugh. Why would you pee on a kaz—"

Awareness dawns on his features and he freezes.

"It's not a kaz-oboe, is it?"

I shake my head even though he can't see me, practically swallowing the word, "No."

I'm laughing so hard my sides ache. This is not going how I expected it to.

"Paloma… what are you trying to tell me?"

"I'm sorry," I say, trying hard to not hyperventilate. "I thought it would be cute to make you guess."

He yanks the scarf off his head and stares at the pregnancy test in his hand, blinking repeatedly. Then he lifts his gaze to me, spreads his mouth into a big, open smile and says, "Ha ha! Yes!"

He springs from the chair, wraps his arms around me and snuggles me into his chest.

"I did it! I put a baby in you."

"Whoa whoa, there, stud. It was a joint effort."

"I'm a manly man." His voice is low and gruff.

"There was never a doubt in my mind," I say.

He pulls back, just enough to look into my eyes and tuck his fingers under my chin.

"And you are all woman. Such an amazing, beautiful woman."

His lips brush over mine in a tender kiss.

With tears in his eyes, he says, "How did I get so lucky?"

"Oh, I don't know. I still think you put some magic spell on me. Hypnotized me with your wicked guitar playing."

His eyes glitter as he rakes his gaze over my face. Then his bright smile turns into a grimace.

"You didn't clean the part you *peed* on?"

"I put the lid on it."

"I got pee. On my tongue."

"Oh come on. It's not like we don't exchange other bodily fluids."

"You're going to pay for that, Paloma."

My eyes go wide seeing the wild look on his face. "What are you going to do?"

He grins devilishly and tightens his arms around me like a vice. But in a gentle way.

"Mateo? I'm pregnant, remember? You have to be nice to me."

"Oh, I'm not going to hurt the baby. But what I'm about to do to you is anything but nice."

A million thoughts fly through my mind. Some of them a little naughty. But I'm completely surprised by what he does next.

He licks my face. Like a Great Dane. One big, flat-tongued slobber from my jaw to my eyebrow.

I squeal, wiggling in his arms.

"You are really gross," I say, even as giggles escape me.

"And you're having my baby." He beams, perfectly straight teeth on full display. He's glowing so much, he might be radioactive.

"*Our* baby," he amends. "Or babies. It's too early to tell."

"I'm not having a litter of puppies. Just one baby."

He nuzzles his nose on mine and kisses me softly.

"For now."

Can't get enough of Mateo and Desirée?

Then you're in for a treat, because there's a surprise chapter JUST for Gigi Blume's newsletter subscribers.

Go to *www.subscribepage.com/jabonus* for immediate access.

Then turn the page to read a teaser from Dante's point of view.

Thoughts of
DANTE

I never thought I'd still be babysitting Mateo while my parents go to Costco well into my thirties, but here we are.

My brother's trigger-happy finger is one click away from buying a plane ticket to South Carolina, and subsequently making an enormous fool of himself. Not to mention pissing off his girlfriend's parents.

If he shows up on their doorstep after Desirée told him

she needs space, I'm pretty sure Mr. Grant, Mrs. Grant, and Desirée's brother, Ian, will subject Mateo to Guantanamo level waterboarding.

My brother is a lovesick fool–the quintessential tragic poet. I feel sorry for the kid.

Kid. Ha. Look at me. Feeling old. I'm only seven years his senior. And yet, every single one of my thirty-five years is creeping up on me like miles on a used car.

I suppose that was the reason I decided to sell my towing business to my friend Elvis. I'm tired of the conflict from people who come to the tow yard, angry and irate because they parked in the wrong place or had their vehicle repossessed.

Sure, we *do* get work from the auto club. There is that side of the business where we're able to help someone whose car won't start. But mostly, the job is one big ball of stress.

I want to do good for a change. Make a difference in this world. Help people. Save lives instead of transmissions.

That's why I enrolled in the EMT training program. But before classes start, I need to get everything squared away with Elvis and all the paperwork that goes with transferring a business over to someone.

Elvis is a good guy, but he was getting on my nerves today. So when my parents asked me to come over, worried about leaving Mateo alone at the house, I welcomed the distraction.

Until now.

If my brother whines any more about missing his girl-friend, I'm going to throw something at the wall.

"Mateo, I'm warning you," I say.

"She hasn't called."

"She called you three days ago."

He makes a mopey face and slumps his shoulders over. It makes me glad I've never had a serious relationship with a woman. At my age, the chances are slim I ever will.

Which is fine by me.

When Enrique and January arrive, I'm ready to pass off the babysitting duties to them and get myself some lunch. But they're no help. January has a soft spot for Mateo, and now she's helping him find a chartered plane from one of her rich friends.

Oh, and she brought over five dogs she'd rescued from a puppy mill because that's such a January thing to do.

Now, I somehow find myself the new owner of a fluffy golden retriever pup. Unless I can convince Francesca to keep it.

What is it with dogs in this family? My parents take their Yorkie everywhere, even though Mom has to sneak her into Costco inside an oversized purse.

They're going to get kicked out one of these days and then where will they buy their giant packs of toilet paper?

In the end, I'm glad I came over if only to clear the air of Mateo's emotional farts. I'm not the type of guy that likes to talk about *feelings*.

I'll leave it to artists like Mateo to wear his heart on his sleeve. All I can offer him is to be present. So that's what I'm doing.

After a heart-to-heart that felt more like a root canal, Mateo finally comes to terms with the situation and abandons his asinine plan to fly to South Carolina.

But just when I think I can have the rest of the day to

myself, I get a call from Elvis. It's a routine request. No big deal.

But what I don't realize is that this call will change my life.

Whether the change is for better or for worse is still to be determined.

***

Dante meets his match in book four of the Precio Brothers series. Subscribe to Gigi's newsletter for news of the title reveal and release info

www.subscribepage.com/jabonus

THE GIGIVERSE

FOMO?

Social media more your thing? Follow me in all the places. (Hint: Instagram is my favorite)

- facebook.com/gigiblume
- instagram.com/gigiblume
- amazon.com/author/gigiblume
- bookbub.com/authors/gigi-blume
- youtube.com/@gigiblumeauthor

facebook.com/gigiblume

instagram.com/gigiblume

amazon.com/author/gigiblume

bookbub.com/authors/gigi-blume

youtube.com/@gigiblumeauthor

ACKNOWLEDGMENTS

Carina Taylor! Once again, you saved my butt. Thank you for helping me brainstorm ideas to make Mateo the lovable guy he turned out to be and not the brat he was originally.

Julie Christianson: What would I do without you? Thank you for your incredibly helpful feedback. To think, this book could have made a nose dive without you. XOXO

Kristyn Fortner: If I wasn't convinced before that you're Superwoman, I am now. There are no words to describe how grateful I am to have you in my corner. Also, how do you DO all the things you do?

KG Fletcher and Craig A Meyer: I'll never forget our happy hour chat in Long Beach and later, the fun time having dinner with your band. I couldn't jot down notes fast enough when you were trying to explain all about the touring life. If I completely misrepresented it, that's on me. Also, you totally rock.

Leah Brunner: Thanks for critiquing the rough draft I sent you and also for making me laugh while we rant about author life. Cheers with a giant margarita.

Desirée Call: I waited a long time to be able to use your name for a book heroine. Thanks for lending it to me. It's readers like you who encourage me to keep writing.

ABOUT THE AUTHOR

Gigi is a USA TODAY bestselling author and hopeless musical theatre nerd who has perfected the art of lolly-gagging.

Former professional wedding singer, Gigi lives in Southern California with her personal chef (AKA husband) and two weird and awesome kids who have grown into wonderful, artisticly talented young adults.

Quoting movies, Shakespeare, and pop culture with her kids is one of her favorite pastimes. A Hufflepuff and die-hard Whovian, she's convinced magic is really a thing, still believes in Santa Claus, and finds miracles everywhere.

When Gigi's not writing about swoony book boyfriends and the women that bring them to their knees, she likes to re-read Pride and Prejudice, embarrass her offspring, and get distracted by her dogs.